TOM BROWN'S BODY

Gladys Maude Winifred Mitchell – or 'The Great Gladys' as Philip Larkin described her – was born in 1901, in Cowley in Oxfordshire. She graduated in history from University College London and in 1921 began her long career as a teacher. She studied the works of Sigmund Freud and attributed her interest in witchcraft to the influence of her friend, the detective novelist Helen Simpson.

Her first novel, *Speedy Death*, was published in 1929 and introduced readers to Beatrice Adela Lestrange Bradley, the heroine of a further sixty-six crime novels. She wrote at least one novel a year throughout her career and was an early member of the Detection Club along with G. K. Chesterton, Agatha Christie and Dorothy Sayers. In 1961 she retired from teaching and, from her home in Dorset, continued to write, receiving the Crime Writers' Association Silver Dagger Award in 1976. Gladys Mitchell died in 1983.

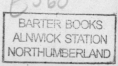

GLADYS MITCHELL

Tom Brown's Body

VINTAGE BOOKS
London

Published by Vintage 2009

4 6 8 10 9 7 5

First published in Great Britain in 1949 by Michael Joseph

Vintage
Random House, 20 Vauxhall Bridge Road,
London SW1V 2SA

www.vintage-books.co.uk

Addresses for companies within The Random House Group Limited
can be found at: www.randomhouse.co.uk/offices.htm

The Random House Group Limited Reg. No. 954009

A CIP catalogue record for this book
is available from the British Library

ISBN 9780099526230

The Random House Group Limited supports The Forest Stewardship Council
(FSC®), the leading international forest certification organisation. Our books
carrying the FSC label are printed on FSC® certified paper. FSC is the only forest
certification scheme endorsed by the leading environmental organisations,
including Greenpeace. Our paper procurement policy can be found at
www.randomhouse.co.uk/environment

Printed and bound by
CPI Group (UK) Ltd, Croydon, CR0 4YY

CONTENTS

Preamble

What a dickens is the Woman always a whimpring about Murder for?

John Gay – THE BEGGAR'S OPERA (*Act 1, Scene 4*)

THE village of Spey is delightfully situated. It has woods and a river to the north, and to the south and west the undulations of its open fields meet the gorse and heather of the moors. It has a blacksmith, livery stables, a haunted Priory, and a witch.

The manor house of Spey was built in 1730, and in 1829 it became a public school. Nowadays the Headmaster, his wife, and, when they are at home, his two daughters, live in one wing of the manor, and the School House boys, some of the masters, the Headmaster's servants, and his butler's budgerigars, occupy the rest of the building.

Around the eighteenth-century mansion, like satellites around a noble planet, courtiers around a king, or his family of sheaves bowing down to Joseph the Dreamer, are other and lesser Houses which, with the mansion itself, make up the School.

There are twelve of these lesser Houses, and they are so discreetly situated – having been added one at a time as the School increased its numbers – that they do not impair the prospect of the original mansion. Unfortunately, together with Spey itself, they come to the number of thirteen, and, by superstitious boys and masters, that lesser breed, the parents, and that influential hierarchy, the Old Boys, to this mystic number has been attributed the dire misfortune which fell upon the School soon after the conclusion of the war.

The School, in short, has added to its other traditions the dubious one of a murdered junior master.

1. *French Leave*

*

We run great Risques – great Risques indeed.

IBID (*Act 3, Scene 6*)

ON Wednesday afternoon in the middle of a delightful and mild October, Merrys and Skene were about to make a plan to be A.W.O.L. It was their reaction to the unjust and unreliable behaviour of their seniors. In other words, Merrys had had a row with his form-master, and Skene had been put down to play in the House Third instead of the House Second, where he considered that he belonged.

'And if that ass Cartaris thinks he can sack me in favour of that ass Timms, he can jolly well get his head looked at with X-rays, because it just means we shall lose to those asses in Mayhews,' said Skene. 'Just because I happened to fumble the ball once – and only once, mind you! – and that ass Scallamore picked up and just happened, by the most fearful bit of luck – and I'm not sure he wasn't offside at that! – to drop a goal, Cartaris needn't think I funked. He practically said I did, and I practically called him a liar, and, anyhow, I'd been kicked over the heart – that ass Felles did that; I hacked his shins for him in the next scrum; and, anyway – '

'Yes,' said Merrys, who had been waiting with some impatience for this tirade to end, and now deemed it best to interrupt it, 'and if Conway thinks he can shove me in D for not being able to translate a lot of rot which nobody would have got up to if that ass Micklethwaite hadn't been put on first and rattled off all the bits everyone knew without even stopping to breathe – '

'Oh, Micklethwaite!' said Skene. 'He'll get a Balliol. Everybody thinks so.'

'More likely to get a brick in his ribs,' said the vengeful sufferer from Micklethwaite's virtuosity. 'Anyway, I'm

about fed up with this place, and I'm going to do something
about it. I've jolly well made up my mind.'

'There's not much you *can* do,' said Skene, 'without
getting gated or lammed.'

'I'd just like to *show* them!' said Merrys, who was seriously
annoyed with Mr Conway. 'Fancy shoving me in D when I
was down for my turn of the Roman Bath!'

'Hard cheese, of course,' admitted his friend, realizing
that the core of the grievance had been reached. 'Let's go
and have a look at it,' he added, 'and bung a brick at
Micklethwaite. He's *always* there! Nancy gets him extra
turns, I think.'

'Nancy's a – !' stated Merrys. 'Come on, then, if you want
to fag over there. But we mustn't be late for tea!'

They strolled off towards the far end of Deep Field, to
where the ground dropped to what had once been a little
stream.

Here there was a high board fence reinforced at every fifth
yard by a post made of concrete. Behind the fence the scene
changed. A great rectangular hollow had been delved from
an outflanking spur of the moor, and within the hollow was
the Roman Bath referred to in bitter tones by Merrys.

All of it was under cover. Inside the Bath were frescoes
copied faithfully by a famous modern cartoonist from Roman
models; was a beautiful piece of tessellated pavement,
modern, but so skilfully copied from the one discovered on a
Roman site not very far from the school that even experts
looked at it twice before they realized that it was not the
original; was a Latin inscription inviting the rich, the
virtuous, and the learned to bathe in the health-giving waters
blessed by Priapus (a strange god to introduce into a world
of boys, some thought), and dedicated to the gentler Glaucus.

Beyond the Roman Bath was the School boundary, and,
beyond that again, a moorland road which led ultimately to
the village of Spey and on to the town.

The Roman Bath was the apple of Mr Loveday's eye, and
in his House Merrys and Skene had been nurtured for the

past two years. Unlike most such loves, this one happened to appeal as strongly to the public as to its originator. Good boys – that is to say, boys who had not been detected in wrong-doing – were always put on a rota by Mr Loveday at the beginning of the Christmas Half, and, whilst the river was too cold for comfort, these good or – it cannot be over-emphasized – undetected boys had a turn in the warmed Roman Bath, and regarded this as a privilege not to be despised, particularly as it was restricted to the members of Loveday's House.

The building had been constructed under the fanatically zealous eye of Mr Loveday, partly by professionals and partly by means of forced labour recruited amongst his boys. The plans and blue-prints he had made for himself one winter after he had visited Pompeii and Herculaneum.

He had employed workmen to instal the heating system, but even this, his chief pride, was on the Roman model, and the completed building included a *caldarium*, a *tepidarium*, and all such other adjuncts as archaeology and the Latin authors suggested. Mr Loveday had had the most enormous fun over his Bath, and had spent some years on the plans and in saving money to carry them out. The Roman Bath had become one of the show-pieces of the School, and rivalled the Chapel and the Headmaster's garden in interest and importance.

The names of naughty boys, unwashed boys, late boys, and lazy boys were sternly removed from the rota by the august hand of Mr Loveday himself, and were only rein-serted after a period of penitence and atonement.

Due for their turn, therefore – and not more than five of them were ever allowed to use the Roman Bath at one time, and that time was from four o'clock until five on first Thursdays – boys were apt to slink about doing evil with much more circumspection than usual, or even, to the irritation of boys in other Houses but in the same form, to eschew evil together for a season. Merrys, therefore, whose piety had become lately a matter of fury to his co-mates and

brothers in exile, was naturally more than incensed at the
mean trick played by fate and his form-master Mr Conway
in doing him out of his turn. Fate was in baulk, but upon
Mr Conway he desired vengeance.

'Of course, *you* can rag in form, and take it out of Conway
that way,' said Skene, when they had satisfied themselves
that the place was locked and that the virtuous, favoured,
and erudite Micklethwaite was nowhere to be seen. 'But
what can *I* do? I can't rag Cartaris. I'd only get my bottom
tanned, and there isn't much future in that.'

'There isn't much point in ragging Conway, either,' said
Merrys. 'He'd only shove me in D again. No, we've got to
do something to sort of give ourselves uplift. You know – rise
on the stepping-stones of our dead selves to higher things,
and at the same time, get our revenge. That's what we've
got to do. The thing is – how?'

Skene, a pale-skinned, hazel-eyed, reddish-haired, chunky
boy – one of the more easily-recognizable Scottish types –
looked at his friend with anxiety.

'You're nuts,' he said.

'No, I'm not. I read about it in the hols,' explained
Merrys. 'You sublimate things. For instance, if you get
tanned, you think of being an early Christian martyr, and
decide to live a good life – well, you might do that in any
case, but, well, you know the sort of thing; or – well, it's not
easy to explain, but – oh, well, we've got to *do* something.
We've got to get on top again, and atone to ourselves for this
bally sucks about the Bath, and you, I suppose, about getting
shoved into House Third instead of House Second – although, if you ask my opinion – '

'Well, I don't!' said Skene, giving his friend a vicious and
indignant kick.

'All right! All right!' said Merrys, rubbing his ankle.
'What I was saying was to buck ourselves up, and look the
whole world in the face, for we owe not any man because
we've got our own back on Fate and what-not, if you can
get that idea into your fat head.'

'Yes, I see that, all right. But what *can* we do?'

'It's got to be something that hasn't been done before,' said Merrys solemnly. 'Otherwise it isn't much good.'

'Don't be a silly owl. Everything worth doing *has* been done before.'

'Not quite everything,' said Merrys, mysteriously, glancing round the rapidly-emptying field, as boys began going in to tea.

'What do you mean?' demanded his practical friend.

'Swear you'll come in with me if I tell you?'

'Well, all right, then. But I don't believe – anyway, spit it out pronto, or we'll be late in, and all the potted meat will be gone.'

'Look here, then. We'll go to the Dogs.'

'Go to – Oh, but we'd never be able to sneak out of footer to do that! It's always House Practice on Wednesdays.'

'I'm not talking about the afternoon Dogs, chump. I'm talking about the evening Dogs. They don't start until eight, and it's dark by the time Prep's over. We could easily –'

'What about Call-Over and supper?'

'We can manage those. We'd better not miss supper. After that, well, Albert-Edward's got a bike, and it's got a step. We could take turns at riding the bike and standing on the step. We could get to the place by nine, see two or three dog-races, nip back again on the bike, and so home by about eleven.'

'And suppose we get nabbed? We'd be sacked at once.'

'You can't be sacked unless you're out after midnight. I know that for a cast-iron fact. Besides, we shan't be nabbed. How can we be? Who's to nab us?'

'Things might go wrong. Besides, the bike! Think of the frightful row there'd be if Albert-Edward knew we'd pinched his bike! He may be an ass, but he *is* a Housemaster.'

'Oh, rot! He never even looks at the bike. He only had the thing for the war when he was in the Home Guard. It's just shoved inside that little place by Jack the Ripper's toolshed. I expect Albert-Edward's forgotten he's got it by now. Beaks are always absent-minded about property.'

'The tyres'll be flat.'

'Oh, well, it's sure to have a pump on it. Tell you what! Let's get Jack the Ripper to pump it up, and tell him to see that the lamps are O.K. He'll do it for a bob, and once he's taken the bob he'll have to keep his mouth shut for his own sake. What do you say?'

'We'll have to go out past Spivvy's cottage, remember.'

'What odds? Ten to one, he'll be up in the masters' Common Room when we go, and asleep by the time we get back. Now you *said* you'd come – '

'On condition that you get the bike, then.'

'All right, then, although I think – '

'And that the lamps and the tyres are all right. I'm not going to break my neck.'

'All right, then, but they *will* be all right. And who cares, anyway, about your bally neck?'

'*And*,' said Skene, with sudden cunning, 'that if we win anything on the Dogs, we split it fifty-fifty. You're always much luckier than I am.'

'*Win* anything on the – Gosh! I'd never thought of that!' said Merrys, startled. 'I say, though, that *would* make a stink if it came out! Do you think – ?'

'It's my last condition,' said Skene, who now saw a ray of hope that the expedition, of which he was thoroughly nervous, might, after all, be abandoned. 'Unless you bet, and we split your winnings, I'm out. I don't mind subbing up half your stake if you lose,' he added handsomely.

'You're a blasted Shylock,' said Merrys. 'All right, then, fifty-fifty.'

Hope died in Skene's loyal but cautious breast.

'All right, then,' he agreed despondently. 'I'm on, I suppose. Let's do it soon and get it over.'

*

Merrys was not the only person who was disgruntled that he had missed a visit to the Roman Bath. Mr Loveday (Albert-Edward to the members of his House) was a mild and scholarly gentleman of advanced views, particularly on what is called, erroneously, discipline, but as a rule he reserved these views for the eyes of editors of educational journals. On this occasion, however, he felt that he had been cold-shouldered to the point of insult, for Mr Conway had not seen fit to inform him that he was keeping back one of his candidates for immersion, although there was evidence that the boy had pointed this out.

'It's time we thought of some better way of managing boys than by beating them and putting them in Detention,' he observed bitterly in the Common Room, after his roll-call for the Roman Bath had failed to elicit a response from Merrys. 'I don't complain, of course. Those are the recognized ways of keeping order, especially by people whose brains and personalities are deficient in the vital qualities which go to make a schoolmaster. Nevertheless' – he glared at the back of Mr Conway's neck – 'I am suffering from – '

'Another overdose of Neill magnesia?' said Mr Conway, turning his head only slightly. He was young enough to despise Mr Loveday wholeheartedly. He thought it was quite time that the Headmaster dispossessed some of these senile Housemasters – got them to take Orders and push off into rural England – so that their legitimate successors (himself primarily) could afford to marry and settle down. 'Go and work it off somewhere else, Loveday, old dear. I can't help it if your whelps aren't given a chance to do their Prep, and so fall down on their classwork.'

'I don't believe in all this Prep,' said Mr Loveday, his fingers angrily clutching the bowl of the pipe that was in his jacket pocket. 'With competent teaching it is quite unnecessary. As for keeping boys in when they should be taking exercise' – he broke off to glare across the room again at the thick-set, aggressive, black-haired Mr Conway, who, unfortunately, again had his back to him and was earnestly discussing the respective merits of pre-war light ales with a master of his own age and tastes – '*then*, I say, it is time to

consider whether the principle of granting and withholding
privileges is not very much to be preferred.'

'It's what they try at Borstal Institutions, isn't it?' said
Mr Conway, suddenly swinging round. 'Why don't you get
a job at one of them?'

Mr Loveday, who was a genuine reformer and therefore
did not make quite such a mess with his theories as a less
sincere man might have done, said that, in his view, the
system, Borstal-based or not, was the right one. He then
referred (mistakenly) to the success of his Roman-Bath privileges and their abuse by incapable form-masters, and received in reply a long and spirited denunciation of his boys
from Mr Conway, who referred to their sins of omission and
commission, their furtiveness, their impudence, their lazi-
ness, their slackness in form and on the games-field, their
unwashedness (Roman Bath or no Roman Bath), and their
general and unrelieved wrong-headedness.

'In other words,' said Mr Conway unpardonably, 'they're
governed by a couple of elderly women, and they know it.'

Mr Loveday turned very white, and another master said,
quietly, 'Steady on, Conway,' but, beyond his ebbing colour
and a sudden intake of breath as though something had
sharply hurt him, Mr Loveday made no attempt to challenge
the insult. He gave Conway a straight glance, and walked
out. It had been a mild Common Room joke for years that
Mr Loveday's sister, who was his housekeeper, wore the
trousers, but it was a joke so far made in Mr Loveday's
absence.

*

Mr Kay, referred to by Skene as Spivvy and as possessing a
cottage which the Dog-fanciers would have to pass on their
way out from school, was the only married member of the
staff who was not a Housemaster. He was too newly-joined
to have been given a House, and, a cottage falling vacant
upon the cricket professional's retirement to his home town
in Yorkshire (and no other professional having been ap-

pointed), Mr Kay had been granted the use of this cottage for himself and his wife. He paid no rent, but had given Mr Wyck, the Headmaster, an undertaking that he would keep the cottage garden tidy without pressing the Headmaster's gardener into service, and would vacate the place if another pro were appointed.

Mr Kay was not very popular with the boys, and some of the masters despised him. He was yellow-faced, black-eyed, and claimed to be half-Portuguese – his mother had been born in Brazil – and Mr Conway, who had a sharp but accurate tongue, called him Louis the Spiv, for Mr Kay taught French to the lower forms and Economics on the Science side. Thus Mr Conway's nickname for him was sufficiently descriptive to be considered worthy of Common Room use by some of the younger masters. It had also become known to the boys, a fact of which Mr Kay had been apprised by a Fourth Form clerihew, which he had been handed, cheekily, in place of a French exercise. It ran:

> Louis the Spiv
> Had not the right to live.
> Like every other skunk,
> He stunk.

It had also leaked out (again through Mr Conway, who interested himself unkindly in other people's affairs) that Mr Kay had taught for a time at a grammar school somewhere in the Midlands, and had left hurriedly in the middle of a term. He was, in consequence of Mr Conway's discoveries and verbal allusions, a solitary man, not even very happily married, and as soon as his duties for the day were over, he was in the habit of going home to his cottage for the evening and night, and shutting himself up with his work. He did not return to School until nine-thirty on the following morning.

The pious argument voiced by Merrys, therefore, that Mr Kay would be in the masters' Common Room when the truants departed for their illegal outing, was based on a fallacy. Mr Kay was not only in his cottage when the boys went by, but he even heard the sound of the bicycle wheels on the gravel drive near his windows.

The sound did not disturb him in the slightest. Merrys and Skene were far too wary to risk talking to one another while they were so near the School, and Mr Kay, hearing the bicycle's somewhat laboured progress, merely concluded that it marked the entrance or exit of the postman, who must be rather later than usual. He did not draw aside his curtain to glance out. He did not listen for the postman's knock. His wife was away from home, and he had heard from her by the morning delivery. He was not expecting any other letters.

Merrys and Skene had found it unexpectedly easy to borrow Mr Loveday's bicycle. They did not even have to take Jack the Ripper – Mr Loveday's knife-and-boot boy – into their confidence. It was Merrys who had done the actual borrowing. Skene had insisted on this.

'You got me to promise to come,' he said. 'It's up to you to do the rest.'

'Cold feet?' asked Merrys, in accents calculated to embarrass and wound the hearer.

'Yes, if you want to know, I *have* got cold feet,' said Skene, firmly. 'But I *said* I'd come with you, so I'm coming. But that's *all* I'm going to do.'

'All right, then,' said Merrys. 'I only wish it was Conway's bike, though,' he added, in a different tone. 'The silly, sickening, unfair beast! I'd jolly well smash it up for him as well as borrow it, if I had it.'

'No, you wouldn't, chump. There'd be a row, and everything would come out.'

Merrys did not contest this, but went off to spy out the lie of the land with a view to sneaking the bicycle. Mr Loveday's potting-sheds, garage, and kitchen premises were out of bounds to his boys, but there were ways and means of circumventing this law.

'I say, Stallard,' said Merrys, presenting himself before his House captain as that august man was dismembering a bloater which he had just cooked for himself over his study

fire, 'I'm awfully sorry, but I've dropped a gym shoe out of
the dorm window, and I think it's got caught in a bush.
May I go round and pick it up?'

'How the devil *could* it drop out of the dorm window?'
demanded Stallard, irritated, for a bloater must be eaten
hot, in his opinion, or not at all. Fagging was not part of the
official system at Spey, and he did not want the trouble of
cooking another bloater if this one grew cold and, in his
view, inedible.

'Please, Stallard, I had cleaned it, and shoved – put it on
the window-ledge to dry, and, as I went to move away, I
suppose I must have caught it with the edge of my hand,
sort of, and – '

'Oh, go to hell and get it!' said Stallard, hitching his chair
nearer the table and picking up a fork and a bit of bread.
'And no messing about, do you hear!'

'Oh, yes, Stallard. Thanks a lot.'

Merrys then ran round to the forbidden territory, found
the coast clear, collared the bicycle, hid it in the bushes and
rejoined his comrade. Both were studious during Prep, both
ate large suppers of bread and margarine, both responded
to Call-Over in the hearty, trumpet-voice of virtue, and both
(having sworn the two boys in their dormitory to secrecy)
descended on to the roof of Mr Loveday's outhouse, crept
past a chimney-stack, slithered down a drainpipe, and so
gained the kitchen garden unheard, unseen, and unthought-
of, at exactly ten minutes past nine.

Mr Loveday kept no watchdog. Their progress was neither
stayed nor interrupted. Merrys dragged the bicycle from the
bushes and wheeled it up a concrete path and then across Mr
Loveday's lawn. Soon Skene had mounted to the step,
Merrys was in the saddle, and the boys were on the main
drive and zigzagging towards Mr Kay's cottage and the
School gates.

The new dog-racing track was distant some seven miles
from the School. With optimism which proved to be mis-
placed, Merrys had allowed half an hour each way for the

journey. Winter Call-Over was at nine, and boys of the age
of the heroes were expected to put lights out at half-past.
Talking was then allowed until a quarter to ten, and silence
was anticipated from that hour until half-past six on the
following morning. Housemasters made their own rules, and
these were the rules of Mr Loveday.

It was therefore a little after nine-fifteen when Skene and
Merrys reached the road beyond the School, and half-past
chimed from a church tower when, the School two miles or
so behind them, and the bicycle careering merrily down a
steep hill, the lads left care in the background and began to
enjoy the escapade.

'I say, this is wizard!' observed Merrys. Comfortably
seated – for Mr Loveday was not a tall gentleman and
Merrys was a long-legged youth – he was allowing the
bicycle, still zigzagging a little, to cut out a good pace along
the moorland road.

'Smashing!' agreed Skene, although he was still not so
wholeheartedly enthusiastic as his friend. In addition, his
position on the vehicle was not particularly comfortable, as
anyone who has ridden on the step of a bicycle will know. In
fact, it was not so very long before he suggested that it might
be a good idea for the two of them to change places.

Almost as soon as the exchange was made, he thought
better of it, for the flattish half-mile of lonely countryside
which had succeeded the downhill glide gave place to a long
hill up which the bicycle ground its way to the agony of both
its passengers.

The dog-racing track came in sight at last, however, and
the boys, secreting their – or rather Mr Loveday's – machine
in an alley, walked up to the gates and sought admission.
They were daunted by the discovery that it was necessary to
pay half a crown each before they could pass the turnstiles.
Merrys looked at Skene, and Skene said, with gloomy
doggedness, that he was hanged if he was going to fork out
half a crown for the doubtful pleasure of watching a couple
of races, which was all they could possibly find time for.

Merrys was inclined to agree. The man on the gate took no
notice of them, except to suggest that they had better make
up their minds, or the crowd would be out, anyway, before
they got inside.

'Why, what time is it over?' asked Merrys.

'Last race about half-past ten,' replied Aeacus. The boys
looked at one another again. Then Merrys turned away,
and, followed by the faithful but greatly-relieved Skene,
took up the bicycle and pushed it disgustedly into the main
road to make for home. Suddenly he changed his mind.

'I say, we needn't go back *yet*,' he suggested.

'Better not, perhaps,' agreed Skene. 'The beaks won't be
in bed yet, and we don't want to get nabbed by somebody
walking across the quad.'

'Besides, we've got to put Albert-Edward's bike to bed,'
said Merrys, 'and it won't do to sneak round there if there's
any chance of anybody hearing us. Tell you what! Let's go
through the town on to the bypass and use the cycle track as
far as Belling cross-roads. Then we can cut across the moor—
it's quite a good surface, I expect – and get back into the
village by Double Corner. It's not so hilly that way, either.'

The cycling track alongside the bypass brought the ad-
venturers all too soon to the cross-roads at which they were
obliged to turn eastwards. After the broad, well-lighted road,
the little white track across the moor looked narrow, lonely,
and frightening.

'I say, I almost wish we'd gone the other way,' said
Merrys. His knee, on the mudguard, had grown (he believed)
a corn, and his foot, on the step, had gone to sleep. 'What
about *me* pedalling now?'

'Steady, you ass!' cried Skene, as his friend attempted to
alleviate the discomfort of his position. 'You'll have us into
the heather! Count 500 out loud, and then we'll change.'

His friend obeyed; they stopped the bicycle, changed
about, and the moor grew larger all round them. The road
was eerily lonely, the night grew blacker and blacker, and

the journey, which had become more and more uncomfortable, now seemed disagreeably long.

'I should have thought we'd have been in sight of the
village by now,' said Skene, at last.

'Well, I don't know,' said Merrys, who (secretly) had been
thinking the same thing for the past quarter of an hour.
'Come to think of it, you see, all the lights would be out by
now. You know how early villagers go to bed. We won't
know we're in the village until we get there. We shall
suddenly come to the pub. That's the first building, going
by this road.'

'I suppose,' said Skene, 'we haven't missed Double
Corner in the dark?'

'Good Lord, no, of course not!' said the startled Merrys.
'How *could* we miss it, you ass?'

'Easily, I should think,' said Job's comforter, now on the
step. 'The trouble would be to see it. Except for our front
lamp, it's as black as your hat all the way.'

At the end of another quarter of an hour the horrid truth
had to be faced. The Corner must lie some miles in the rear
of the cyclists. These, however, were not free from the unreasonable human conviction that to go on is better than to
go back.

'We're sure to come to somewhere soon,' said Merrys.
'Ten to one, if we rode back, we'd only miss it again, and be
no better off. We don't want to find ourselves back in that
bally town.'

It was at this point that they saw a light ahead of them.
Both boys were greatly relieved. They took it for granted
that they had come to the inn. Once through the village, a
little over a mile would bring them to the gates of the
School – or, rather, to where the gates had been. They had
been seized for scrap, and the governors had not replaced
them.

The bicycle lamp, however, showed a broken fence painted
in some dark colour, a ragged hedge, and a glimmering path
between bushes.

2. *Witches' Brew*

*

Why are the Laws levell'd at us? – are we more dishonest than the rest of
Mankind?

IBID. (*Act 2, Scene 4*)

MRS BEATRICE ADELA LESTRANGE BRADLEY had long
cherished the notion of writing an account of an ancestress
of her own, one Mary Toadflax, who bore the early seven-
teenth-century reputation of having been a witch.

Finding herself with some welcome leisure one summer,
Mrs Bradley therefore had begun her researches into this
fascinating history, and had progressed far enough to be able
to pass the results on to a specialist in such matters.

He was able, at the end of eighteen months of painstaking
work, to direct her to the village of Spey, where, in the
possession of an old woman named Lecky Harries, was a
book of spells and charms which, he had reason to believe,
might have been the property of Mary Toadflax in her hey-
day and which, for some unknown reason, had escaped the
fire which consumed its owner.

The details which he was able to supply tempted Mrs
Bradley to leave her clinic in the care of her chief assistant,
and travel north and east to the cottage where the book
reposed. She had no adventures on the way. Spey was clearly
marked on the Ordnance map, and she arrived there without difficulty under the guidance of her chauffeur George.

Enquiry by George at the village public house set them
upon the road which led to the cottage, and at about three
in the afternoon of a bright October day Mrs Bradley was
knocking on the door of Lecky Harries.

'But she's a witch,' they had told George at the inn. 'Better
not take any risks. If thy lass won't have thee, try another.
Old Mother Harries might give thee the wrong brew!'

'After which, madam,' said George, describing the incident, 'there was bucolic mirth of a Miltonian type. I purchased a round of drinks for my informants, and, as it was almost closing time, escaped a return of hospitality.'

Mrs Bradley was not more superstitious than her levelheaded factotum, yet she felt a keen stirring of interest when the door of the cottage was opened by a pale-faced but darkcomplexioned man with greasy black hair and yellowringed black eyes who asked her, none too civilly, what she wanted.

'Your paramour, incubus,' said Mrs Bradley brightly. There was a senile, shrill chuckle from the opposite side of the room, and a little, bent, bright-eyed old woman got up from the chimney corner and, grasping hold of a long stick, sagged forward over the carpetless floor to greet the visitor.

The dark gentleman slammed the door behind him, and was gone.

'Come you in, my pretty,' said the hag unnecessarily to Mrs Bradley, 'for I can tell you're a woman by the pattern your posy of fingers makes on my heart.'

'You can't see me?' Mrs Bradley enquired; for the bright eyes were as brilliant as her own.

'I can see nought, nor haven't, this twenty years,' pronounced the sibyl, 'but I can tell by your voice how warm you are. Burning for love, eh, my lassie? Come to old Mother Lecky for a wee small drink, have you? Sit down, and tell your grandma your troubles.'

'I want facts about Mary Toadflax,' said Mrs Bradley distinctly. She could have sworn that the bright eyes searched her face. Then Mother Harries nodded.

'You shall have them,' she said. 'But first you must stay here a night and a day, and give me the knowledge that you have in you – the knowledge of men and of things. You vibrationing thing, then! You are warm! You have long life before you – a great expectation of days. But I know now that you are old as the fools count age. Speak: will you stay, and exchange with me secret for secret? For secrets you have in your heart.'

'I will stay until dusk and return after dark,' said Mrs Bradley, imitating the witch's oracular delivery.

'Wait till I wet the pot, then,' said Mother Harries, 'and we will drink tay together.'

'You've been on the stage,' said Mrs Bradley suddenly. Mother Harries, who was hobbling towards the door which led to the kitchen of her cottage, turned her head, and again gave the impression that she was looking Mrs Bradley straight in the face.

'Until my sight was reft from me,' she said. They drank very sweet black tea with a good dollop of gin in it, and then Mrs Bradley mentioned again the purpose of her errand. She not only wanted details of the life and exploits of Mary Toadflax; she wanted to see her magic book.

Lecky Harries did not deny that there was such a book, and she did not, in so many words, admit that she had it in her possession.

'Next time you come we will speak of it again,' she said; and Mrs Bradley could get no more out of her. There were several built-in cupboards in the two downstair rooms of the cottage, and others, Mrs Bradley surmised, in the bedrooms. One of them must house the precious book. She had a pretty good idea of its market value, and she was prepared to put on top of this a contribution which would satisfy the sentimental value that the book would have for her. She did not desire a bargain. She was aware that bargains were usually fraudulent either to the purchaser or the vendor.

' "Take what you want," says God, "and pay for it," ' she suddenly observed, with a chuckle. 'Next time I come, I should like, at any rate, to *see* the book. I should also be interested to hear how it came into your possession.'

'I inherited it,' replied Mrs Harries.

'Then we must be related.'

'Oh, I knew that directly you came in,' said the sightless old woman with conviction. As there was neither proof nor disproof of this statement, Mrs Bradley paid it the perfunctory attention of a 'Really?' and prepared to take her leave.

'Another cup?' said her hostess. Mrs Bradley declined gracefully. Very strong tea laced equally strongly with gin was not her usual afternoon beverage.

'I hope, madam,' said George, respectfully aware of something preoccupied in his employer's manner when she returned to the car, 'that your researches are about to be blessed.'

'Cursed, George,' said Mrs Bradley, as he arranged the rug over her knees. 'That elderly woman has the local reputation, didn't you tell me, of a witch?'

'That was pub talk, madam.'

'She also claims to be a relation of mine.'

'I wouldn't be greatly surprised at that, madam. I have often been aware of the eldritch in you.'

Mrs Bradley gazed at her man as stout Cortez gazed at the Pacific. George had often surprised her, but never more so than at this particular moment.

'George,' she said solemnly, 'you have hit it. And now, since there is not only the eldritch in me but a particularly nauseous witch's brew of strong sweet tea laced with gin, get me back to the house at once, and have the car ready again at ten o'clock to-night.'

*

'Well, go on, knock,' said Merrys. Skene tapped delicately on the cottage door with his bare and, by this time, cold knuckles. There was no reply.

'It isn't any good,' he said. 'I expect they've gone to bed.'

'There's a light downstairs, you ass.'

'I expect they left it on by mistake,' said Skene, who disliked the whole aspect of the situation in which they found themselves.

'Oh, rot. Here, let me try,' said Merrys, covering his knuckles with his school cap and then pounding vigorously on the door.

'I say, you know, they'll be pretty sick if they *have* gone to bed,' said Skene, nervously.

'Be your age,' retorted his friend; and pounded again. This time the sound of footsteps rewarded the bold effort. The door was opened by an old woman carrying a candle.

'Come in,' she said. 'The candle is to light you, not me. I require no illumination ever contrived by man. Step past me into the house, and sit down. When you have sat you may cross my palm with silver, if you will.'

Suddenly, over her shoulder, there appeared the face of another old woman; a yellow face with brilliant black eyes and a little beaky mouth now writhing back its lips in silent laughter.

Merrys turned, cannoned into his friend, gulped, and, cramming his cap on to his head, raced back to the hedge beside which they had left the bicycle. Just as they gained it a man loomed up in front of its headlamp and took the path through the open gateway between the ragged bushes.

'Good Lord!' said Merrys. 'Did you see who that was?'

'Of course I did,' said Skene, with the nervous anger of extreme dismay.

'He didn't recognize us, did he? Do you suppose he can pick us out in the morning?'

'Don't know. Hope not. We didn't have our caps on.'

'I did! I pulled it out to knock on that beastly door, and shoved it on when we bolted.'

'I say, you *are* an ass!'

'Well, who would expect to run into a beak out here at this time of night? Come on. It's no good beefing about it now. I don't honestly think he saw us.'

This opinion, delivered roundly, slightly comforted Skene. They ran with the bicycle down the dark road until they were out of breath.

'Ease up!' gasped Merrys, at last. 'He isn't following us. Where the heck do we go from here?'

They dropped to a walk and then were about to stop and mount when Merrys said, his hand to the breast-pocket of his jacket inside his waterproof coat:

'I've lost my fountain pen!'

'You've probably left it in your locker,' said Skene. 'Come on.'

'No, I haven't, you ass! I had it clipped into my pocket. I always carry it there.'

'Well, it'll have to stay lost,' observed Skene unsympathetically. 'I'm not going back to that beastly cottage to look for a fountain pen, and perhaps run into Spivvy again. Besides, we'd never find it in the dark.'

'But it was a jolly good pen. I had it for Christmas. I'm almost certain I must have dropped it in that garden. I had it out just before that, because it's got a torch at the end.'

'Well, hang it, we *can't* go back there again!'

'But if the Spiv finds it, we're sunk. It had my name on it, on a band round the barrel, and even an ass like Kay – '

'Oh, Lord!' said Skene, disgusted by this revelation. 'You really *are* an ass! Oh, well, come on, then. I suppose we'd *better* go back.'

But when they reached the cottage there were further terrors in store. The light in the little room seemed brighter, and in front of it they could see in silhouette a fiercely gesticulating figure, whose waving arms were casting a gigantic shadow on the blind. Suddenly an arm went through the window. There was the sound of the breaking glass, and then a voice, rough with fury.

'If I have to *hang* for him, I'll finish him, the swine! Here! Who the devil's that outside? I could swear I heard – oh, blast! I've cut my arm!'

The boys turned tail again.

'Did it sound like the Spiv's voice?' asked Skene, when they were well away from the house. 'Do you think that's who it was?'

'I suppose it must have been. I say, come on! Let's pedal as fast as we can along this road. It must lead *somewhere*, mustn't it?'

'Shouldn't think Kay would be the sort to talk about finishing people,' observed Skene, when the fever of fear and excitement had cooled with the difficulties of making progress uphill on the sandy and interminable road. 'Still, you can't tell, I suppose. After all, he's really a Dago. They do have funny tempers and all that.'

'Oh, those weak-kneed sort of asses always threaten what they're going to do, but they never dream of doing it. Always saying they'll report you to the Head, but they never do. I say, I wish we'd found that cursed fountain pen!'

The culprits, with the luck of the undeserving, came into the village at last, and, anxious now to get back to the House and to return Mr Loveday's bicycle, they were soon at the School gate.

'Better walk the bike past Spivvy's cottage, just in case,' muttered Skene.

'In case of what, you ass?'

'Well, in case anybody should hear us.'

'Be your age. There's nobody there to hear us. They don't keep a proper servant, and his missus is still on holiday. Issy told me. And we know where Spivvy is, anyway.'

'He might have got back himself by now.'

'Pigs might fly, but *he* didn't,' said the bold Merrys, still pedalling on. He stopped the bicycle as soon as they drew near the School buildings, however, and the two boys crept like cats towards Mr Loveday's kitchen garden.

They restored the borrowed property to its shed, and were rounding the side of the House preparatory to climbing into the dormitory when they saw a surprising sight. From the direction of Mr Loveday's Roman Bath, which lay at the far end of Big Field, could be seen two lights which might have been rather powerful will o' the wisps, or, mundanely, a couple of lanterns or electric torches.

'I say, what do you think that is?' asked Skene.

'I don't know. Somebody playing the fool. A.W.O.L. like us, I shouldn't wonder.'

'Would they use lights? Anyway, the water would be beastly cold. They only stoke it up two days a week, ready for first Thursdays, you know.'

'I *don't* know, then. Think we ought to go over and have a look?'

'No, I jolly well don't! It can't be burglars, because there's nothing to steal. Perhaps it's Nancy the Nark having her weekly tub!'

Merrys giggled at this well-worn and libellous jest, and the two boys, having skinned their knees but come to no other harm in climbing up to their dormitory, soon rejoined Eaves and Meyrick, the other occupants of the room.

'What was it like?' whispered Eaves.

'All right. Dry up,' responded Merrys.

'I say!' whispered Skene, raising his head from the pillow. 'Aren't we in luck? Hear that?'

What he had heard was the swishing down of the rain.

'Missed it by less than five minutes! Golly!' said Merrys. 'Been dashed awkward if we'd had to account for soaked clothes. I never thought of it raining! Did *you*, Skene?'

Skene said nothing. He took off his shoes, socks, and jacket, left them on the floor, and went to bed in his trousers. Merrys found pyjamas and struggled into them in the dark. 'Tell you in the morning,' he whispered as he crept between the sheets. 'We think there *might* be a murder.'

'At the Dogs?' was the excited, anticipatory response.

'No, of course not. Dry up. You'll wake somebody. Good night. The Dogs are a washout. You have to pay half a crown just to go in.'

'But what about the murder?'

'Nothing, you fool! I was only pulling your silly fat leg. And, look here! Don't you two go shooting your heads off in the morning!'

'What do you think we are!' said the injured pair.

'Often wondered,' responded Merrys. '*Pax*, you damned idiot! You'll bring old Albert-Edward! Oh, *damn* you! That was my knee-cap! Shut *up*, you fool!'

'Tell us about the murder, then!'

'There *isn't* any murder. It was only that we heard the Spiv having a frightful row with someone.'

'His missus, I expect. They do row. Elkins told me so. His people know her a bit.'

'Elkins is a cad.'

'Yes, he is, rather. What did the Spiv say?'

'Oh, nothing much. It wasn't his cottage, anyway. He jammed his fist through a window. . . . Don't chortle, you ass! You'll bring somebody up! Shut *up!* And it *wasn't* his missus, either. She's still away. But the whole thing was rather rummy, and if you'll swear not to tell a soul, we'll tell you about it in the morning.'

*

'I was born under Taurus,' said Mrs Bradley complacently, 'or so I am led to believe.'

'I should like to cast your horoscope,' said Mrs Harries politely. 'But you wanted to see my book. There is just time to show you a little of it before my client appears.'

Mrs Bradley had scarcely hoped for such luck. She glanced at her watch. It showed twenty-five minutes to eleven. She had been in the cottage less than a quarter of an hour. She had sent George and the car packing, with orders to return for her after breakfast, for she anticipated a long and interesting session with the sibyl from whom she hoped to purchase Mary Toadflax's treasury.

'I am indeed curious to see the book,' she agreed. 'Did you read it?'

'No,' said Mrs Harries, who had given up the rough speech of the countryside and reverted to her natural enunciation. 'I might be tempted, so I left it alone. I would be glad to be rid of it. I think perhaps I will give it to you as a symbol of sisterhood. What was your maiden name?'

Before this interesting secret could be disclosed there came a very muffled tap at the door.

'Drat!' said Mother Harries. 'There he is already! Too early. Let him cool his heels for a bit.'

'The man I saw before?' Mrs Bradley enquired.

'The same. He pesters me. He is a foreign man. He came

on a night wind. I think that he, too, has wind of Mary Toadflax's book.'

The knock was repeated, very much more loudly.

'Are you sure it is he?' asked Mrs Bradley, whose ears were keen. 'It sounded to me as though there were voices, very young voices, outside.'

'No one but he would come,' pronounced Mrs Harries with an air and in a tone of omniscience. The knock came again, louder still. Mrs Harries picked up the candle, upon whose supporting saucer she laid her aged hand with sure instinct, and shuffled her way to the door. Mrs Bradley had conceived the impression that she *could* see, although possibly only dimly. She followed her and stood at her shoulder.

The candle lighted the young, strained, pallid faces of a couple of fourteen-year-old boys, who, upon perceiving the countenances of their receptionists, turned in terror and fled. The expected visitor arrived some two minutes later, and must have met the boys at the gate. He knocked softly.

'If you wouldn't mind going into the kitchen,' suggested Mrs Harries, 'I think you might hear something of interest.'

Mrs Bradley obediently retired, and the new arrival was admitted by the witch.

'Parcae,' she pronounced solemnly.

'Three-fold Hecate,' replied the dark man.

'And three Dianas,' said the witch.

The session having thus been declared open, there followed a heavy ritual in which various demons were invoked and the One Morer referred to, and then the visitor broke out in an impassioned, hysterical diatribe against some unknown enemy upon whom he threatened vengeance.

Mrs Bradley came out of the kitchen just as he put his fist through the glass of Mrs Harries' front room.

'Either get rid of him or put him to bed,' said she. 'He is your client, I know, but, if he goes on like this, very soon he will be my patient.'

The man under discussion decided matters for himself.

'Two of you? Two of you?' he said suddenly and loudly.

'I don't believe in your witchcraft! I don't believe in your witchcraft!' He rushed out of the cottage, banging the door behind him.

'What did you tell him?' Mrs Bradley enquired.

'Of nails and the wax,' said the witch. 'He will try both, never fear.'

Mrs Bradley, who had long held the view that the victims of witches and warlocks, fortune tellers, necromancers, and the like, deserved what they got, merely resumed the subject of Mary Toadflax and her book.

The book which was produced at four in the morning proved to be without value. It was an expurgated French nineteenth-century copy of the life of Simon Magus.

'I'm sorry,' said Mrs Bradley after she had glanced perfunctorily through its pages, 'but I am not interested in this book.'

It was the most definite statement that she had made for fourteen years. Mrs Harries smiled.

'You know what it is?' she demanded.

'Oh, yes,' Mrs Bradley answered. 'And it is neither what I expected nor what I want.'

'As I thought,' said the sibyl contentedly. 'And now I will tell you something interesting. That young man will see bad trouble in the future.'

'If you encourage him to commit murder he will certainly see trouble in the future,' said Mrs Bradley. 'He is in a sad state of mind.'

'You think he needs *your* services, not mine,' said Mrs Harries, 'but you are wrong. It does him good to come here and shout away his hate.'

Mrs Bradley agreed with this view, but only cautiously, and returned to the subject of the book.

'Is that the only one you possess?' she demanded.

'You may rummage for yourself,' said Mrs Harries. 'I know that if you discover anything worth while you will tell me. I trust you as I would trust myself. I shall go to bed now. Take the candle and try your luck.'

'Thank you. I have my torch,' said Mrs Bradley.

'Then my house is at your disposal. Search until daylight, but do not touch the elm that grows under the stairs.'

Mrs Bradley bade her hostess good night. She went to the cupboard under the stairs, but the only thing she found there was a birch broom. She did not touch it. She assumed that the handle was made of elm, sometimes called wychwood. There was no trace of the book she sought in the cottage. She satisfied herself of this, and wondered what Mrs Harries had done with the black-letter spells and charms of Mary Toadflax. She did not, however, wake Mrs Harries and ask her. Instead, she sat in the chimney corner of the cottage and spent the rest of the night wide awake, alert to all sounds and uncomfortably aware of a sense of danger.

George came, according to orders, in the morning, and she slept in the car whilst George drove her back to the rooms she had taken in Spey village. Her hosts were the local doctor and his wife. They knew of her errand, and were glad to see her at breakfast. She retired to her room when she had made a frugal meal, and was interested to find a large toad, with eyes which reminded her somewhat of those of Lecky Harries, squatting amiably on the middle of the counterpane.

She suspected the doctor's young son of a practical joke, and, removing the toad to the front garden, she decided to challenge the child at midday.

The little boy denied all knowledge of the toad, however, and asked to see it, but although he and Mrs Bradley searched the garden, no trace of it was to be found.

Mrs Bradley returned to Mrs Harries and gave her five pounds, all in silver. The blind woman – if blind she was – seemed pleased with the present. She returned a florin 'for luck,' and wished Mrs Bradley well.

'Come again in the dark of the moon,' she said. 'Who knows? The luck may have changed.'

3. *'Mr Perrin and Mr Traill'*

*

A Lawyer is an honest Employment, so is mine. Like me too he acts in a
double Capacity, both against Rogues and for 'em.

IBID. (*Act 1, Scene 1*)

SPEY SCHOOL was well endowed; so well endowed, in fact,
that Education Acts passed it by and government grants
were as pointedly ignored by its trustees as though they had
never existed.

It was not an expensive school, as schools go, and had not
increased its fees since 1909, when it had become so much
sought after that the governing body had decided upon a
slightly discouraging scale of fees although they did not need
the extra money.

Scholarships to Spey were not numerous, but there were
more than a dozen bursaries offered every year to clever
boys of the school who wanted to go to Oxford or Cambridge
in what a sadly undemocratic deed of gift referred to as a
'gentlemanly manner'.

The School was very well staffed and the masters were
very well paid. Once appointed, they were expected to work
for their living, and it was understood (and an article of their
signed agreement) that the Headmaster would present a
written report on each of them to the governors on every
twenty-fifth day of November.

There were so many masters that cliques and parties
formed as naturally among them as among a large band of
courtiers.

The younger masters at Spey were divided into two main
sections. There were, of course, cross-sections, permutations
and combinations, pairs, special interests and occasional
changes of allegiance, but, speaking generally and in a broad
way, there were two main sections, one under the leadership

of Mr Conway, and the other under the leadership of Mr Semple.

Mr Semple was an Old Boy. He was modest, firm, and popular, and had destined himself to take a wife and, later, a House. He was a good fellow, a bit of a prig, and more than a bit of an athlete. He had been a double Blue, for he was a footballer and a runner.

He disliked Mr Conway very much, but rarely upset himself about this because Mr Conway was, in point of fact, afraid of him, and so left him alone. He was not subjected to such witticisms and rudeness as made some of the older masters and one or two of the young ones feel like murder, but he was a decent fellow in his rather prim way, and it gave him a feeling of discomfort when Mr Conway's malicious shafts were directed towards others.

When, therefore, Mr Kay, of the doubtful antecedents and unprepossessing appearance, appealed to him to 'come out for a run one morning before breakfast' he was disposed to accede to the request. Mr Conway had been particularly offensive that day, not to Kay, in whom Mr Semple was not interested, but to Mr Loveday, who, although an old dodderer (in Mr Semple's opinion), happened also to be Mr Semple's old Housemaster.

Mr Semple, therefore, accepted the invitation in no uncertain voice, and exchanged an enquiring and challenging stare for an exclamation of mirth from Mr Conway. Mr Conway then went out of the Common Room, and Mr Semple was moved to enquire, in a very loud voice which he knew Mr Conway could hear:

'You're not the Kay who did one fifty-nine point four in the Inter-Clubs, are you?'

'I'm afraid it was some time ago,' replied Mr Kay modestly, 'and, of course, it was a very fast track.'

This settled the question of early morning running, and, after that, Mr Semple turned out, on an average. three times a week for a spin, sometimes on his own, but more often in Mr Kay's company.

The two men became no more intimate because of this, but Mr Semple was glad of someone to run with, and Mr Kay felt less of an outcast than he had done before Semple consented to join his morning pipe-openers.

In the winter the two men sometimes put on dark shorts and football jerseys, and punted a Rugby ball about. Mr Semple was a more than useful three-quarter, and had long cherished an ambition to play a team of masters against the Old Boys. As it was, he himself always turned out for the Old Boys against the School, but no other master was qualified to do this, and there were six or seven good men on the staff who would form the nucleus of quite a useful fifteen if he could find enough others to put with them.

Mr Kay's game was Soccer, another reason for his slight unpopularity in what had always been a Rugby-playing school, but Mr Semple had high hopes of Mr Kay as a Rugby player, for he had safe hands, an intelligent mind, and was developing a 'feel' for the independent and unpredictable foibles of the elongated, egg-like ball.

On the morning following the outbreak by Merrys and Skene, therefore, Mr Semple decided that he would run down to Kay's cottage and see whether he was prepared to turn out early for a punt-about. Accordingly, at just after a quarter to seven he quietly left the School House (where he lived at the end of a corridor for whose order and quietness he was responsible), and walked briskly towards Mr Kay's cottage near the School gate.

He was a little earlier than usual, and, from the School drive, saw the curtains of the cottage were not drawn back and that there was no sign of Mr Kay. He did as he usually did on such occasions. He called out Mr Kay's name twice, and then trotted on to the grass at the verge of the drive, leaned against a tree, exchanged his football boots for his spikes, and then called again.

A window on the ground floor was thrust open, so that the curtain swung out, and an unshaven and shock-headed Kay invited him to trot round for a bit, as he himself had overslept.

'I'll be out in five minutes,' he said.

The morning was scarcely come, the air was chilly, and Mr Semple was soon on the running track. He trotted round it four times, then took off his track-suit, sprinted a little, and then put on his track-suit and cantered back towards the cottage.

'Are you coming or not?' he cried encouragingly, and, not wishing to continue his exercise alone, he exchanged his spikes for his football boots, and walked briskly through the School gate. At least, he was about to do so when he heard Kay calling from the cottage side of the railings, and they both saw the body of the black cock at the same moment.

It was lying half on to a flower-bed in front of the railings, and it was not very pretty to look at. There was no sign of the head, and the general appearance of the tufty neck suggested some rather sickening possibilities.

Semple looked horrified and disgusted. Kay licked his lips and smiled in an embarrassed manner like a man who recognizes an insult and is too timid to challenge it.

'Takhobali, should you think?' he enquired.

'I don't know,' Semple replied. With an effort of will he took the cock by one leg and carried it to the end of Kay's garden. Here he laid it down. 'Get a spade, would you?' he said. 'I don't want any boys to see this.'

'Oh, boys aren't squeamish,' said Kay; but he went off at once to his toolshed. 'Ever read that thing by M. R. James?' he asked casually, as he dug a deep hole in the flower-bed.

'Which one?' Semple enquired, trying hard to take his mind off the ritual killing of the corpse and his eyes from its interment.

'Why, the one about young Lord Saul.'

'Oh, that! It wasn't James, though, was it? I thought it was Lord Dunsany.'

Mr Kay made no reply. Methodically he finished shovelling back the earth, then he smoothed it all over and stepped away from the small bush which he had been holding back with his body. The bush sprang back and the spot where the digging had been done was hidden from sight.

'I shall tell Mr Wyck,' said Mr Semple, after they had walked on to the turf of the School field. 'I don't think I'll stay and punt about, after all, this morning. It's getting late and I've got a First Fifteen list to go over with Cranleigh. I'd forgotten all about it. Sorry to have got you out under false pretences.'

*

Mr Wyck, the Headmaster of Spey, was, like all great headmasters, a law unto himself. That is not to say that he was an autocrat; in fact, any type of dictatorship was extremely repugnant to his mind. But Mr Wyck was an original thinker and had his own methods – usually unexpected by the boys – of dealing with every school situation as it arose and of solving its constituent problems almost before others had realized what these were.

He had a sixth sense which kept him informed about events, conversations, and loyalties in the Common Room, too, and he was not surprised, therefore, when, before breakfast on the day of the burial of the black cock, the elderly Mr Loveday came to him and tendered his resignation.

The Headmaster did not accept it; neither did he ask for an explanation. He merely said:

'Sit down, my dear Loveday, and tell me how your sister likes the new boiler you have installed in your delightful Roman Bath.'

'It is about my sister – it is because of my sister – that I wish to resign my post,' said Mr Loveday, refusing to be side-tracked.

'She is well, I trust?' said Mr Wyck, who had the actor's gift of altering face and tone at will.

'Yes, yes. Annette is always well, I am thankful to say. But I am too old a man, Headmaster, to be subjected any longer to the gibes and insults of puppies!'

'Oh, you mustn't take too much notice of Conway,' said

Mr Wyck. 'He is a conceited fellow, but useful, you know, quite useful over the games. He and Semple, between them –'

'Oh, I've nothing against Semple,' said Mr Loveday. 'And it isn't connected with the games. I have been insulted in open Common Room, and my sister with me.'

'Unintentionally, unintentionally,' said Mr Wyck.

'I do not agree. Besides, there's another thing,' said Mr Loveday, his face growing even darker. 'Why should my boys be differentiated against?'

'In what way?' Mr Wyck enquired. 'I know Conway is a trying sort of fellow and has a habit of keeping boys in at inconvenient times, but I am afraid we must uphold him, you know. He will learn as he grows older. We've all been through the mill, my dear fellow, and must suffer the tyros gladly.'

'It's not my Roman Bath this time,' said Mr Loveday, mollified by the Headmaster's implication that he was a better disciplinarian than Mr Conway, although he knew that this was not so. 'It is the boxing. My boys have begun to complain. It takes a good deal to make boys complain of one master to another –'

Mr Wyck knew better than this. He was well aware of the genius of boys for fomenting quarrels between masters either for their own advantage or for their own lawless amusement.

'Boxing?' he said, raising his eyebrows to emphasize that this was a new departure. 'How do you mean?'

'Well,' said Mr Loveday, his untidy moustache beginning to bristle, 'it's like this, Headmaster. Last year my boys were allowed the use of the gymnasium on second Tuesdays for boxing practice, but last week Cartaris came to me and explained that the House boxing had had to give place to School boxing coached by Mr Conway. I saw nothing against this. The School, naturally, must come before any individual House. But what do I find? This week Cartaris informs me that other Houses are allowed their full practice time. It is only on *my* day that the gymnasium is required for a full School practice.'

'Wait a minute, though, Loveday,' said Mr Wyck. 'Wait just a minute, my dear fellow. Which of your boys are in the School boxing team?'

'I – I really could scarcely say,' said Mr Loveday, looking nonplussed. 'Cartaris, I suppose, and – and – '

'Heavyweight, Cartaris of Loveday's,' said Mr Wyck impressively. 'Middleweight, Stallard of Loveday's. Lightweight, Edgeley of Lovedays. Featherweight, Takhobali of Loveday's. You know, it does seem to me, my dear fellow, that as there are so many Houses to be fitted in and only the one gymnasium into which to fit them, that your House is getting its practice time, even although it is not called House practice but School practice. Still, perhaps if you had a general word with Conway – '

Mr Loveday could have snarled with disappointment and fury. Mr Wyck smiled sadly and shook his head. He did not like Mr Conway, but he thought that a man of Mr Loveday's age and experience should have been able to manage him. Mr Wyck disliked dissension and loved harmony, but on a big staff there must be some misfits. Unfortunately, in many ways Mr Loveday, fussy, pedantic, old-maidish, was more of a misfit than the presumptuous and arrogant Mr Conway. Mr Conway was at least a reliable history specialist and a useful games coach. Mr Loveday was an out-moded Housemaster and an anachronism in the form-room.

Mr Loveday did not realize, until he had reached his own front door, that the core of his grievance, the slighting reference to himself and his sister as two elderly ladies, had not been quoted in detail. He wondered whether it was worth while to go back to Mr Wyck, but he decided that the Headmaster (as had happened frequently lately) was in an unsympathetic mood.

He was glad, however, that the Headmaster had taken no notice of his request to resign his post. The Roman Bath had taken most of Mr Loveday's savings, and continued to

absorb a surprising and perturbing amount of his income.
Boys did not come to his House as readily as they had done
some twenty years previously. There were even vacant
places . . .

Besides, it had perhaps given an impression of lack of
keenness when he had not realized how many of his boys
were being coached for School boxing.

'I must get myself abreast of these things,' thought Mr
Loveday. 'But, dear me, there seems so much to do and to
think about these days! Food, the rationing system, a cater-
ing licence, the constant supervision of coal supplies, the cost
of electric light . . .' Depressed, he shrugged off his gown,
and then pulled it on again. He was due in form in ten
minutes' time and had mislaid his mark book.

*

'Hook him, man, hook him with your right!' said Mr Conway. Damn that old idiot Loveday! If only he could be
persuaded or forced to retire, there might be some chance of
putting in for his House and getting married. The governors
did not approve of their junior masters getting married, but
they wanted their Housemasters to be able to import unpaid
housekeepers! 'Now push out your left! That's better. No,
keep away from him, idiot! He's heavier than you! Feel for
it! *Feel* for it! Now – ! Ah! That's the stuff! Jab! *Jab!* Good
Lord, you're not patting a dog! Hit out, man! Ah, serve you
right! You ran right on to that one. All right. Gong them,
Carter. That'll do. Get a quick shower and a good rub
down, and then get some clothes on, both of you.'

That old idiot would have complained by now to Wyck.
And there was that yellow swine Kay. *He* was married already. The boys did not like him much, it was true, but he
ran his blasted O.T.C. pretty well, and the governors liked
it. Fine old crusted Tories to a man, and liked the thought of
boys playing at soldiers. And Semple, pious prig, was on his
side. And Semple's uncle was chairman of the governing
body this year. And Semple was fond of old Loveday and

had looked pretty sick last night in the Common Room. Damn Semple! He was after Marion, too. It might turn into a sort of comic-opera rivalry between them. 'You can't have the man and the money too!' Ah, but you *could* have the woman and the House. And Marion, as old Pearson's daughter, would be smiled upon, without doubt, by the governing body. Whoever got her would certainly get Loveday's House when the old fool thought fit to retire.

Yes, he'd been wrong to play Semple's game by taking a rise out of Loveday. Marion would be sure to hear of it and would think it rather a rotten thing to do. Perhaps it was, in a way. The old man could not help being three-quarters senile.

Mr Conway kicked a pair of gym shoes irritably under a balancing form, pulled off his white sweater, and put on his pullover and a jacket. He exchanged his sneakers for walking shoes, and went off to have his tea.

Just as he reached the gymnasium door a handsome and beautifully built boy of about fifteen came crashing into him.

'Sorry, sir!' he gasped. '*Beastly* sorry, sir!'

'You bring me a hundred lines and look where you're going next time!' yelled Mr Conway.

'Yes, sir. Please, sir, could you come, sir? There's a cad outside, sir, trying to throttle Scrupe.'

'Why on earth couldn't you say so at first?' demanded Mr Conway. He broke into a run, the youth cantering lightly at his heels.

4. *Noblesse Oblige*

*

Depend upon it, we will deal like Men of Honour.
IBID. (*Act 3, Scene 6*)

In nearly every school there is at least one licensed eccentric. Martin, of *Tom Brown's Schooldays*, is a classic example. The position of school madman – envious in its way – was held at Spey by Scrupe, of Mr Mayhew's House. Scrupe was sixteen and a half, and owing to the fact that he found it impossible (or so he had informed Mr Conway, who taught the subject) to concentrate on Latin because he had been brought up to speak Spanish, he had been removed from the Classical side and set to study Economics with Mr Kay and Mathematics with an unorthodox little man much beloved by the Old Boys.

This gentleman's name was Mr Reeder. He was apt to become bored during Maths lessons, finding boys slow and their imaginations limited. As a rule, therefore, he could be relied on for entertainment. The red herring was seldom dangled before him in vain.

'Sir,' said Scrupe to Mr Reeder, during the week following the outing of Merrys and Skene, 'what are the statistics for murder in this county?'

'They will increase by one, if you ask silly questions,' said Mr Reeder. 'And, by the way, what is all this about you and a stolen cockerel?'

'Oh that, sir?' said Scrupe easily. 'Yes, that was very unfortunate. The farmer was under a misapprehension. It was not I who stole his cockerel.'

'Why should he have fastened on you, then?'

'I happened to be passing the farmyard, sir, and I stopped to admire his dog. A handsome pedigree animal, sir, and, if I am any judge – '

'Sit down,' said Mr Reeder. Scrupe, who seldom obeyed orders from masters without questioning them first, said plaintively:

'Sir, I am sure the farmer mistook me. Do I remind you of anyone?'

'Yes,' said Mr Reeder, who was tired of the lesson and welcomed the chance of a diversion, 'Thurtell and Hunt.'

'Please, sir, who were they?' enquired Biggs, in response to a meaning kick from Scrupe.

'Your education seems to have been neglected,' said Mr Reeder, whose hobby was criminology; and he proceeded, to the ecstasy of the form, to recount a sordid and unedifying history which he terminated only in time to set the boys some preparation before the bell went.

'What *was* all that about Scrupe and a cockerel?' he enquired of Mr Semple when they met in the quad before lunch. Mr Semple, looking thoroughly uneasy, replied that he had no idea, but that Scrupe, in his opinion, was born to be hanged.

'Oh, I don't know,' argued Mr Reeder, taking the words literally for his own amusement. 'When one goes over the records, don't you know, there seems nothing in Scrupe's character to indicate his bent for a life of crime.'

'Murder isn't a crime,' said Mr Semple, scowling. Marion Pearson was meeting Mr Conway for lunch in the only respectable hostelry the town boasted and was going to play golf with him afterwards. It was Mr Conway's afternoon off, and Mr Conway had taken pains to acquaint the Common Room of his plans.

He kicked the edge of the turf angrily, but Mr Reeder, launched unexpectedly upon his favourite topic, disregarded his companion's state of mind, although this was obvious.

'Interesting that you should say that,' he said, bending to light his pipe which he then took out of his mouth in order to stab into the air the substance and import of his remarks. 'I find that people vary enormously in their approach to murder. Of course, the known motives for it are few, and I must say that I don't find myself in agreement with those who incline to believe that one murder begets another.'

'Don't you?' said Mr Semple, who was in so evil and unusual a frame of mind that he would cheerfully have added Mr Reeder's murder to that of Fate's darling, Mr Conway, could that have been achieved by wishful thinking.

Mr Reeder, unaware that his doom would have been sealed but for Mr Semple's upbringing and inhibitions, babbled cheerily on, and again, unwisely, introduced the subject of Scrupe and the stolen cockerel. At this, Mr Semple snorted with rage and left him, and Mr Reeder had to wait until nearly nine o'clock at night before he obtained the information he required.

'I say, what do you think of Scrupe and the cockerel?' he demanded of Mr Conway, who was proud of his own participation in the riot outside the School gateway.

'Scrupe is a most infernal boy,' interpolated Mr Loveday, 'and I cannot think it was wise to interfere to the extent of indulging in fisticuffs – as I understand a junior member of the staff did – in defence of the lad.'

Mr Conway laughed and made a show of lazily stretching his arms.

'Oh, I don't know,' he remarked, without letting his eyes rest on Mr Loveday. 'Some of us, perhaps, have the courage of our disillusionment. I loathe Scrupe – always have! – but I dislike to see an unequal fight – always have! So, of course, one joined in – from the purest of motives, Loveday, of course – rescue of the perishing and all that. One hopes that one made oneself – '

'Damned conspicuous,' said Mr Semple, neatly.

'What did the Headmaster say?' enquired Mr Tuttle, another of the junior masters and Mr Conway's chief toady rather than crony. Mr Conway threw back his head and laughed loudly.

'Commended my courage and deplored my lack of discretion,' he said. 'He has also interviewed the farmer. I have no further information.'

'It doesn't sound like Scrupe – chicken-stealing,' said Mr Reeder. 'Wonder what his idea was?'

'I think the farmer's barking up the wrong tree,' said Mr Conway who, for all his conceited ill-nature, had a fair understanding of boys. 'Having snatched the young idiot from sudden death, I questioned him. He denies all knowledge of the bird, and, whatever opinion one may hold of his mental powers, I'd say he's no liar.'

'Scrupe is a curiously clever boy,' said Scrupe's Housemaster belligerently.

'Operative word "curiously", I should imagine,' said Mr Conway with lazy scorn. He disliked all Housemasters on principle, and regarded them as a race of nincompoop partisans where their boys were concerned.

'Indeed!' said Mr Mayhew, Scrupe's particular partisan. 'Allow me to point out to you, Conway – '

'Here's the Old Man!' said Mr Reeder, in what he evidently regarded as an almost inaudible whisper. 'Oh, no! It's only Pearson. Come in, Pearson, old man!' Mr Pearson, the woodwork master, came in.

'Gentlemen,' said he, perfunctorily, and as though he did not believe what he was saying.

'Good evening, Pearson,' said Mr Loveday who, as the oldest member of the resident staff, came forward to do the honours. 'This is a very great pleasure.'

'Thank you,' said Mr Pearson, this time as though he did not believe what Mr Loveday was saying. 'I come not as guest, but as host; only, as your Common Room is considerably more spacious than my drawing-room at home, I trusted that it would not appear out of place for me to request the comfort of your domain for a small – a very small celebration.'

He moved aside, and, to the stupefaction of the entire Common Room, he was discovered to be followed by the Headmaster's butler, parlourmaid, and secretary, all bearing bottles of champagne, and by his own housekeeper, his housemaid, his kitchenmaid, and his jobbing gardener, all carrying trays of glasses.

'Th-thank you very much, Pearson. A very great pleasure, I am sure,' stammered Mr Loveday, feeling that he must be dreaming. 'To what are we indebted – that is to say – '

'It is to say,' said Mr Pearson, with a ghastly attempt at lightheartedness, 'that I desire to felicitate that dear fellow Conway there upon his engagement to Marion, my daughter. I understand that the marriage was arranged yesterday afternoon, and that it was because of his understandable joy and self-esteem that our good Conway interested himself in a dispute from which, I am given to believe, he emerged with great credit. Gentlemen,' concluded Mr Pearson, almost in tears, 'permit me to invite you all to join me in my hearty felicitations.'

Mr Semple and Mr Conway stood with their winking glasses like two men in a dream. Then their eyes met, and they suddenly drained their glasses. Neither tasted the champagne. Mr Kay put his glass down on a side table, and murmured a teetotaller's arrogant, insufferable excuses. Mr Pearson opened another couple of bottles and splashed the wine into the glasses.

'You know,' said Mr Reeder, 'I'm still not satisfied about Scrupe and the cockerel. Wasn't it *before* Conway went out that he had the fight with the farmer?'

'What on earth does that matter?' enquired Mr Sugg. 'He laid the fellow out, I'm glad to say.'

'Yes – yes, I did,' stammered Mr Conway. All eyes were turned on him. 'Any-anybody else would have done the same. Fellow had a cart-whip, you know, and while I've no doubt a damned good hiding would do Scrupe a world of good, I didn't like the look of the instrument, as the regulations so tactfully call it. So I – well, just sailed in and laid the chap out. That's all.'

'Enough, too, conceited puppy,' growled Mr Loveday to Mr Mayhew, to whom (although they were great rivals as

Housemasters) he had turned in the knowledge that Conway was a favourite with neither of them.

'Quite agree, quite,' said Mr Mayhew. 'I've no doubt that Scrupe could have taken care of himself. My boys are not accustomed to molly-coddling.'

Mr Kay muttered something under his breath and walked out.

'I say,' said Mr Reeder in a confidential undertone to Mr Sugg, 'Conway doesn't look as though he'd ever heard of his own engagement until Pearson mentioned it. Did you ever see a fellow more taken aback?'

'I expect he wanted it kept dark for a bit, you know,' said Mr Sugg. 'The governors don't like the men to marry young. They expect them to be at least on the short list for a House before they embark on the holy estate.'

'Ah, that would be it,' agreed Mr Reeder. 'Wonder what made Marion tell her father? Secretive, hard-headed little piece. Always has been, from childhood.'

Mr Semple remained just long enough in the Common Room for his going not to excite comment, and then quietly made his way out. He went straight to Kay's cottage. He knocked at the door, obtained no answer, went round to the window and tapped on that.

There was no light in the room except firelight, but the curtains had not been drawn together, and he could make out some curious object dangling on a string over the hearth. He could not make out what it was, but the glow of the fire lighted up a dripping pan into which fell something which sizzled as it dripped.

Mr Semple went round to the front door again and knocked; but there was no response. Moodily he turned away and went back to School. He did not re-enter the Common Room. He went straight to the School House and up to his room. There was Rugby football going on at the end of his corridor. Mr Semple knocked two boys' heads together and kicked the bottom of a third. Feeling slightly better after thus rationalizing his feelings for Mr Conway, he went into **his** room, filled a pipe, and, forgetting to light it, sat and sullenly brooded.

He went to bed later than usual and slept well, although he had imagined that he would lie awake all night and grind his teeth in jealous anguish over the treachery of women. It was not until two mornings later that he got up early to rouse Kay for their morning exercise.

5. 'O Weep for Adonaïs'

Where shall we find such another Set of practical Philosophers?

IBID. (*Act 2, Scene 1*)

ON the edge of Mr Kay's garden, just in front of the railings, they saw the body, this time of a man, and neither had the slightest doubt whose body it was, although it was lying on its face.

'Good Lord! It's Conway!' exclaimed Semple. 'Surely he's not . . . ?'

'Surely he's not!' reiterated Kay, going up close. 'Good heavens! He must have been lying here for hours! He's soaked right through from the rain!'

He stopped down by the body and was about to turn it over when Semple said:

'What about a doctor? Just in case there's something that could be done. Anyhow, I wouldn't touch him. If he's got any broken bones you'll do more harm than good. Perhaps we could just loosen his collar. I'll do it while you send for a doctor.'

'Right. I'm on the phone,' said Kay, immediately straightening. 'Could you go over to Mr Wyck? I think he ought to know about this. I'm sure poor Conway is dead. Don't you think we should get Mr Wyck as soon as we can?'

'Yes, I do,' replied Semple. 'And I'll have to make certain no boys are likely to come this way. When you've telephoned for a doctor, I think we ought to get the police. Conway's been attacked, I rather think. Come and look at this deep mark on his neck! It looks as though someone tried some thuggery on him. I'm going to suggest to Mr Wyck that we call the police!'

He walked quickly out of the cottage garden – for he had stepped over the fence to look at the body – and then he stepped on to the turf and began to run. Mr Kay went into the cottage and picked up the telephone receiver.

*

Mr Wyck made no attempt to disguise his incredulity at the report brought by Mr Semple.

'Conway? Dead? Killed? – or suicide? Oh, nonsense!' he said. Then he added, 'It's quite impossible.'

'I'm afraid it's happened, sir,' said Mr Semple patiently. He accompanied the Headmaster to the cottage, where Mr Wyck was able to satisfy himself that matters were as dreadful as Mr Semple had indicated.

'We must have a doctor at once,' he said.

He stood looking down at the sprawled figure of Mr Conway from a point of vantage which gave him a view of the sinister deep red line which seared the young man's thick neck, and he realized at once that no doctor could make any difference.

'Mr Kay has telephoned, sir,' said Mr Semple. 'Here he comes.' Mr Kay came out of the cottage as the Headmaster looked up. He was very pale, but he greeted Mr Wyck in his usual tones, and with the accepted formula.

'Good morning, Headmaster.'

The Headmaster lifted gloomy eyes to Kay's face. He nodded an acknowledgement of the greeting but did not reply to it. After a few moments of brooding upon Mr Conway's body, he murmured:

'Terrible, terrible! Poor fellow! I wonder what possessed him? I had no idea of this! No idea at all. He must have been in some trouble we did not know of.'

'You don't really suppose this was suicide, sir?' asked Mr Semple incredulously. 'Look at the mark on his neck! You can see it plainly, even without turning him over. And then, sir, who cut him down? And where is the rope or weapon – or anything?'

'Come further off, my dear fellow,' said Mr Wyck, 'and explain to me what you mean.'

'Well, sir,' said Mr Semple, when they were at what Mr Wyck apparently regarded as a seemly distance from the body, 'I saw a bit of dirty work during the war . . . I was a Commando, as I think you know . . . and if ever I saw a man who'd been set on, I'm afraid it's poor Conway. Besides, he was the very last type to make away with himself. He was far too conceited, although I don't want to criticize him now.'

'I don't believe you are right about that, you know,' said Mr Wyck soberly. 'He had the kind of character which I have often associated with suicides. Still, there is the other violence you mentioned. If the poor fellow has been set on and robbed, you had better keep all your information for the police. I will telephone them immediately, and then we had better all three wait until they turn up. Fortunately it is still very early. We shall not be missed for an hour or more yet. You will both keep silent upon this subject, of course, as long as you possibly can. Rumours will spread soon enough. I wonder – there was that farmer, a brutal, uncontrolled person – '

By this time Mr Kay, who had been looking anxiously up the road for the first sign of the doctor's car, had joined them, and the Headmaster turned to him, and seemed to scrutinize him closely. A flush rose beneath the yellow colouring of Mr Kay's sallow countenance, and he said, in a tone to which Mr Wyck was unaccustomed:

'There is no need to look at me like that, Headmaster! I can assure you that, although the circumstances look particularly black against me, I had no hand whatever in this deed!'

'I beg your pardon, Kay,' replied Mr Wyck equably to this outburst, although his eyebrows had risen and he looked grim. 'And I think perhaps you should ask mine. I had no thought in my head about the blackness of the circumstances except in so far as they affect poor Conway himself. I take it that you are concerned to find him like this within the bounds of your garden?'

'I most certainly am!' replied Mr Kay, with the same explosive energy as that to which the Headmaster had already objected. 'And I'm concerned to think of the attitude the police will adopt towards this business! I am bound to be involved, and I dislike the thought very much.'

'Well, you had better take another short stroll along the road, and see whether anyone is coming,' said Mr Wyck, perceiving that Mr Kay was really overwrought, and that there was nothing to be gained at the moment from discussing the tragedy with him.

Mr Kay, without another word, stepped over the low fence which separated his cottage garden from the School drive, and walked out through the gates.

'Unstable, unstable,' muttered Mr Wyck, who was feeling overwrought, too, as his active brain began to realize the magnitude of the disaster which had fallen like a blight upon the School. 'Now what can he know about it, Semple? No, don't answer, my boy! That is a most improper question for me to ask. And keep an open mind, my dear fellow, and a still tongue. And remember that farmer.'

'Of course, sir,' said Mr Semple, who, as an Old Boy, had never learned to call Mr Wyck by the title in use by the rest of the staff.

At this moment there was the sound of a car, and the doctor arrived from the village. He was the School doctor, and knew Mr Wyck well. He was shown the body and he knelt on the wet earth beside it. His examination was brief.

'Bad show,' he said, standing up and looking down at the sticky mould on the knees of his trousers. 'Better not brush that off until it dries. Yes, he's dead, I'm afraid. All his own work, do you suppose? . . . Don't answer that. It couldn't be. No weapon. And, unless I'm a half-wit, the fellow's been drowned. Post-mortem will settle that, though. Don't touch, him. Have you sent for the police? . . . Don't answer that either. Sorry for you! Damned sorry! Somebody didn't like him very much!'

His hearers were much too honest to challenge this last statement.

*

'No sign of the rope, either? Well, I think I'd like a word with the owner of the cottage,' said the local Superintendent of police, when the official photography was over, and permission had been given for the body to be removed to the mortuary. 'There will be an inquest, of course, but meanwhile . . . Mr Kay, isn't it, sir?'

The yellow-faced Mr Kay came forward at once.

'But I don't know anything about it, you know,' he said. 'The full extent of my knowledge is the same as your own and that of Mr Semple, who was on the spot, actually, a little sooner than I was myself.'

'I see, sir. So Mr Semple, then, was the person who may be said to have discovered the body. Perhaps, Mr Semple, you would just let me have the details.'

'Oh, Lord!' thought Mr Semple. 'I wish I'd never let myself in for this! Might have known there was something fishy about a Dago! The little tick means to rat. Oh, well, here goes!'

He accompanied the Superintendent into the cottage and there gave an account of himself and of the discovery of the body. It had been seen, he averred, by himself and Mr Kay at approximately the same instant.

'Mr Kay, then, was left here while you went up to the School to inform the Headmaster, Mr Semple?' said the Superintendent. 'How long, sir, do you think you were gone?'

'I couldn't tell you to within a minute or so, but I should think I was gone about ten to twelve minutes. I ran to the School House, but walked back with Mr Wyck.'

'And when you returned the body was, of course, sir, in the same position as when you left it?'

'Oh, Lord, yes, so far as I'm aware. You don't suppose Kay turned it over and faked the evidence, do you?'

'I don't suppose anything yet, sir,' replied the Superintendent in tones of reproof. 'I believe it was Mr Kay who sent for the doctor?'

'Yes, it was, but we agreed upon it, of course. It was just that it was his telephone.'

'Then if you will kindly step outside, sir, I had better speak to him in here.'

Mr Wyck had already returned to the School House, leaving word with the police that he would be grateful for a word with the Superintendent when he had finished with Mr Semple and Mr Kay.

Mr Semple, who had retrieved his spikes, ran after the Headmaster and caught him up at the entrance to the School House garden.

'I need not repeat my request to you to keep all this to yourself for the present, Semple,' said Mr Wyck.

'Of course, sir.'

'What puzzles me,' continued the Headmaster, as they went into the House by the side door from which they had left it, 'is what on earth poor Conway could have been doing at Kay's cottage. I thought they avoided one another as a usual thing.'

'The doctor didn't say anything in our presence as to the time it all took place, sir, did you notice?'

'I had not realized that. But, yes, the time of death would make a difference, no doubt, although I cannot see, at this stage, quite what difference. The whole business is black; very black. I am completely puzzled. One would have supposed that if a miscreant had attacked poor Conway, Kay would have heard some sound of it. And in any case, what was Conway *doing* there? That is the immediate problem.'

'The last I saw of Conway yesterday was at just after eleven,' volunteered Mr Semple. 'I was in the Common Room talking to Saville and Manley when Conway came in. He saw us, and went straight out again. I knew the time, more or less, because Manley suddenly looked at his watch and said that it was past eleven and he would be locked out if he did not go. As soon as he went, Saville and I went to our rooms, and I went to bed. I should think I was in bed by about a quarter to twelve.'

'But why on earth should Conway have gone out to the cottage so late at night?' asked Mr Wyck, perplexed. 'He didn't even *like* Kay, did he?'

It was after this that the rumours flew round the School, and the voice of surmise and suspicion was heard in the land.

'I say!' said one pop-eyed Lower Boy to another. 'There's been a murder! Somebody has cut Mr Conway's throat, and there's pools of blood all over Mr Wyck's garden.'

'I say,' said Meyrick to Eaves. 'You don't think – you didn't think – I mean, you don't suppose Merrys and Skene murdered Mr Conway, do you, while they were A.W.O.L. again?'

'Good Lord, no,' said Eaves, horrified. 'And don't you start saying things like that. In fact – look here – ' They went into a guilty huddle, and did not hear the bell for the next lesson.

His Housemaster sent for Scrupe.

'Er, Scrupe,' said Mr Mayhew. 'That is – Mr Reeder tells me – I feel it cannot possibly have any bearing, but – '

'You mean the statistics for murder in this county, sir?' said Scrupe helpfully. 'No, sir. Not an inkling. Just ornery curiosity, sir, I assure you.'

'Just – ?' said Mr Mayhew.

'Ornery – a low-grade American adjective indicative of something repellent or undesirable, governing the word curiosity, noun, abstract, neuter gender, deriving from – I'm afraid I don't know any Latin, sir, but in Spanish it would be *curiosidad*, and therefore I deduce that it would have a Latin root, but, of course, as I don't take Latin any more, I am probably wrong, sir. I say, sir,' he added, in his natural tones, 'I'm awfully *sorry* about Mr Conway. You know, he rescued me from that beastly farmer.'

'Oh, not at all, Scrupe. Thank you, thank you,' said Mr

Mayhew hurriedly. 'I just sent to ask you – to make quite certain – '

'Of course, sir, I may be psychic,' suggested Scrupe, disappearing again behind his protective façade.

'Oh, I hardly think so. I hardly think so,' said Mr Mayhew, even more hurriedly than before. 'But you're sure you don't – didn't – that is, of course not! Of course not! Thank you, Scrupe. You will not, of course, repeat this conversation.'

'Just as you say, sir,' said Scrupe. He went straight to the two boys who shared his study and informed them that Mayhew obviously had a guilty conscience.

'I say, Tar-Baby,' said Everson of the School House to the most picturesque member of Mr Loveday's, 'I suppose your natural instincts didn't get the better of you during last night?'

'Yes, please, Everson?' said Prince Takhobali, the goodtempered but temperamental scion of a West African royal house. He had been called Tar-Baby, needless to say, since the first mention of his name coupled with the sight of his dark face. He had been ragged very little since his introduction into Mr Loveday's House, for he accepted everything English with the same unconquerable, gleaming, ritual, fatalistic smile, and was apt to indicate his opinion of his questioners with a different sort of relish.

'Mr Conway's been murdered,' explained Everson, 'so, of course, we thought it might be you.'

'I heard that Mr Conway was drowned,' agreed the Tar-Baby. 'It is great luck for some persons.'

'You're telling *me!*' said Everson, with vigour. 'Although of course he wasn't drowned. He's been knifed. And I should say it *is* luck for some persons. Were you one of them?'

'I? Oh, no. I do not need to be lucky. I am good,' said the Tar-Baby simply, his smile widening. He caught Everson's flying foot and landed him flat on his back. 'You should not kick good men. And he *was* drowned.'

'Dash it!' said Everson, rubbing the back of his head. 'He *wasn't* drowned, you ass! He was murdered.'

'Drowned *and* murdered, yes,' agreed the Tar-Baby. 'Drowned *and* murdered, Mr Everson.'

'How do you know? Did Issy tell you?'

'Nobody told me. I found out for myself. Mr Conway was choked round his neck, and then he was put in the water.'

'What water, image?'

'Mr Loveday's bath,' replied the Tar-Baby.

*

'I say,' said Merrys to Skene, 'what are we going to do?'

'Do?' said Skene. 'Be your age. What the hell *can* we do?' He was paler even than usual, and looked dogged. His doughy face was puffy.

'We could say we knew Mr Kay was at that house that night, and was threatening to do someone in.'

'What good would that do? Yes, and where would it land us? Hang it, Conway wasn't murdered at that house! Besides, we don't know anything about the *time!*'

'I know. But he was found in Spivvy's garden, and we heard what was said about somebody hanging for somebody.'

'Somebody said Mr Wyck's garden, but it wasn't. As a matter of fact, I heard he'd been drowned in the Roman Bath. He wasn't found in Spivvy's garden at all. So you see that lets Spivvy out.'

'Good Lord, of course it doesn't! If Spivvy did it, the last place he'd choose would be his own garden. Don't be a fool.'

'Well, why does everybody say it *was* Spivvy's garden, then?'

'Because of the blood. I wish we hadn't mentioned murder to Meyrick and Eaves, all the same, though. They'll think we *know* something. And, after all, we don't, really. We can't be *sure* that it was the Spiv who said anything, and, anyhow, it was days ago!'

'I don't like it much, though,' said Merrys. 'Say what you

like, Spivvy was there when hanging was being talked about,
and it was Spivvy's garden where the blood was found –
though chaps still say it was the body. I asked Stallard what
would happen next, and he said he supposed the police
would have to be brought here.'

'They've been here already. Issy saw them. He sees everything. They'll trace our footprints and the marks of Albert-
Edward's bike, I suppose,' said Skene gloomily. 'And there's
your beastly fountain pen. If anybody finds *that* – '

'Well, I *did* say I wanted to find it. It was you that – '

'Well, never mind that. It's a beastly nuisance, anyway.'

'Yes, I know. Perhaps I didn't lose it in that garden, after
all, though.'

'That wouldn't matter particularly. Wherever it's found,
we're sunk. The police are like bloodhounds. They never
let go when they've got their teeth in you.'

'That's bulldogs, you fool. Anyway, let's wait till the pen
is found. Better still, let's find it ourselves before the police
do. Hang it, we've got the start of them. And, whatever you
do, don't you go blabbing your head off. It won't do any
good, and it'll mean we'll be sacked for certain. And my
father's ill. I don't want to go home and say I'm sacked. It'd
be perfectly beastly. Swear you'll keep your mouth shut.'

'That's all very well, and of course I shall. But, hang it all,
it was *your* idea. I say, that cottage was a bit weird, you know.
I heard that a witch lives there, and those women who
opened the door were sort of *queer*. Honestly, what do you
think we ought to do?'

'Nothing!' said Merrys, too much afraid now to take the
risks he had previously advocated. 'It was ages ago, anyway.
It couldn't have anything to do with Conway, could it? Do
you know what I think? I think that farmer's got something
to do with it.'

'What farmer?'

'Why, the one that swore Scrupe had taken one of his
cockerels and killed it.'

'Why him? He wouldn't know Conway.'

'Well, Conway sailed into him all right when he went for Scrupe with his cart-whip.'

'I expect he's had his revenge, then.'

'The police will soon find that out. They'll trace his footprints.'

'Do you think footprints would be clear enough, with chaps barging in and out from the gate and all that?'

'There might be blood on his boots.'

'I say, shut up! Look here, let's keep quiet about the cottage. We don't want to get mixed up in things. Murder or no murder, we'd still be sacked if it came out where we'd been. And I don't see why we should tell. It's nothing to do with us, really.'

'As long as Spivvy didn't recognize us we're all right; but the thing is, did he?'

'If only you hadn't been chump enough to wear your school cap and drop your beastly fountain pen!'

'Well, I couldn't help it, you ass!'

'You can be had up for being an accessory, you know,' pursued Skene. 'You can get seven years, I believe.'

'We'll have to chance that. What strikes *me* is that if we go about blabbing we may find ourselves in Queer Street. A bloke who would murder Conway wouldn't be inclined to stick at *us*.'

'But you don't honestly think Spivvy did it? Hang it, he wouldn't stand a chance against Conway.'

'Not if Conway knew, but Issy says that Conway didn't know. He was set on and – and finished off, before he knew what was happening. Look here, I'll tell you what! If Spivvy is arrested, we shall know it's all right. But if anybody else is arrested – one of the beaks, I mean – we shall have to tell.'

'You said just now – I thought we agreed – '

'That can't be helped. If somebody got hanged and we hadn't said anything, we'd be murderers ourselves.'

'I wouldn't mind being a murderer. Look at Landru.'

'Well, we'd be just the same as the cads, then. *They* never stick their necks out.'

'Why should *we?*'

'Oh, be your age!' said Merrys irritably, already again beginning to regret his unusual lapse into chivalry. 'We've jolly well got to, that's all. Besides' – his face brightened – 'don't you see? Spivvy won't split on us.'

'No, but what about him murdering us?'

'We can't keep on going over that. Are we going to say anything or aren't we?'

'Let's see what happens,' said Skene. Rumours and counter-rumours continued to infest the School. They were not resolved into truth and falsehood until after the report of the inquest, but this was not yet. Mr Kay began to shun his fellow men, and, after dark, he crept down to Mrs Harries's cottage again.

6. *Policemen's Feet on Ida*

*

Murder is as fashionable a Crime as a Man can be guilty of.

IBID. (*Act 1, Scene 4*)

'WELL,' said Mr Preedy, the School bursar, 'the police will be here again this afternoon.' He was addressing Mr Reeder and Mr Semple, who had waylaid him on the way out from lunch.

'It was odd about that boy Scrupe,' said Mr Loveday, who had overheard the remark.

'I don't see that at all,' said Mr Mayhew, who was with him; and he launched into a lengthy defence of Scrupe which no one heeded.

'I hope that the police will soon turn their attention from the scene of the crime to the home of its perpetrator,' said the Bursar. 'Not enough is being done by them, in my opinion. Not that I – or, I imagine, any of us – can give them any further information. I'm afraid the whole thing is going to be muddy, *very* muddy. So bad for the School. And I do not see what Mr Wyck is going to say to the boys, yet something must be said to them. That is clear. We can't have them spreading unhealthy rumours. Why, one boy even thought the body had been found in the Headmaster's garden instead of in that of Mr Kay!'

'The whole thing is a damned nuisance,' said Cranleigh, captain of football, to his cronies Keithstone and Murray. 'Just on the eve of the Helston match, of all senseless times to choose for a first-class stink! I suppose the old man will make me scratch, as Conway took some of the games.'

This, however, was the last thought in Mr Wyck's worried mind. Much better, he thought, particularly as it was an away match, to let the School go over to Helston and enjoy themselves. The motor coaches had already been ordered, and the best thing the School could do was to pile into them, get away from a morbid atmosphere for a bit, and shout their heads off on the Helston playing-fields.

'I say, I suppose it's all *right* to have Spey here?' said one infant Helstonian to another. 'As long as they stick to murdering their beaks one doesn't mind much, but supposing they start in on us?'

'You won't be missed,' said his comrade.

*

'We should wish, sir,' said Superintendent Beadle of the county police, 'to leave your boys out of it for the present, and concentrate upon what your gentlemen can tell us.'

'Leave the boys out for the *present?*' said Mr Wyck. 'Oh, but surely, Superintendent, you can dismiss the boys *and* my staff from your enquiry! We have told you all we know, and I am absolutely certain – '

'Quite so, sir,' said the Superintendent, in the comforting tones which the Headmaster already knew so well and was to grow to dislike so much. '*Quite* so. Only, you see, since that affair at – '

'Oh, but that was a Home Office school,' said the Head-master hastily. 'One can scarcely compare those young hooligans with a school of this type, surely!'

'Boys will be boys, sir. Young savages, most of 'em are. That's our experience, anyway. Get carried away. Panicky. Do anything in the heat of the moment, however much they might come to regret it later on. But at the moment I would like to have another word with your Mr Kay, sir, thanking you, and with your permission.'

Mr Kay, looking hot and bothered in spite of the wintry chill of a bitter November afternoon, faced the Superintendent across the Headmaster's sitting-room carpet.

'Sit down, sir, please,' said the Superintendent kindly. 'Now you say you heard nothing at all after the postman passed your window at about a quarter past nine?'

'Nothing at all, Superintendent.' Mr Kay was emphatic.

'Very well, sir. But it may interest you to know that the postman did not call at the School last night.'

'But I heard the sound of his bicycle wheels on the drive. He went past the windows of my cottage. Yes, and the same thing happened some days ago. I remember it quite distinctly.'

'You may have heard the sound of bicycle wheels, sir, but not those of the postman's bicycle. We have made very careful enquiries, and the postman did not come nearer the School than the Vicarage, a mile and a half away.'

'But I'm *certain* I heard the wheels,' Mr Kay protested. 'Who else could it be but the postman?'

'One of the boys doing a mike?' suggested the Superintendent. 'I suppose they break out sometimes and go on the spree?'

'I shouldn't think so,' said Mr Kay, betraying to the trained eye of the Superintendent distinct traces of nervousness, however. 'Besides, the boys are not allowed to keep bicycles at School.'

'Perhaps one of the servants, then?' suggested the Superintendent.

'I couldn't say. You had better ask the Headmaster.' Mr Kay sounded decidedly flustered now. He had taken a charm off his watch-chain and was twisting it between his thumb and finger.

'I shall do that, sir. Now, your story as to finding the body. You say this was at half-past seven this morning, just as it was beginning to get light. You also say that Mr Semple was with you, and that he may have seen the body before you did.'

'That is so. I was going out for my usual morning exercise. But I've told you all this before.'

'Just so, sir. But a relevant fact might emerge.'

'I don't see how it can,' said Mr Kay, peevishly. 'I've told you every single solitary thing I know. Semple came to call me up – I'd overslept for some reason – '

'For what reason, should you suppose, sir?'

Kay looked baffled and furious.

'How on earth should I know for what reason? My wife not being there to wake me, I suppose,' he answered. 'Anyway, Mr Semple went over to inform Mr Wyck, and that is all I know, except that I first rang up the doctor.'

'You did not touch the body, sir?'

'I told you, last time, that I did not. We all read detective stories nowadays, and naturally I know better than to touch anything. Semple loosened the collar and disclosed the marks on the neck, and there was no sign of the rope with which, presumably, the job was done. Neither have you found that rope in my possession. There really isn't anything else I can do for you.'

'I wonder whether we might have one more look over your cottage, sir, after I have interviewed the other gentlemen?'

'Of course, if you think it's any good.'

'Thank you, sir. Sergeant, get Mr Loveday. You'll be over here at the School for some hours, I take it, sir?'

'For my sins, no doubt I shall,' said Mr Kay.

'Until about six o'clock, sir, may we take it?'

'Oh, yes, until about six this evening. I shan't return to my cottage and destroy all the evidence of my guilt before you get there again,' said Mr Kay irritably. 'Rope doesn't burn very easily.'

The Superintendent smiled indulgently and welcomed Mr Loveday, who nodded briefly to Mr Kay as they passed one another in the doorway.

Mr Loveday had news and views. The latter were ignored, although tactfully, by the Superintendent. The former received consideration.

'Your bicycle, you say, sir? What makes you think it had been tampered with?'

'As soon as I heard of the crime, I set to work to search my premises.'

'Exactly with what object, may I ask, sir?'

'With no particular object. Simply as a precautionary measure.'

'What precautions did you need to take, sir?'

'Come, come, Superintendent. I merely wanted to make certain, I suppose, that my House could present a clean slate.'

'Had you any reason to suppose it would not have been able to do so, sir?'

'No, no, of course not! But there it is. One's natural anxieties as a schoolmaster are not easily grasped by the public.'

'I see, sir. You searched your premises and discovered that someone had tampered with your bicycle. I need hardly remind you, sir, that this piece of evidence may be of the utmost importance. Mr Kay heard a bicycle going past his cottage at a time when no bicycle, so far as we can find out, had any reason to be doing so. What led you to suppose that your machine had been used, sir?'

'Well,' said Mr Loveday judicially, 'I *think* – perhaps I had better confine myself to that verb – I *think* that my tyres were in perfect order when last I used the bicycle, but there is no doubt that the back tyre has now sustained a severe puncture. My knife-and-boot boy – an expert in his way – has diagnosed the rent in the outer cover as having been caused by a large nail.'

'Indeed, sir? May I ask how long it is since you yourself used the machine?'

'Oh, I could hardly say. In 1945, perhaps.'

The Superintendent shook his head.

'Unless you've more evidence than that to offer me, sir, I'm afraid I could scarcely regard it as certain that your bicycle had been used.'

'I applaud your caution, Superintendent. My additional evidence is that my knife-and-boot boy swears that the machine was not where he left it; also, I myself can declare to having seen three sets of tyre marks on the dust of the floor in the shed where the bicycle is stored, proving that it had, at any rate, been moved.'

'Interesting, sir, and I don't say not valuable. But perhaps

I could speak to the servant in question later on, and also have a look at the machine.'

'Of course,' said Mr Loveday. 'Still, one cannot quite believe that the miscreant who killed poor Conway would have required to cycle to the School gate and back. It is not a very great distance.'

The Superintendent agreed, and recalled Mr Kay.

'Look here,' Mr Kay began angrily.

'There is just one point, sir,' said the Superintendent smoothly. 'It seems you heard this bicycle going past your windows at, roughly, nine-fifteen. Now, sir, when did you hear that bicycle coming back?'

'Not at all. Besides, you are assuming that it was going *away* from School when I heard it. I simply heard it pass, that's all. For all I know, it might have been going *towards* the School.'

'I take it that you remained in your cottage from then on, sir?'

'Certainly,' said Mr Kay, showing no hesitation and looking the Superintendent firmly in the eye.

'You are quite sure, sir?'

'Of course I'm sure! What do you take me for? – a cat on the tiles?'

The Superintendent, who, so far, had left all note-taking to the sergeant, now discomfited the witness by taking out his own notebook from some secret pocket and recording this answer in longhand.

'I should wish you to read that over, sir,' he said impressively, 'and sign it, if you will be so good.' He offered the notebook to the Schoolmaster. Mr Kay made no attempt to take it.

'I shan't sign anything whatsoever,' he said flatly, 'except in the presence of a solicitor. You can't make me do so, and I protest at being asked.'

'Very good, sir. Perhaps you would just give me your opinion, then, by word of mouth, that I have written down your words as you would wish them to be used in evidence.'

'If you are charging me, you had better do so in a proper manner,' said Mr Kay.

'Come, come, sir,' said the Superintendent briskly. 'I'm sorry to have offended you. I can take it as definite, then, that you heard the sound of a bicycle at about nine-fifteen, but nothing later, and that you did not leave your cottage until half-past seven in the morning?'

'Exactly right,' said Mr Kay, very shortly.

'In that case, sir,' said the Superintendent smoothly, 'was old Mrs Harries mistaken in thinking that you visited her cottage last night between the hours of ten o'clock and one?'

'Yes,' said Mr Kay. 'I don't know any Mrs Harries. She sounds to me like a criminal lunatic. Did she give you my name?'

'No, sir. But the description fits, and we do happen to know you weren't at home at half-past ten last night because one of the other gentlemen came to borrow a book from you, and another of the gentlemen accompanied him.'

'I must have been asleep when they knocked,' said Mr Kay, suddenly wiping his face, a sign of agitation which impressed the Superintendent deeply.

'Very good, sir,' he said woodenly. Mr Kay wiped his forehead again when the Superintendent had gone. He did not go far, however. He went to interview Jack the Ripper, alias William Dobbs.

'Ah. Bin rode, that there boike had. Put moi 'and on she and I knows,' said Dobbs, without hesitation. 'Ride her moiself I 'ave, see?'

The kinaesthetic sense was no new thing to the Superintendent. He believed in it. It was not concrete evidence, to be sure, but he did not need to have read John Drinkwater's *Little Johnny* to feel certain that touch can be, at times and with certain persons, one of the least deceptive of the senses. He understood that Dobbs had 'borrowed' the bicycle and ridden it on more than one occasion.

'O.K., Dobbs,' he said briskly. 'I believe you.'

'So well you moight,' said the redoubtable William, 'bein'
as 'ow I knows.'

'Well, now for the bicycle shed,' said the Superintendent.
But the shed yielded nothing in the way of concrete evidence.
There was no doubt that the bicycle had been moved. For
one thing, Mr Loveday and Dobbs had both moved it
during their amateur investigation of the crime. Whether it
had been moved on the night of Mr Conway's death was, in
the opinion of the Superintendent, incapable of direct proof.
He put away his notebook and went back to Mr Kay's cottage.

Mr Kay's cottage still yielded no surprises, and was in no
way remarkable, except that it was on the telephone. It did
appear, however, that Mrs Kay occupied a bedroom on the
first floor, whereas Mr Kay had a bed in his study on the
ground floor. The Superintendent, naturally, made no refer-
ance to this domestic arrangement, but he tabulated it
mentally all the same.

'And now, sir,' he said to the fermenting Mr Kay whom
once again he had recalled for questioning, 'I must ask you
one thing which, don't misunderstand me, I shall be putting
to every one of the scholastic gentlemen in turn, including, I
may say, the Headmaster himself. What were your relations
with the deceased?'

'With the – oh, I don't know.' Mr Kay looked suddenly
troubled, but he did not hesitate. 'Not altogether happy, I'm
afraid. He had a sharp tongue, and I'm by way of being a
bit of a black sheep here, of course.'

'Black sheep, sir?'

'Not an Oxford or Cambridge man,' Mr Kay explained.
'Not one of the ones. Educated in, as a matter of fact, first, a
primary school in Manchester until I was eleven, then in
Brazil, and then at a provincial university in the Midlands.
And then I always think people see straight through me to a
Eurasian grandmother.' He caught the Superintendent's
look of surprise, and added, 'Oh, yes, that's my heritage. I
call it Portuguese, and I had a Portuguese mother and an
English father, but, all the same . . .'

'And very nice, too, I'm sure, sir,' said the Superintendent awkwardly.

'You needn't tell anyone else,' said Kay at once, lifting his chin.

'Certainly not, sir, if it's against your wishes. It could have no possible bearing, so far as I can see, on the enquiry.'

'Don't you be too sure,' said Kay bitterly. 'The inferiority complex is responsible for making more criminals than ever came up to the Old Bailey. And now, if you don't mind, I'm due in class.'

'I say,' said Norris, of the Science Side, in an audible aside to Scrupe, 'Spivvy looks a bit green about the gills. I bet he's Suspect Number One.'

'That would surprise me very much,' replied Scrupe in an even louder tone. 'I don't think he has the guts to commit a serious crime.'

'Murder isn't a crime,' said Biggs, whose father was a well-known barrister. 'The only crime is being found out.'

Mr Kay did not even lift his head from the essays he was correcting. Lewis, another member of the form, raised his hand and dexterously flipped a note on to Scrupe's open exercise book.

'His missus has left him for good,' Lewis had written. 'I bet it's only a matter of days before he's arrested.'

Scrupe scribbled on the bottom of this note:

'Then his missus is a heel. Fancy deserting a man at the foot of the gallows!'

He flipped this back so clumsily that it fell on the floor. Lewis bent to pick it up. Mr Kay lifted his head.

'Bring it here, Lewis, please.'

Lewis, as in honour bound, took out a piece of paper not completely innocuous in that it bore a reasonably recognizable cartoon of the Headmaster, and laid it on the desk. Mr Kay glanced at it, and then said quietly:

'I am afraid, then, Scrupe, that I must trouble you for a verbatim report of what Lewis wrote to you and what you replied to Lewis.'

'I can't quite remember, sir,' said Scrupe. 'But, roughly speaking, it was an estimate of your chances with the police. I should not have thought of telling you this in cold blood, sir, but since you ask me – '

'I see,' said Mr Kay. He corrected a couple more lines of an essay on economics. 'I am afraid, Scrupe, that I must trouble you to see the Headmaster.'

'Be not afraid with any amazement,' said Scrupe, 'and I regret this as much as you do.' He rose, and went quietly out.

The news that Scrupe had been flogged for telling the Headmaster that Mr Kay ought to be hanged had spread round the School before nightfall.

'Did you really, Scrupe?' asked an admiring member of his House. 'And did the Old Man really tan you?'

'My dear fellow,' said Scrupe loftily – for the news had enhanced his prestige – 'the major prophets have always been subject to ill-usage, calumny, and lies. In this case, I was subjected to a certain amount of ill-usage, and am on view Tuesdays and Thursdays, on presentation of a visiting card. However, Mr Wyck and I parted on cordial terms, as gentlemen of honour, whatever their passing differences, always may, and I still steadfastly maintain – '

'But did you *really* say Kay ought to be hanged?'

'Certainly not. I indicated to the Headmaster that I was not prepared to say what I thought. And what I think is your guess, and your guess is as good as another's. And now I have a letter of apology to write, and could contrive to word it better without so much babbling.'

'But what do you *really* think, Scrupe? Do you *really* think Kay's got it in him?'

'I think the Headmaster is a sensible and discreet man, my dear fellow, but that, in my time, I shall make a firmer Headmaster than he does. I shall hit harder, for one thing.'

'You *are* an ass,' said his interlocutor, in even more admiring tones than before. Scrupe shrugged, and settled to his task.

'Dear Mr Kay,' he wrote, 'I regret that any ill-considered words of mine should have added to the harassing nature of your thoughts. Yours sincerely, P. W. Scrupe.'

The Headmaster did not pass it on. Neither did he send for Scrupe again. It is not only in the East that madmen are feared and respected.

*

Mr Kay's troubles were not only caused by impudent and unkind boys, the Superintendent's patient, polite but incessant thirst for information, and the somewhat odd glances he received from his fellow masters.

During the evening of the day succeeding the death of Mr Conway he telegraphed to his wife to suggest that she should return home at once.

She had not left him; that was merely a romantic interpretation put upon her absence by some of the boys. Their relationship, although not a happy one, had not been so far strained that Mrs Kay was inclined to neglect her duty.

She was a cheaply-smart, ignorantly-sophisticated woman of twenty-nine, good-looking, selfish, as extravagant as Mr Kay's not unlimited means would allow, but generous enough to return at once when she heard that her husband was in trouble.

When she heard the particular nature of the trouble, she was, not unnaturally, horrified. What upset Mr Kay, however, was her doubt, somewhat baldly expressed, as to his innocence.

'You did hate the poor perisher,' she said. 'Couldn't you make it accidental death in a fight?'

'But I *didn't do it, Brenda!*' yelled her exasperated husband. 'Get that into your head, for goodness' sake! If I'd felt as bad about the fellow as all that, I'd have got another job! Good heavens, one doesn't go about *murdering* people! Whatever next!'

'Oh, well, sorry I spoke,' replied his wife, tossing her head. 'But if you didn't do it, and if Johnny Semple was with you when you found him, what have you got wind-up about?'

'Look here, Brenda,' said Mr Kay, dropping his voice, 'you've got to stick to me over this. The trouble is . . .'

'Well?'

'The trouble *is*,' said Mr Kay unhappily, 'that – oh, well, never mind.'

'Well, really!' exclaimed Mrs Kay, with justifiable fury. 'Of all the misleading, contemptible idiots. You mean you *did* do it, don't you? Why not be a man, then, and say so? *I* shan't give you away. I've too much self-respect.'

'Brenda,' said Mr Kay desperately, 'listen to me. I did not kill Conway. The trouble is, though, that I did tell someone I should.'

'Who?'

'Sanderson,' replied Mr Kay, referring to a retired Indian Civil Servant whom he sometimes visited.

'Well, what of that? He won't give you away, either. You've let off hot air to him before. He's not a bad old stick.'

'I know. It isn't Sanderson I'm afraid of. But while I was there one night two boys came to the house, and I shouldn't be a bit surprised if they overheard what I was saying. I know hanging came into it – or was that after they'd gone?'

'What two boys?'

'That's the trouble. I don't know.'

'Boys from this School, do you mean?'

'I don't even know that, for certain. It was pretty dark, and they didn't stay a minute. It was all over and done with very quickly.'

'I can't see what you've got to be afraid of. I don't suppose the boys recognized *you*, any more than you recognized *them*.'

'Don't you think so?'

'No, I don't. It's no use your getting cold feet. Apart from that, why should anyone suspect you?'

'It isn't just anyone. It's the police. I don't see why they should, but I think they do.'

'Then make a clean breast of everything. Tell them you yelled out in a temper, and may have been overheard. Get Sanderson to confirm what you say.'

'It would look pretty black if I did. It would be playing straight into that Superintendent's hands. He's found out I hated Conway . . .'

'Well, you weren't the only one.'

'No, but . . . oh, well, I'll have to wait and find out what happens, that's all there is to it.'

'You're sure it was Sanderson you went to see?'

'Why, yes, of course.'

'Pity he wasn't at home. I happen to know he's on holiday in Cornwall,' said Mrs Kay sweetly and with venom. 'If you're going to trust me, trust me. If you're not going to trust me, take your dirty lies elsewhere and get somebody else to save your filthy neck for you.'

'Brenda!' called Mr Kay after her retreating figure, as she stepped on to the School drive. 'Brenda, for God's sake . . .'

His wife stopped, paused, and then came back to him.

'Who were you with?' she said, with a calmness more threatening than her outburst of spiteful fury.

'Oh, go to hell!' said Mr Kay, also changing his tactics. He had his own reasons for not mentioning Mrs Harries.

*

'I say,' said Merrys to Skene, 'are you coming with me to find that confounded fountain pen?'

'No,' said Skene roundly. 'I'm not. If you're ass enough to have lost the thing, you can jolly well be ass enough to go and find it. You know we've all been gated except for the Helston match.'

'That's the point,' said Merrys, who was pretty sure that his friend would not finally fail him. 'I thought we might manage. The train stops at . . .'

'We're going in motor coaches, fool.'

'Oh, well . . . oh, well, I hadn't thought of that. Any chance we could sort of drop off the coach, and . . .?'

'Good Lord, no! There are to be at least a couple of beaks in charge of each coach.'

'I . . . see . . . yes . . . hm! Well, I shall have to think it out.

I *must* get that bally pen back. Can't *you* think of anything?'

'No, I can't,' said Skene crossly. 'And if I could, I jolly well wouldn't.'

'Well, hang it, I've got to find it. It simply isn't safe to leave it all over the county for Kay to pick up.'

'Well, what about telling him you've lost it? I should think he'd be as keen as anyone to get it found and returned.'

'Don't be an ass!'

'But I'm not being an ass,' said Skene, earnestly. 'Can't you see? It's what we said before! Spivvy won't want us going to the police about him, and if he doesn't want that, he's jolly well bound to help us. Then he'll know we'll keep our mouths shut.'

The criminal content of this idea shocked and disconcerted Merrys.

'But that's blackmail!' he exclaimed; and then exploded the ethical force of this observation by adding: 'And you can get about fourteen years for blackmail.'

'Suit yourself,' said Skene. 'It's your pen.'

The wretched Merrys gloomily agreed that this was so, and racked his brains to discover some method by which he could discover the whereabouts of his pen without breaking the School rules or his country's laws. He was not successful, and the pen remained undiscovered until after the Helston match.

This game was played on a Wednesday afternoon on a skating-rink of thin mud and amid tumultuous battle-cries. Spey were weak behind the scrum but had a formidable pack, and, coached to this end by Mr Semple when he perceived how the weather was going to turn out, they kept the ball at their feet and gave the Helston three-quarters little chance. If a Helston man did pick up the ball he was ruthlessly tackled or rudely thrown into touch. The only try of the match was scored by Murray, of the School House, the left-wing three-quarter of the Spey fifteen, who picked up an awkward pass from Keithstone and fell over the line almost on the corner flag.

Spey failed with the kick, but, putting out every effort, they kept Helston from their line. Cartaris, to his own satisfaction, played a sound and safe game at full-back, and the School returned in the dusk to taste the pleasures of victory. Cartaris, in fact, was in such mellow mood – besides being tired – that Merrys felt emboldened to put to the test a last desperate plan for the recovery of his pen.

'I say, Cartaris,' he said, when the House was lining up for evening Chapel, 'do you think the Old Man would give us a Saturday half in spite of the gating? If *you* asked him, I think . . .'

'Think again,' said Cartaris. 'Think of your skin, and hop it while you've still got a whole one, you cheeky little beast!'

'Er . . . yes. Thanks, Cartaris,' said Merrys. 'Sidey brute!' he added vengefully afterwards to Skene; for hero-worship is not as potent as it was. 'Anybody would think it was *him* that scored the try.'

'He,' said Skene, with the automatic grammatical accuracy of a Scotsman.

'Funny ass!' said Merrys, bitterly. '*How am I going to find my bally pen?*'

This question exercised his mind day and night, to the obstruction of learning and the confounding of sleep.

'Merrys is sickening for something,' said Miss Loveday to her brother. 'Have you noted him?'

Mr Loveday noted nothing that had not been noted previously by somebody else, unless his Roman Bath was in question.

'No,' he replied. 'I think I shall have to reconsider a thought I had. I had made up my mind to let boys who had been detained by Conway have a turn later on in the Bath. But now that the poor fellow is dead, it seems like speaking ill of him to do so. What do you think?'

'If you had made up your mind to do it before the death, I don't see that the death makes any difference,' replied Miss Loveday. 'But the Roman Bath must come second to Merrys's health.'

This was obviously a new idea to Mr Loveday. He considered it with scholarly detachment, and committed himself to its justness.

'Yes, yes, I suppose so,' he said. 'Well, then, I think perhaps I will grant Cartaris an extra turn. He played well against Helston, and upheld the credit of the House.'

'Isn't that treating him as if he were a *little* boy?' enquired Miss Loveday.

'Doubtless,' her brother agreed. 'Very well. I will not mention it . . . although . . .'

'But *I* shall,' said Miss Loveday at once. 'I shall request him to test the temperature by going in. I shall say that I do not trust the furnace man to keep the water at seventy degrees. This will ensure that he is rewarded in a manner consistent with his dignity.'

Mr Loveday reflected, without bitterness, that his sister was the better Housemaster. This thought brought with it, however, the sound of a hateful voice. Was the House governed by two elderly women, himself and his sister? He put the point at dinner.

'Would you say the House is governed by two elderly women?' he enquired.

'Shades of Gerald Conway!' exclaimed Miss Loveday. 'What else did the wretched youth say?'

Mr Loveday, who had not even known that Mr Conway's Christian name was Gerald, made no reply for a moment. Then he said:

'Did it ever occur to you, Annette, that John Semple might have been crossed in love?'

Miss Loveday stared in amazement at this suggestion, which at first appeared to her fantastic in the extreme, but soon she collected herself sufficiently to retort:

'Not, at any rate, by me! But there is something in what you say. I believe Gerald Conway had cut him out with Marion Pearson. But you don't suppose that modern youths kill their rivals in love? What surprises me is George Pearson's attitude.'

They stared at one another, fascinated by the thought which had come into both their minds.

'Nonsense!' said Mr Loveday loudly. 'Nonsense! Nonsense! Nonsense!'

'Considering the bottles of champagne, and the public announcement, no doubt you are right,' said his sister. 'But George detested Gerald Conway, and now Gerald Conway is no more.'

7. *Dead Men Speak Dutch*

*

But, hark you, my Lad. Don't tell me a Lye; for you know I hate a Liar.

IBID. (*Act 1, Scene 6*)

THE inquest on Mr Conway was held on the Saturday morning in the village schoolroom. The police had asked for an adjournment following the identification of the body and when the medical evidence was concluded. The latter turned out to be interesting and curious.

The coroner sat in the head-teacher's chair on a small platform or dais. The schoolroom was acrid with the smell of a coke stove and draughty from the open panes in the otherwise ecclesiastically air-proof windows.

The public included Scrupe, who had argued successfully with his Housemaster on the desirability of his being present at the inquest.

'But, as a pupil of Mr Conway, sir, I must see justice done. Just suppose, sir – '

'Nonsense, Scrupe. Justice has nothing to do with a coroner's court. Have you no general knowledge at all?'

'But, sir, out of *respect* – '

'Nonsense, Scrupe.'

'Sir, you are being cruel, sir. Just because I don't choose to show my feelings, that's no reason – '

'Nonsense, Scrupe.'

'No, but really, sir,' said Scrupe, in what masters believed to be his natural voice, 'I should be awfully glad of the chance. I shall be spending the rest of my life in the Argentine, sir, on my father's ranch, and I do think I ought to take out with me the tradition of English liberty. After all, sir – '

'Go, go, *go!*' said Mr Mayhew, out-talked as usual, and,

as usual, annoyed by this fact. So Scrupe was among those present at the inquest, and listened with grave attention, a virtuous air, and great detachment, to the evidence.

Also present (apart from those such as the witnesses who were compelled to attend and did so most unhappily), were Mr Pearson, wearing a black tie, his daughter Marion (a pretty but shrewd-looking girl of about twenty-three) wearing a black hat, Mr Mayhew (not from choice but with a dim idea of keeping an eye on Scrupe), Mr and Miss Loveday, the latter wearing her usual garments but flourishing a black-edged handkerchief and nursing a pair of unworn black kid gloves, the Second Master, whose name was Regison, Mr Reeder, the School bursar, the School secretary, Mr Sugg, and a Housemaster named Mr Poundbury who had his own reasons for being an interested party.

Mr Semple and Mr Kay were called as witnesses, and Mrs Kay had turned up to support her husband. The other witnesses were the Headmaster (who, in the absence of any relatives, had perforce accepted the responsibility of identifying the body), the police, and the local doctor.

The doctor's wife had also come along, and had brought with her a black-eyed, beaky-mouthed, yellow-skinned, reptilian old lady whom Merrys and Skene might have recognized and whom Mr Kay obviously knew. He went very pale when he saw her come in, but to his relief she did not appear to notice him, and by the time he had to give his evidence he was so anxious to make a good impression that he had forgotten all about her.

The proceedings began in formal style with the assembled company standing up at the instigation of the Coroner's officer. This ceremony was followed by the official call-over of the jury. There were eleven of these and they were sworn in rapidly and efficiently. After this they sat down, very uncomfortably for the most part, in the schoolchildren's desks facing the Coroner's dais.

The Coroner then addressed them. He informed them that only a few witnesses would be called, and these in order that the body of Gerald Aloysius Hugo Conway might be buried.

He outlined, after this, such facts as the police did not object to having made public. The body of Gerald Aloysius Hugo Conway had been discovered outside a cottage just within the boundaries of Spey School. It was obvious that death was unlikely to have been from natural causes. Mr Wyck, the Headmaster of Spey, would be the first witness.

'Your name is Esmé Christopher Wyck? You live at Spey School? You are the Headmaster of that School?'

Mr Wyck gravely and quietly replied in the affirmative to these three questions.

'You have seen the body? You identify it as the body of Gerald Conway? Will you tell the Court when you last saw him alive?'

'I cannot answer that with any exactness,' said Mr Wyck, 'but I think it would have been in the School chapel at about half-past nine on the previous morning, that is, on the twenty-third of October.'

'When did you see him next?'

'At about a quarter to eight on the morning of October the twenty-fourth. He was then, I thought, dead.'

'Did you have subsequent reason to revise that opinion?'

'Unfortunately, no.'

'Any questions?' said the Coroner to the jury. There were no questions. Mr Wyck sat down, and Mr Kay was called. He described the finding of the body. He was not questioned; this seemed to surprise him, for he retired reluctantly. Mr Semple followed, and corrobated Kay's evidence.

Then came Dr Neilson. His evidence was interesting if only because it disposed of rumour, although all the rumours added together approximated to the truth.

The doctor agreed that his name and address were as the Coroner stated, and he agreed, too, that in addition to being in what was still called private practice he was the police doctor, the School doctor, and honorary physician and surgeon to the local football club. He then gave his evidence.

The body of Gerald Conway had been dead for about four hours when he examined it. Pressed closely, he amended this to between three and five hours. Death had been brought about by drowning. The marks on the neck were undoubtedly caused by a rope, and there was a superficial head wound, but both these injuries together had been insufficient to have caused death.

The police evidence was short and simple. It was obvious that the body had been removed from the water and had been taken to the spot where it was found. The rope had been removed from the neck. There was no sign of the rope in the vicinity of the body. There was no sign, either, of any instrument which could have caused the scalp wound.

The Coroner's jury had no hesitation in coming to the conclusion that Conway had been murdered by a person or persons unknown.

*

'Queer business,' said Doctor Neilson to his wife and their guest, when they were home again after the inquest. 'What did you make of it, Mrs Bradley?'

'Nothing much,' replied the saurian visitor amiably. 'What did you?'

'I can't make head or tail of it. I can't see, for one thing, why the body was moved. Why not have left it in the water? Surely it was a very risky thing to have pulled it out and taken it into the School grounds? I can't see any sense in that.'

'It depends where the water was, doesn't it? Perhaps if we knew where the drowning occurred we should know why the body had to be moved.'

'You say "*had* to be moved". You think it was essential to the murderer's safety? Yes, that seems the explanation. But I know of no water near here deep enough to drown a man except the river, although that's not far from the School, of course.'

'There is poor old Mr Loveday's Roman Bath,' said his wife.

'Oh, but – ' The doctor laughed and shook his head. 'You're not going to tell me that that diffident old ass killed a man of Conway's youth and strength!'

'No, of course not. I only meant that the Bath has water in it deep enough to drown in.'

'That is very interesting,' remarked Mrs Bradley. 'I should like to see this Bath. I am acquainted with Mr Wyck. I wonder whether I could persuade him to show me over the School? The trouble is that he probably doesn't want visitors until this matter is cleared up. I shall await my opportunity.'

That afternoon she went off to Mrs Harries's cottage. The blind crone was seated in her kitchen counting onions. Mrs Bradley opened the front door and announced herself.

'Come through,' called Mrs Harries. 'I was passing the time until you came.'

'You expected me, then?'

'Yes, indeed I did. You went to an inquest this morning.'

'Who told you?'

'Milking Meg.'

'Indeed? And did she tell you what was said there?'

'She told me of drowning and dragging, of cock-fighting, bear-baiting, and rabbit-coursing.'

'Talking of cocks,' said Mrs Bradley quickly, 'who is Mr Kay's enemy? Whom does he propose to kill?'

'That's my dark gentleman. He has named no names. He had the sheep's heart of me, and I told him where to buy the loaf of wax. My own black-headed pins he had, and that's all I know. Their quarrels are none of my business. It's only their silver I ask.'

She refused to say more, but went on mumblingly counting her onions until Mrs Bradley left the house. At the gate Mrs Bradley looked back. The witch was standing in the front doorway mopping and mowing like an idiot. Then she straightened up and ran her thin talons through her grey hair until it stood up all over her head.

'I wonder what she *does* know?' thought Mrs Bradley;

and she repeated the observation that evening in describing the scene to the doctor and his wife. But neither of them could enlighten her.

'She's a queer old party,' said the doctor unnecessarily. 'And she's cured some of my patients who did not respond to the recognized methods of treatment. There's something uncanny about her. She's an educated woman, for one thing, although occasionally she chooses to talk like the villagers, or else in some gibberish of her own.'

'She's been on the stage,' said Mrs Bradley.

'I loathe and detest her,' said the doctor's wife. 'She foments mischief in the village. The vicar's wife has told me more than once of quarrels which she's blown into flame so that she can sell her magical rubbish. Some years ago the vicar had to deal with an outbreak of devil-worship, and it was all traced back to her. And do you know how it began? – all because they wouldn't put her vegetable marrow in the most prominent place at the Harvest Festival!'

'I wish I knew why Mr Kay goes to her cottage. I think I must ask him,' said Mrs Bradley. This she did that same evening. She walked the two miles from the doctor's house to Kay's cottage and tapped at the door. She knew that someone was in, for she could see the light in the window, but some moments passed before the door was opened.

Mr Kay himself stood there.

'Who is it?' he asked nervously. Mrs Bradley cackled, and he shrank back. 'You?' he said.

'If you mean Mrs Harries, no,' Mrs Bradley replied; and at the sound of her voice he came forward again, and peered at her hesitantly.

'What do you want?' he enquired.

'I am making a regional survey of village superstitions,' said Mrs Bradley, poking a large black notebook almost into his eye. 'And as I have seen you at Mrs Harries's cottage, I thought you might be able to help me.'

Mr Kay gave a short laugh.

'Come in,' he said. 'We seem to be fellow workers. I'm

writing a book on village magic. Perhaps we can help one another.'

The cottage was beautifully kept. He led her into a room lined with books, many of them in Spanish and Portuguese. There was only one picture, but that, Mrs Bradley thought, was a Murillo. The furniture was simple, modern, and almost new. She took an armchair by the fire and looked expectantly at her host, although she could not help wondering where his wife was.

'Mrs Harries is, of course, a survival,' he said.

'On the contrary, she is a charlatan,' said Mrs Bradley firmly.

'A convincing one, then.'

'Yes, probably. How did you get on with the loaf of wax?'

'Oh, she told you about that, did she? It's rather odd, really. I tried it for Conway. Well, he's dead, of course, but he died the wrong way. He was murdered. That doesn't come into it, does it?'

'Isn't it murder, then, to achieve one's end by magical means?'

'Yes. If he'd pined away and drooped into death, I might have believed that I'd killed him. But he didn't. He was attacked and then drowned. It doesn't fit.'

'But you did wish him dead.'

'Of course.' He looked rather surprised. 'The fellow was the bane of my life.'

'And you plotted his death?'

'Certainly not. I am doing research.'

'Into witchcraft?'

'Yes.'

'Why?'

'Oh, just that I am interested. Nothing more. I had no intention of killing Conway by witchcraft, if that is what you mean.'

'I don't mean that. There is only one way of killing a person by witchcraft. It is the way by which people are killed by it in Africa. The subject must *believe* that he will be killed. I don't think Mr Conway was the kind of man to believe that witchcraft could kill him.'

'No, he wasn't. That lets me out, I think.'

'And I think it might,' said Mrs Bradley, retailing this conversation later to the doctor and his wife. 'I don't believe that witchcraft can kill anybody who doesn't believe in it.'

The doctor agreed.

'On the other hand,' he said, 'it has been proved, surely, that witchcraft can be assisted. If the hated person doesn't die by witchcraft, he can be *assisted* to die by more ordinary and mundane methods. I don't feel inclined to suspect Kay less than I did.'

'Very true,' Mrs Bradley answered. 'But there are other, equally interesting, theories. While I was at Mrs Harries's cottage one night, two boys turned up. They were witnesses, I think, to Mr Kay's extraordinary outburst of temper during which he put his hand through Mrs Harries's sitting-room window.'

'Two boys from the School, do you mean?'

'I imagine so. They had not the voices of village boys. I was there when they arrived. I suppose that means that they were breaking School rules, for the time was well after eleven.'

'And Kay put his hand through the window? – deliberately, do you mean?'

'Well, not exactly deliberately. He was gesticulating very freely, and accidentally punched the window pane.'

'Oh, I see. And you think – ?'

'I think that, one way and another, Mr Kay may have been able to sublimate his hatred. His compensation-mechanism functions well. He punched a hole in the window and he has tried to remove Mr Conway by magical means.'

'You're not serious?'

'I don't know how serious I am. I know the facts. Mr Kay has melted a wax image before his fire at home, and he has stuck a sheep's heart with black-headed pins.'

'The man must be crazy.'

'Not necessarily.'

'But you don't believe in magic?'

'Not in wax loaves and sheeps' hearts, no.'

The doctor shook his head and laughed.

'As time goes on, we shall know what you do believe, I suppose?' he said. Mrs Bradley nodded slowly and rhythmically.

'I certainly believe that Mr Kay's visits to Mrs Harries may prove to have some bearing on the death of Mr Conway,' she said, 'but what that bearing may be is entirely dark to me at present.'

'Did you hear that Conway had just become engaged to be married?' the doctor enquired. Mrs Bradley looked interested.

'To whom?' she asked.

'To the daughter of Pearson, the woodwork and metal-work master,' replied the doctor. 'He is a visiting master. He lives at the other end of the village. He is a widower with this one daughter. From what I've heard, it seems pretty certain that Pearson wasn't in favour of the match, but he turned up at the School on the night before Conway's death and gave quite a party.'

'Champagne and oysters?'

'Champagne, anyway. And the news must have come as a bit of a blow to another of the masters – young Semple. It's been obvious for some time that he's been hoping to marry Marion Pearson, and we think he must have taken an awful knock when old Pearson turned up with the champagne.'

'I like Mr Semple,' said the doctor's wife.

'And I like the sound of Mr Semple,' Mrs Bradley observed. 'I like the sound of Mr Kay, Mr Semple, and, of course, Mr Pearson. They are three of the liveliest suspects I have encountered for years.'

'Suspects? You think one of those murdered Conway? But it's incredible!'

'Yes,' Mrs Bradley agreed. 'It's incredible to you because you know them. But the incredible is not necessarily the impossible, and I, you see, am not acquainted with any of them, which makes it easier to say what I think.'

'Then one of those three, in your opinion, killed Conway?' asked the doctor. 'I don't believe it!'

Mrs Bradley shrugged.

'Well, which one?' said the doctor challengingly.

'It would be immoral of me to tell you,' said Mrs Bradley, 'although I am most interested in what you've told me.'

'I don't seem to have told you very much.'

'Oh, but you have! You say that Mr Conway himself seemed surprised when his engagement to Miss Pearson was announced, and you say that it was supposed that Mr Semple might have married her and that Mr Semple was angry and upset when he heard the news, and you say – '

'Oh, heavens!' said the doctor, laughing. 'I seem to have said more than I thought I had!'

'Yes,' said Mrs Bradley cheerfully. 'By the way, I suppose *you* had no reason for wanting to be rid of the young man?'

'*I* hadn't, but I know who *had*,' said the doctor suddenly. 'And that's Poundbury, whom, so far, you haven't met. He was present at the inquest – a vague-looking, tall fellow about forty years old. Teaches Latin, and has a very beautiful young wife. He hated Conway like poison, and with good reason. Still, he wouldn't have murdered him, you know.'

8. Nancy's Fancies

*

A Lawyer is an honest Employment, so is mine. Like me too he acts in a double Capacity, both against Rogues and for 'em.

IBID. (*Act 1, Scene 1*)

As the first week passed by, Mr Kay's popularity climbed (in his own view) to undesirable and embarrassing heights. The theory, now current in the School, that he might at any moment be arrested and charged with the murder, caused boys who, so far, had attended his lessons under protest and who had got through the hour as best they might, to seek him out not only in the form-room but in Extra-Tu (before-time a hated imposition reserved for the backward and the unwary) with requests for information with regard to imports and exports, inflation, vicious spirals, price controls, hard and soft currencies, the regulation of wages in industry, statistics of various kinds, and other, less obviously relevant subjects, so that they might pursue him, later on, to his cottage and feast their eyes upon the scene of the crime.

As his cottage had been placed out of bounds to all but his own pupils, these enjoyed a notoriety in the school to which they were unaccustomed and of which they took full advantage.

There was another popular member of the School besides Mr Kay. The rumour that he had stood up in form and advised Spivvy to escape while the going was good, and to take refuge on Mr Scrupe's Argentine cattle-ranch from which extradition was not possible, had raised Scrupe to the ranks of the bloods. His opinion was sought, his witticisms received the tribute due to them, and, most significant of all, his style of dress was copied by his admirers.

To do him justice, Scrupe took almost no notice of this evanescent fame.

Mr Mayhew had sent for him within an hour of his interview with Mr Wyck.

'I am sorry, Scrupe, that you should have been sent up to the Headmaster.'

'Yes, sir, so am I,' replied Scrupe, meditatively rubbing his bottom, an action calculated to infuriate his Housemaster, and in no sense failing of this purpose.

'I trust that your conscience is now clear,' said Mr Mayhew, raging, but speaking calmly.

'My conscience, sir, is never less than clear. I envisage every act before I embark upon it, and, my being in, it is up to the opposed to beware of me.'

'I believe him,' said Mr Wyck, when he heard of this conversation. 'I hope that Scrupe will not underestimate his opponents, though. The boy has a brilliant future, if a future exists for any of us. I think I had better take a General Assembly in the morning.'

The Headmaster had considered carefully how best to address the boys on the subject of Mr Conway's death. His first move had been the natural and unexceptionable one of a memorial service in the School chapel. After that, he had not referred to the subject for a day or two, but, once the first inquest had been held, and his business with the police had been temporarily suspended, it was no longer possible for him to keep silent. Parents harried him, several boys were withdrawn without notice, and the Governors had convened a special meeting.

The Headmaster was glad to be quit of the police for a bit. They seemed to have been everywhere. He had even surprised one youthful constable up among the branches of the cedar tree on his lawn, making notes on the contents of his study. Other policemen were apt to bob up out of shrubberies without preliminary notice, and the Superintendent had interviewed Mr Kay a third time and to such effect that Mr Reeder had observed, over coffee in the Headmaster's drawing-room, that whether that poor fellow Kay had murdered Conway or not, he would have Mr Reeder's sympathy if he murdered a few policemen.

The School, which had felt slightly affronted that there

had not been, so far, a General Assembly, was rather pleased when Mr Wyck kept them in the School Hall on the Wednesday morning after the inquest, and addressed them on the subject of Mr Conway's death.

'You are not children,' observed the Headmaster, 'and it is time that you should be taken into my confidence. This is a most unhappy term – '

'I don't know so much,' muttered Cartaris to Cranleigh. 'We beat Helston all right, didn't we?'

– 'But I do not wish to dwell upon the past. It is the present and the future which concern us. Now it seems to me' – he scanned the ranks before him, and many a young boy for whose innocence any one of the masters would have gone bail stirred uneasily under his gaze – 'that some boy or boys before me must know something more about this dreadful affair than has yet come to light. If there is such a boy – or if there are such boys – I should wish to have imparted to me this knowledge. Much may be forgiven a culprit who, by a recital of his own misdeeds, helps to shed light upon the strange and shocking circumstances in which we find ourselves. I shall, boys' – he paused, and even the Sixth Form slightly shifted their feet – 'I shall confidently await the course of events.'

'How much do you think the Old Man knows?' asked Merrys agitatedly of Skene. He had still been able to make no plan for retrieving his fountain pen, and was scared.

'Nothing, you ass! Be your age,' said his friend. 'He's only fishing.'

But Merrys was not reassured, and his acute anxiety soon became apparent, particularly when Mr Kay was given special leave three days later.

'Merrys,' said Miss Loveday to her brother, 'is a sensitive boy. This awful murder is preying on his mind. He would be all the better for an airing.'

The expression that a boy would be all the better for an airing was a favourite one with Miss Loveday. A boy needed an airing if she thought he needed dosing, thrashing, coddling, translation to a study, an extra turn in the Roman Bath, inclusion in the House cricket eleven (in which she took a deep, religious, and, to the boys, embarrassing interest), a term-time visit to the dentist, a hair-cut, or, indeed, anything which came outside the routine of the form-room. 'I should like Merrys to see a psychiatrist. I suppose his parents ought to be approached. I will see to it.'

'Yes, they must be approached. Some people are odd about psychiatry,' said Mr Loveday, who was accustomed to taking up his sister's suggestions without argument. 'For my own part – '

'Your own part doesn't matter,' interposed Miss Loveday. 'Your subconscious mind is no particular nuisance.'

Glad to be reassured on this point, Mr Loveday approached the Headmaster, and obtained Mr Wyck's consent to bring a psychiatrist into his House, provided that the Headmaster chose the psychiatrist himself. Mr Wyck had his own reasons for making this otherwise extraordinary stipulation.

Merrys's parents, who did not find Miss Loveday's writing very easy to read (she had an old-fashioned idea that to type letters to parents was discourteous), thought that the operative word was physicist, and, not being able to attach any meaning to the letter, they wrote back to agree with it because they did not think that anything could alter their son for the worse. They then forgot all about it and went to Torquay. They were, from Mr Loveday's point of view, ideal parents, for parents who take undue interest in their boys are the bugbear of all Housemasters.

Merrys, apprised of his fate, accepted his new role with philosophy.

'I believe Albert-Edward thinks I'm bats,' he confided to Skene. 'He talked about my reflexes. I thought he meant my biceps at first, but it seems not.'

'Reflexes are serious, you ass,' said Skene comfortingly. 'Criminals have them. I should say Albert-Edward is on to something.'

'More likely Nancy,' returned Merrys, discomfited. 'I believe she's mad herself. Madmen always think everyone else is.'

'She may not be far wrong in your case,' said Skene, amiably.

*

Miss Loveday had already rung up the doctor when the Headmaster informed her brother of his decision to choose the psychiatrist himself; therefore the doctor lost no time in communicating to his guest the welcome tidings that there was now no reason why she should not visit Spey School.

He had telephoned the Headmaster, and had received a cordial invitation from Mr Wyck to bring Mrs Bradley along at the earliest possible moment. He remembered their previous meeting, which had been at an Educational Conference some years previously, and it was with relief, he confessed, that he could at the same time accede to Mr Loveday's request and be certain that a reputable and sensible person would be invited to take charge of Merrys's conscious and subconscious mind.

'And she could have a look at the rest of the boys in that House,' said Mr Wyck to his wife, when he had put the telephone receiver down. 'I am not satisfied with matters there. It is really quite time that Loveday retired, although I haven't the heart at present to suggest it.'

'I'm longing to meet Mrs Bradley,' said Mrs Wyck. 'What is she like to look at?'

'As far as my memory serves me, singularly unprepossessing,' replied Mr Wyck judicially. 'But a character. Yes, certainly a character. And, of course, an exceptionally brilliant woman.'

But Mrs Wyck was accustomed to unprepossessing people in the persons of the masters, their wives, and the parents of the boys; and she had met so many brilliant people that one more or less made no difference.

'I suppose she will live at Loveday's,' she remarked.

'I expect Miss Loveday will invite her to do so.'

'Then we will have her to dinner once or twice, if that will do.'

'When she's examined Merrys and so forth, I'm going to ask her to stay on at the School until we get this awful business cleared up,' said Mr Wyck, suddenly. 'She has had some success, I believe, in such cases, and she may be able to cope with the police. They've already trodden twice on my rock garden.'

Mrs Bradley, quite as anxious to get to the School as Miss Loveday and the Headmaster were to have her there, burst upon Mr Loveday's astonished House at supper time, although she had arrived in time to pay an afternoon call upon her hostess.

At supper she sat upon Mr Loveday's right and scanned the ranks of Tuscany with interest. Her bright black eyes took in all details whilst she listened with every appearance of interest to Mr Loveday's conversation, for Mr Loveday, shying away from the point at issue, was giving her an earnest account of the construction and heating of his Roman Bath, so that comments and interjections on her part were redundant, which, with her usual intelligence, she had realized at the outset that they would be.

Miss Loveday, at the foot of her brother's table, conversed with the prefects Stallard and Compton (who agreed noncommittally with her views and proffered none of their own) upon the House's chances of lifting the cricket cup next season. Of football Miss Loveday had less knowledge than of cricket, but football she referred to during May and June. She had a theory that it made boys nervous to have the current game discussed at meal-times, and she thought that this nervousness gave boys indigestion. She was known to the House as Nancy the Nark, a sufficiently descriptive nickname, and one which had wounded her when first she heard it, but it had resulted in a certain amount of ironic popularity which she learned to enjoy. Her brother placed her second only to his Roman Bath in his affections, and gave way to her lightest whim. Mild and easy-going as he was, he was known to have thrashed a boy severely merely for bouncing a tennis ball against the wall beneath her bed-room window whilst she was taking her afternoon rest. He was, in point of fact, afraid of her, a mental state which is apt to result in affection.

After supper the House prefects were summoned to Mr Loveday's drawing-room to be introduced formally to the guest with whom they had sat at supper.

'Stallard, my head boy, Cartaris, captain of football, and the School full-back, Compton. Here, also, are Edgeley and Findlay,' said Mr Loveday. 'Boys, this is Mrs Lestrange Bradley, of whom, no doubt, you have heard.'

The prefects looked obstinate, a sign of shyness, and Mrs Bradley, grinning, gave Edgeley, who was near her, a poke in the ribs. He yelped involuntarily, and the others laughed with embarrassed heartiness.

'Well, now that Edgeley has taken the edge off things,' said Miss Loveday (adding to the slight hysteria of the gathering by her awkward choice of nouns), 'we can get down to brass tacks, as you boys say.' The prefects, who would not have dreamed of employing this metaphor, maintained their previous expressions. 'Mrs Bradley,' con-tinued Miss Loveday, 'has come to turn you all inside out, so here is your chance to show your guilt.'

'I don't want the House to be informed of this,' interposed Mr Loveday hastily, 'but you five, as House prefects, are to be taken into our confidence. Now, you must all begin by feeling thoroughly at ease.'

'Thank you, sir,' said Stallard, not knowing what else to say, and feeling anything but at ease. 'We – I think we understand what you mean.'

'That's that, then,' said Miss Loveday. 'Now, find seats. Findlay, the most lissome, had better sit on the floor, and Edgeley, his friend, may join him, and then we will all eat cake and drink sherry. I encourage the boys to like sherry,' she added to Mrs Bradley, whilst Mr Loveday busied himself with the decanter and Stallard handed round cakes, 'because I think it is so much better for them than the gin they all drink in the holidays.'

The boys, who were at the manly age when they were learning to drink beer in preparation for going up to the University, accepted the sherry politely, balanced plates on their knees, or, in the case of Findlay and Edgeley, on the fender, and wished that the social evening was over. It was to prove more interesting, however, than they had expected. After Mr Loveday, in a discouraging voice, had offered everybody a second glass of sherry, he put down the decanter, leaned against the mantelpiece, pulled at his lower lip for a moment, and then came out with it.

'As Miss Loveday has indicated,' he said, 'Mrs Bradley is here on very important business, and I shall look to my prefects to give her all the assistance in their power.'

'Of course, sir,' said Stallard, as this seemed to be expected.

'Certain boys in this House,' Mr Loveday continued, 'are showing signs of nervousness and unrest. These are indications of a disorder with which you prefects are not qualified to deal.' Findlay looked up quickly from his seat on the hearthrug. Cartaris looked down at his fingernails and smiled grimly. The others remained politely poker-faced, wondering what all this was about. 'Oh, I don't mean *that* kind of disorder,' added Mr. Loveday hastily. 'I mean – '

'In other words,' said Miss Loveday, who often embarrassed her brother by acting as his interpreter, 'your Housemaster means that Mrs Bradley is a psychiatrist and that she has come to interview Merrys.'

'You may perhaps wonder,' said Mr Loveday, resuming his position as head of the House, 'why I should take the responsibility of such proceedings. It is, of course, in connexion with Mr Conway's death.'

'Do you mean you think Merrys *knows* something, sir?' demanded Findlay; and the other prefects looked up, interested to hear Mr Loveday's reply.

'No, no. But the boy is in a nervous state, and I – Miss

Loveday and I – think that treatment here might be better than sending him home. His parents concur in this view, and so Mrs Bradley has very kindly consented to examine him. She will place the boy under observation, and – '

'Is he – do you mean he's *insane*, sir?' blurted out Edgeley.

'No, of course not! It is merely – ' Mr Loveday cast about for the most suitable words with which to remove an unfortunate impression.

'By the way, sir,' said Stallard, before his Housemaster could continue, 'that reminds me. I've never thought of it before, but I remember now that the week before Mr Conway's – before it happened to Mr Conway – Merrys came to me with some tale which caused me to give him permission to go round into your garden. I hope that was quite all right, sir?'

'My garden? But – Stallard, you don't think Merrys can have borrowed my bicycle? You know, it *was* borrowed.'

'I don't think anything, sir,' said Stallard uncomfortably, 'but I thought I ought to mention it, that's all.'

'And quite right, too!' said Mr Loveday emphatically. '*Quite* right! What do *you* think, Annette?'

'I picked on Merrys, and it looks as though I was not far wrong,' said Miss Loveday, with great satisfaction.

'You will therefore excuse Merrys from all attendance at football practice if Mrs Bradley finds that the football practice hour is a convenient time at which to interview the boy,' said Mr Loveday, eyeing Cartaris, whom he privately suspected of beating boys who cut football, 'and the rest of you must keep an eye on him without appearing to do so. You must exercise great discretion. *Great* discretion. I would not have the boy know for the world that he is being watched. Miss Loveday and I have felt considerable anxiety as to the possible effects of this dreadful business on nervous and sensitive boys.'

'Merrys walks in his sleep, sir,' said Findlay. 'He frightens the boys in his dormitory.'

Everybody stared at Findlay; his fellow prefects because

they admired his nerve in introducing this (to their minds) extraneous subject of conversation, and the Lovedays because they were genuinely taken aback. Mrs Bradley stared because she was summing up Findlay, whom she suspected of having invented this tit-bit of information for her benefit.

'Really, Findlay? How do you come to know that?' enquired Mr Loveday, excitedly.

'He was being ragged about it, sir. I happened to overhear. I took no notice at the time, but now all this has been mentioned – '

'*Well!*' said Miss Loveday, regarding Findlay with admiration. 'This is really uncanny, is it not? What do you say, Mrs Bradley, to Findlay's evidence?'

'Interesting, instructive, and misleading,' said Mrs Bradley emphatically. Findlay gave her a comical glance. He was an intelligent boy, Mrs Bradley decided, and when she needed help he should help her. He was likely to afford her more assistance than were the earnest Stallard and the ox-like Cartaris, she fancied.

*

She was not at all anxious to interview Merrys when he ought to have been playing football. Apart from the boy's own wishes and he might be fond of football – she had an old-fashioned belief that games – even compulsory games – were not altogether bad for boys.

She had enjoyed meeting the prefects, but it did seem to her that the fewer people – certainly the fewer boys – who realized the purpose of her visit, the greater were her chances of success. She mentioned this to Mr Loveday on the following morning, after breakfast. She did not add, however, that the Headmaster was retaining her in another capacity – that of private detective.

'I tell my prefects everything,' said Mr Loveday. 'I find that it is the only way of inculcating a sense of true responsibility.'

'Who is Merrys's form-master?' Mrs Bradley enquired. It

transpired that one Mr Lamphrey had now shouldered this onerous task. Mrs Bradley walked over to the School House to interview the Headmaster.

'Mr Loveday?' said Mr Wyck. 'Oh, yes, of course. His boys will be scattered in various forms, I am afraid. Merrys? Oh, yes, you may interview him when and where you please. If the boy knows anything about this unhappy business – the whole form? Well, of course, you *could*.' He conducted Mrs Bradley to Mr Lamphrey's form-room. Mr Lamphrey, his gown standing off from his shoulders like the wings of the archangel of doom, was in the act of inviting a boy called Billings to recite the second stanza of Keats's *Ode on a Grecian Urn*. Both he and the boy seemed glad to be interrupted.

'Mrs Bradley', said Mr Wyck, 'would be interested in asking your boys a few questions, Mr Lamphrey.'

'With pleasure, Headmaster,' said Mr Lamphrey, horrified, and gazing for support at his First Boy, who was, of course, the enviable although not universally envied Micklethwaite.

'Gentlemen,' said Mrs Bradley, addressing the form, 'I want you to take a clean sheet of paper, to write your names clearly, and then to put down the first word that comes into your minds when I say – '

'*Binet-Simon* stuff!' muttered Micklethwaite. 'And about forty years out of date.' He said this to nobody in particular. Nobody in particular kicked him, as usual, and there was a slight shuffling as boys took up their pens.

'Right? Murder,' said Mrs Bradley succinctly. 'Blood. Sand. Rannygazoo. Aspidistra. Aunt. Bungle. Spiv. Oxen. South America. Cascara. Beast. Punitive. Matrix. Bicycle. Bluebells. Port Wine. Rabbit. Ink. Hieroglyphics. Dulcibella. Acid. Dogs. Egypt. Herrings. Dulcimer. Wallaby. Bath. International. Haemorrhage. Fitter. Cannibal. Cottage. Indicator. Merchant. Pens down.'

One boy, who had been writing a reciprocal to 'pens down' hurriedly scratched it out, and there was a clatter as of arms restored to an arm-rack. Mrs Bradley requested the first boy in each line of desks to collect the answers to her questions. She looked up at the form when she had looked through the papers.

'I want to speak to Mr Skene,' she said. Skene got up. Mrs Bradley motioned towards the door.

'Mr Skene,' said Mrs Bradley, when they were outside, 'I want the truth, the whole truth, and nothing but the truth. What say you?'

'I don't know,' said Skene. Mrs Bradley clicked her tongue. 'I mean, I don't know what you want to know.'

'Suppose we cast our minds back to the night of the murder?'

'Yes?'

'Mr Skene, confide in me. I am not so foolish as to suppose that you and Mr Merrys murdered Mr Conway, even if you did go out on Mr Loveday's bicycle. Believe me, you must be frank.'

'But we didn't use Mr Loveday's bicycle on the night of the murder!' said Skene, horrified. 'It was like this – but we don't want to be sacked – '

*

'And now, Mr Merrys,' said Mrs Bradley, waylaying the unfortunate youth after morning school, 'what is all this about a fountain pen? Had we not better search for it? Is it possible that it can incriminate us? Exactly where were we when the murder was committed, I wonder? And how vengeful were we towards our Mr Conway? What ill-will did we bear him, and for what reason?'

'We were – well, we weren't *vengeful*,' said Merrys anxiously. 'You see, it was a week before Mr Conway – before Mr Conway – '

'We broke out at night, did we not? And we borrowed our Housemaster's bicycle.'

'I say, you wouldn't tell anybody that?'

'We found ourselves outside a certain cottage.'

'We only wanted to know the way back. We were lost.'

'But at the cottage we found no one to direct us.'

'Oh, I say!' said Merrys, suddenly enlightened. 'It was *you* at that cottage?' Mrs Bradley cackled. 'But, you know, it had nothing to do with Mr Conway. We'd gone to the Dogs, and we couldn't – well, it didn't seem worth it to go in, and on the way back we lost our way, and – well, that's all.'

'Is it?' said Mrs Bradley severely.

'Yes.'

'Then what alarms us?'

'Nothing. We aren't. I mean – '

'We saw and heard.'

Merrys looked at her and saw that she knew it all.

'We *did* hear Mr Kay say he'd like to murder somebody, and we *thought* he put his fist through the window,' he concluded. Mrs Bradley nodded.

'And we know nothing more?'

'No. Honestly we don't.'

Mrs Bradley returned to Mr Loveday's House to receive coffee and a sandwich from Miss Loveday.

'Were Mr Lamphrey's boys discouraging?' Miss Loveday enquired. 'They are said to be difficult. Gerald Conway was their form-master, of course. My brother takes them for Divinity, which every boy is compelled to study, whether he is on the Modern or the Classical side. Even the Army class takes it, although, in their case, the Old Testament only, of course.'

'Gideon and his river-drinkers?' Mrs Bradley suggested, ignoring all other references, which seemed to her completely beside the point.

'A valuable chapter,' Miss Loveday agreed. 'There is nothing to beat the selected minority. King Edward the Third knew that. Crécy depended upon it. There is also the Third Programme of the British Broadcasting Corporation. An admirable thing in its way, although I sometimes think it falls between two stools.'

'In this school, a selected minority would include Mr Scrupe and Mr Micklethwaite, I presume?' said Mrs Bradley, ignoring a challenge.

'They are clever boys, I believe. Of Scrupe I know little except by hearsay, but Micklethwaite is one of our own boys, and it is too bad that he was done out of the Divinity prize by Mr Conway's meanness and treachery,' said Miss Loveday, speaking with warmth.

Mrs Bradley smiled benignly. She had mentioned the two boys' names at random.

'I heard rumours of this,' she said, mendaciously. 'But, surely, if a boy is entitled to a prize – ?'

'You might think so,' said Miss Loveday energetically, 'but, if you do, it means that you cannot appreciate the amount of petty jealousy that there is to be found in a school common room. Mr Conway, for reasons of his own, accused Micklethwaite of cheating in the last Divinity examination at which, most unfortunately (although one does not think, of course, of criticizing the Headmaster), Mr Conway had been appointed invigilator. The boy, touched in his honour, refused to take the prize, and – '

'Do I understand, then, that Mr Conway did not substantiate his accusation by removing the boy from the examination room?' Mrs Bradley pertinently enquired.

'He said nothing – except afterwards to the boy. Micklethwaite is a strange lad. There was no need for him to have made a public thing of it, but he was, it seems, very angry. He attended a co-educational establishment before he came here, and had absorbed odd notions as to his rights. He was much persecuted at first, but I soon put a stop to that. We are, after all, Christians in *this* House, although I would not go bail for some of the others. Well, at any rate, when Micklethwaite refused to accept the prize there was a great fuss, and the Headmaster threatened to cane him for Contempt of Authority.'

'Only *threatened?*'

'Mr Wyck is weak,' said Miss Loveday in low tones,

glancing at the window as she pronounced these treasonable words. 'There was a rumour that the boy had threatened to commit suicide as a protest against the injustice of the punishment, if it was administered, and Mr Wyck thought, I suppose, that he might do it. Commit suicide, I mean. The lad is brilliantly clever and rather overstrung. A pity. I like lads to be manly and only *technically* gifted. Aesthetics have no place in modern life. That is why ferro-concrete has come into its own.'

'I should not think his life here can have been easy,' Mrs Bradley remarked, 'even after you stopped his being bullied. I refer to Mr Micklethwaite.'

'He is a strange lad,' Miss Loveday repeated, 'and a lad of character. He is fearless of pain, and has become an expert in *Judo*. The boys have learned to leave well alone, I believe, and might have done so without my assistance.'

'I must cultivate this boy,' said Mrs Bradley.

'And what progress do you make with Merrys?' asked Miss Loveday, changing the subject. 'His behaviour improved yesterday. I noticed it. He had two helpings of the first course, and threw potato. We do not throw bread now, for motives of patriotism, and should not, for the same reason, waste potato, either. For one thing, there is not too much of these staple fillers for growing lads, and, for another, hunger is a wonderful disciplinarian.'

'So is fear,' said Mrs Bradley. 'You were quite right to deduce that Merrys was afraid.'

'Of what?'

'That is what I am here to find out.' She did not add that she had already found it out, because, although she had heard of the midnight exploits of Merrys and Skene, she had not decided how to make proper use of them. She had decided to go to the Headmaster with her tale before she went to the police, but she wanted further time to study Mr Wyck, and to work out his probable reactions to the tale she would have to tell. Meanwhile, she was not inclined to rely upon Miss Loveday's discretion.

'You have not told me yet of your experiences with the Fifth Scientific,' said Miss Loveday suddenly. 'Did you encounter Whittaker? His father is a platelayer on the London and Great Midland Railway, and Whittaker is one of the Guinea-pig boys. He is a great success. Did he threaten Springer? He loves to learn, and Springer, I think, confounds him.'

'Surely,' said Mrs Bradley, not troubling to explain that she had not yet encountered the Fifth Scientific, 'this School is unique in having boys who desire to learn? My sons never did. Their reports were uniformly scurrilous.'

'Oh, you have sons in the plural? I understood you had only one, the famous K.C.,' said Miss Loveday.

'Ferdinand? He is my son by my first husband, who was of French and Spanish descent. I have other sons, but I much prefer my nephews. Ferdinand and I are unlike, and get on well. He reminds me, in many ways, of his father, and that is welcome, since otherwise I might have forgotten what his father was like. It is some time since we were married,' said Mrs Bradley alarmingly.

Miss Loveday, deflated by this incursion into family history, abandoned the subject, as it was intended she should, and poured out more coffee.

'I suppose it *was* Merrys who borrowed my brother's bicycle?' she remarked. 'I should not like it reported. I know his mother. Where did he go, by the way?'

'To the Dog-racing track.'

'Good heavens! So young a boy!'

'He did not go in. The entrance fee was beyond his expectations.'

'I am glad of that. I see still less need to report the occurrence to the Headmaster. I shall inform my brother, and he will deal with Merrys. I suppose the child was afraid that he might be accused of the murder if it were found out that he is in the habit of breaking out at night. I hope you have reassured him. Nay, I know you must have done. Potato-throwing is always an excellent sign. I check bullying in the

House by it. A lad who throws potato is in spirits, and Merrys threw a good deal.'

'He lost his fountain pen,' said Mrs Bradley conversationally.

'Oh, was it his?' said Miss Loveday, producing a pen from the recesses of her costume. 'I found it on the gravel. He must have dropped it on his way out. You had better take it.'

'Did you not look at the name on it? Merrys had his name on his pen.'

'I saw no name. Would you care to look for it?' Mrs Bradley took the pen. There was no name on it. 'And now,' said Miss Loveday – hastily, it seemed to Mrs Bradley – 'to the business of the visit of the governors. They are said to be against Mr Wyck, who, of course, as a modern Headmaster, has no conception of discipline. I say this in no carping or Communistic spirit, but the facts speak for themselves.'

'In what way?' Mrs Bradley enquired.

'Boys breaking out at night; my brother and I being compelled to heat the Roman Bath by moonlight; John Semple being friendly with Bennett Kay, and so on and so forth,' Miss Loveday economically responded. 'And, of course, all this Common Room champagne. It was sherry when first I came here.'

'The boys who broke out at night were your own boys,' Mrs Bradley was impelled to point out. 'The Roman Bath, which, I must admit, I would very much like to see, is your own and your brother's concern. The champagne, I understand, was in celebration of an engagement, and exactly what bearing the friendship between Mr Semple and Mr Kay can have upon the Headmaster's control of the School, I do not understand.'

'John Semple, although a moron, is not without ancestry of a reputable kind,' pronounced Miss Loveday. 'Bennett Kay is of very mixed blood. In the Common Room, as we knew it of old, a friendship between the two would have been impossible. But tell me more of your experiences. Have you met our dark gentleman yet?'

'Our – ?' said Mrs Bradley startled.

'Prince Takhobali,' Miss Loveday explained. 'Did you think I meant somebody else? And Issacher. A gifted lad, although not, in the strict term, European. A lad with a sixth sense. A lad with eyes in the back of his head.'

Mrs Bradley promised to make Issacher's acquaintance, but before she contrived to do this, further rumours, which turned out to be perfectly true, flashed round the School and were received with considerable acclaim. There was to be a half-holiday for a full Staff meeting at which the Governors would preside; and a C.I.D. Inspector was being sent for from Scotland Yard to help the local police.

9. *An Assembly of the Elders*

*

Where shall we find such another Set of practical Philosophers?
IBID. (*Act 2, Scene 1*)

MRS BRADLEY had not been in and around the School for more than a couple of days when she received a note from Mr Semple.

'Kay and I made rather a curious discovery on the spot, almost exactly, where we found Conway,' the note explained. With anticipatory relish, Mrs Bradley at once wrote a reply, inviting Mr Semple and Mr Kay to meet her as soon as their duties permitted. A room in Mr Loveday's House had been allotted to her as a study, and, with this as a strategic base, she was able to ask them to tea.

Only Mr Semple turned up, however.

'Kay isn't a very sociable bird,' he explained, 'so I've come along on my own. No, no tea, thanks. I've promised to go along and have it with old Pearson. His daughter's out for the evening. I just came to tell you what we found.'

Mrs Bradley summed up her guest, and decided that his looks did not deceive her; for Mr Semple looked what he was – an athletic, games-playing young man, fairly well-bred, obviously simple-minded and equally obviously kind-hearted. What seemed alien to him, therefore, was his bleak-eyed, terrified stare, a slight stammer every time he spoke, and a too-easy assurance and buoyancy with which he was attempting to cover up these nervous reactions.

Enter quite a possible murderer, thought Mrs Bradley, and one with an excellent motive. 'And this discovery of yours?' she said. Mr Semple looked distressed.

'Oh, no bearing, I daresay,' he admitted, 'but Mr Wyck indicated that you were the person to come to, don't you know. It was a headless cock, as a matter of fact. Killed in that Voodoo sort of style. Revolting, actually.'

'Details,' said Mrs Bradley, producing her notebook. Mr Semple looked more distressed than before, but replied and gave the details. They were interesting, and, as he had said, revolting. Mrs Bradley inscribed them carefully in her notebook. 'And what bearing do you suppose all this to have upon the death of Mr Conway?' she enquired. 'Have you heard that a member of the Staff has been visiting the village witch, Mrs Harries?'

'I did hear something,' admitted Semple. 'Why, do you know about that?'

'Oh, yes. I am a frequent visitor there myself. I suppose Mr Kay did not accompany you here because he has met me there.'

'Kay's doing some sort of research for some sort of Society, I believe,' said Mr Semple. 'He's one of these Folk-Dancing sort of chaps.'

Mrs Bradley did not connect folk-dancing and witchcraft very closely, but did not say so. She talked about the ballet – much to the confusion of her guest.

When he departed, she gazed after him with a certain amount of pity. The rejected lover seldom meets with sympathy, she reflected; and rightly so, for he deserves none.

She mentioned this theory to Miss Loveday, who already delighted her very much. Miss Loveday, who had been sewing, put away her workbox with great deliberation, assumed her spectacles (which, to Mrs Bradley's stupefaction, she always discarded when she sewed), and pronounced with deliberation:

'And which of us, my brother or myself, do you suspect of the murder of Gerald Conway?'

'I think (if I thought that either of you had had anything to do with it), that I should suspect the two of you of having been identical accessories,' said Mrs Bradley. Miss Loveday nodded.

'I understand you,' she said, 'and it is, of course, unnecessary to tell you that my brother and I are twins. This

is not generally known, but I tell it to you because I feel
that you knew it the moment you set eyes on us. What say
you?'

'I am dumbfounded,' said Mrs Bradley, 'and, naturally,
much enlightened.'

'I wonder whether you always speak the truth?' said Miss
Loveday. 'I have noticed that doctors, whether charlatans
or not, very seldom commit themselves to direct statements
of fact. Do you suspect our Roman Bath?'

'Certainly,' Mrs Bradley replied. 'Your Roman Bath, the
river, and every bathroom in Spey School.'

'Ah!' said Miss Loveday, nodding. 'You see? An evasive
answer. As for the School bathrooms, with the exception of
those in this House, they are primitive and odd. "They got
them into polished baths and were cleansed." So said blind
Homer. I would not go bail for the cleanliness of the School
House bathrooms, nor for Mr Poundbury's.'

'I am a sybarite,' Mrs Bradley replied. Miss Loveday
studied her face but gained nothing from this scrutiny.

'You are a Sphinx,' she retorted. 'Now, tell me. Have you
come to any conclusions about Merrys?' Mrs Bradley was
on safe ground here, and they indulged in a lively discussion
of adolescent boys for the next hour and a half.

'And now,' said Mrs Bradley, 'tell me all about Mr Semple.
I know he hoped to marry Miss Marion Pearson and I know
he plays games and has championed the cause of Mr Kay,
whom now he despises and dislikes. What else is there to
know?'

'Nothing,' replied Miss Loveday.

*

The meeting convened by the chairman of the governors
had been intended to be a solemn and impressive affair, but
it turned out that the chairman, himself an Old Boy, had
known Mrs Bradley for years, and that they were not only
well acquainted but were old and firm friends.

'Good Lord, Mrs B.!' he said joyously. 'Fancy finding you

here! Come on, and tell me what to say. I suppose it *is*
murder, ain't it? Who did it? Do you happen to know?'

'I *think* I know,' Mrs Bradley replied, 'but that has
nothing to do with your meeting, which, nevertheless, I shall
attend.'

The local Superintendent of Police was also present.

'You know, Beadle,' said the chairman to him con-
fidentially, 'I should call in Scotland Yard if I were you.
Mean to say, it's a bit above your weight, this sort of thing,
unless you're pretty sure you can get your hooks on the
fellow. Who did it, hey? Do *you* know?'

'Not by so much as a hair, sir,' replied the Superintendent,
instinctively following a lead, 'unless, of course, it should
chance to be the gentleman we've got our eye on, and I don't
want to go into that. And Scotland Yard are sending their
Mr Gavin.'

'By the way, Wyck, I suppose we'd better shelve the
question of Housemasters until this confounded business is
settled,' suggested a governor who was known to be a rabid
anti-feminist. 'Wonder who – '

'Couldn't have been a boy, anyway,' broke in a retired
major, another of the governors. 'I know boys out and out.
No vice in 'em. What do you say, Sainsbury?' He turned to
another of the party who was also an Old Boy of the
School.

'Can't concur in your opinion. Boys are all thugs. Got
three of my own, so I ought to know,' replied Sainsbury, a
lively-looking man of forty-five. 'Besides, what about Watt
in '18?'

Reminiscences of Watt led to reminiscences of Pott, and
the talk passed to Bott, Cott, and Gott.

'Talking of Gott,' said Mrs Bradley, seizing her opportunity, 'isn't there a boy at the School named Issacher?'

'Yes, there is an Issacher in Mr Loveday's House,' said
Mr Wyck, looking up from the notes he was writing. He
glanced at her gratefully, for he wanted to get the meeting
over, and all the Potts, Botts, Cotts, and Gotts had been

before his time as Headmaster, and he was not particularly interested in any but his own Old Boys.

'We must interview him,' said Mrs Bradley, at once. 'This boy Issacher, I mean.'

The governors were surprised by this suggestion, but Issacher was sent for hastily by the Headmaster, who now saw a chance of getting on with the meeting. Issacher kept it waiting for fourteen minutes. He was a thick-set boy in a bad temper which his racial background caused him to hide at first. He sidled in, looked at the Headmaster, and bowed to the chairman of the governors, who had been on his father's board of directors at one time.

'Ah, Issacher?' said the chairman.

'Sir?' said Issacher.

'Sorry to have dragged you from your studies and all that,' put in the major, laughing heartily at his own wit.

'I was taking my practice time. I am a pianist, sir,' said Issacher, with deadly meekness. 'Last week I was interrupted for a routine dental inspection when my teeth are perfectly sound.' He showed them. 'This week I had hoped to be allowed at least the hour allotted to me on my timetable.'

'Don't be impertinent, boy,' said Mr Wyck, mildly. 'Stand at the end of the table and reply clearly and exactly to what is asked you.'

'But, sir!' protested the youth, his fine hands beginning to flutter. 'Really, sir, I have done no wrong! I only ask for a little time to practise my music! But no! I am accused and browbeaten! There is no justice anywhere! Of what am I accused?'

'Don't act in this terrified way,' said Mr Wyck. 'You are being foolish, my boy.'

'And talking of accusations,' said Mrs Bradley, before anyone else could speak, 'what of your book, Mr Issacher?'

Issacher dropped his eyes, and there was a pause.

'I don't make a book during term,' he said slowly, his expressionless eyes on hers as soon as he raised them.

'Oh, nonsense!' said Mrs Bradley briskly. 'Tell all, and I'll go bail for you. But, in telling all, be truthful and succinct. We have no more time to lose than you.'

'Very well,' said Issacher slowly, 'I'll tell everything.' He paused again, glanced round at the expectant faces, and then burst out with some suddenness, 'Yes, Merrys and Skene did break out at night! Yes, they did go to the Dogs, but they did no good! Yes, Mr Conway was murdered, but it was nothing to do with me! Yes, I did make a book on whether they would be found out and when! Yes, I made another book on which of the masters did the murder! So what?'

'Go and play the piano, Issacher,' said the Headmaster, still speaking mildly, 'and return to us when you are calm and can speak in a proper manner.'

'And ask Mr Poundbury to spare us a word,' said Mrs Bradley. She wagged her head sorrowfully at Issacher's retreating back.

'Jewish, I suppose?' said the major. 'Artistic race. Wonder who scooped the pool? Whether they'd be found out or not, eh? Not a bad flutter. Intelligent idea.' He developed it, whilst Mr Wyck pretended to make more notes and Mrs Bradley actually did make some. Mr Poundbury was then shown in by the butler. 'Is Issacher in your House?' demanded the major, as soon as the butler had gone. 'Boy's got brains, but he wants a sound thrashing. You'd better see to it.'

'Alas, no, he is not in my House. I wish he were. I can't find a boy to play Hamlet to save my life,' said Mr Poundbury. 'And there's Mr Loveday, who cares for nothing but Roman Baths, and Miss Loveday, who cares for nothing but ferreting out other people's business, with a boy like that on their hands. A genuine talent wasted, wasted, wasted! He is even *fat* enough for Hamlet – "too, too solid flesh" you know. Oh, by the way, did you send for me, Headmaster?'

'Mrs Bradley sent for you,' replied Mr Wyck. 'If you have no objection, I should be obliged if you would answer her questions, keeping closely to the point, if you follow me.'

'I have only one question to put to Mr Poundbury,' said Mrs Bradley, 'and I wish to put it in front of the governing body. Mr Poundbury, what can you tell us about Mr Conway?'

'I?' said Mr Poundbury, surprised. 'Do I know him? – Oh, *Conway!* I'm so sorry! Of course! Conway! What do you want me to tell you?'

'Anything which comes into your head.'

'I scarcely know where to begin,' said Mr Poundbury, smoothing his very sparse hair from his scholarly brow. 'I suppose I had better begin at the beginning. When *was* that? Let me think, Oh, yes, I know. No, I don't . . . What exactly am I talking about?'

'Hadn't we better have our meeting first?' muttered one of the governors, a bishop. 'My train – '

'You are telling the governors all about Mr Conway,' said Mrs Bradley firmly to the witness. 'We should like to hear what you had against him. That is all.'

'Had against him? Oh,' said Mr Poundbury, 'I know! You are thinking of my wife. But I wouldn't rake up past history, if I were you. She's got over it, of course. People do. Not easily, but they do. Yes, yes, there's no doubt of that. They do, do, do. . . . What do they do? Oh, yes – ' He glanced down at his heavily-bandaged right hand.

'And have *you* got over it?' Mrs Bradley enquired. Mr Poundbury shook his head.

'I could have murdered him,' he said simply. Then the meaning of these words seemed to dawn on him. 'Oh, I'm so sorry! Of course, he *was* murdered, wasn't he? I'd forgotten that again for the moment. Well, I must be going, I'm afraid. My wife will get you anything you – Oh, no, of course not. How foolish of me. Really, I do apologize! *What* did you want me to tell you?'

'You've told us what we wanted to know,' said Mrs Bradley.

Mr Poundbury nodded, said, 'Good night, boys. Lights out at ten sharp,' and went out, looking benign. Mr Wyck looked enquiringly round the table.

'An able man,' he said, forestalling criticism. 'Easily the best Classical scholar on the Staff, and with a curious and acceptable gift of coaching the backward boys. No trouble with discipline, either, strange to say. His wife runs the House, of course,' he added to Mrs Bradley. 'She is a gifted person, and is very beautiful. I think you will have to meet her. And, by the way, Poundbury is not usually quite so absent-minded. His wife – '

'What's this tale about her?' demanded the major. 'Nothing scandalous, I hope? Can't have that sort of thing with the boys around. Impressionable age, you know. Once saw that "Young Woodley" thing they put on. Makes you think a bit. I say, you don't think *he* murdered Conway, do you?' he added suddenly. '*I* should call him absent-minded enough to be capable of anything.'

'I don't think absent-mindedness in murderers is a sign of capability,' said Mrs Bradley. 'But I would say that a beautiful wife is excuse enough for anything. An old-fashioned idea, perhaps.'

'But what's this funny stuff about her and Conway?' persisted the major.

'You had better ask her,' said Mr Wyck.

'I didn't think of it in time,' said the major.

'And now, Wyck?' said the chairman. The governors hitched up their chairs. The Headmaster looked at the assembly, glanced at his notes and then gave a short, clear account of what had happened and what steps had been taken after the discovery of Mr Conway's body by Mr Kay and Mr Semple.

'And there is more evidence to be disclosed at the resumed inquest,' he added, 'but you will all appreciate that I am not at liberty to distribute facts which the police do not want advertised.'

'If *I* had anything to do with the conducting of this case,' said the major, 'I should want to know a great deal about that boy Issacher.'

'Poor Issacher! I am afraid he's had an unsatisfactory life, and then, even the best of Jews are upset by the troubles in Palestine, I believe. I don't like the boy as a boy; I'm sorry for him, though. Conway was no friend of his,' said Mr Wyck, thoughtfully. 'I always had a suspicion that he baited the lad. If I'd been certain, Conway would have gone. I won't have that sort of thing. As you know, Conway was held under 18B for a bit at the beginning of the war. They had to release him, of course, and very soon, but you will remember that I was not very much in favour of his appointment.'

'How long had Mr Conway been a master here?' Mrs Bradley enquired.

'Oh, for four years and the fraction of this term that he was with us,' said Mr Wyck. 'I didn't want him, as the governors, I know, will agree, but we were all glad enough to get a master at that time, as you can imagine. As the alternative was to employ a young woman – highly qualified and very charming – from Newnham, I was persuaded to agree to his appointment. But I didn't like it, and I wish now that I had plumped for the girl. At least she wouldn't have been murdered, although' – he smiled sardonically, an expression which gave his face a Satanic and startling charm – 'although I think she might have committed suicide after a bit.'

'That's all very well,' said the major, 'and you may remember I was as dead against Conway's appointment as you were. But what I say is this – '

'You were against appointing the girl, too,' put in Mrs Forrester, the only woman governor. 'You said she wouldn't be able to manage boys.'

'Neither would she!' retorted the major. 'And talking of that – '

'I don't think we had better,' put in the chairman firmly, 'otherwise we shall never get through. Now, Wyck, what further steps are you proposing to take?'

'I should explain first what further steps I have already taken,' said Mr Wyck. 'I have taken the step of inviting Mrs Lestrange Bradley to watch the School for a few weeks. Some boy or boys know something of this unhappy business. That is a fact which must be faced.'

'Just so, sir,' put in the Superintendent, before the major could reaffirm his faith in boyhood generally and in the boys of Spey in particular. 'We have some evidence already that one of the master's bicycles had been used on the night of the crime.'

'Good heavens, man!' exploded the major. 'Think what you're saying!'

'I am well aware of what I'm saying, sir,' returned the Superintendent, with the indulgence often shown by large men to smaller ones, 'and please don't think that we have the slightest suspicion, let alone evidence, that any of the young gentlemen of the School are connected in any way with the crime.'

'I should think not, indeed!' growled the major, in furious resentment of the Superintendent's good-natured attitude. 'I should jolly well think not!'

'However, there's been larks, of a kind, if the Headmaster will excuse the word as applied to his scholars, and what larks they were have got to be found out, and, when found out, sifted and pinned down. Now, I don't say – '

'But I do,' said Mrs Bradley. 'I say that we know the identity of the boys in question, and, although they were out after hours, and although they impounded a bicycle, and even punctured one of its tyres, I am going to ask Mr Wyck, to whom I shall give their names presently, to exercise his discretion on their behalf and to take no action against them, particularly as – '

'I appreciate the necessity of obtaining their evidence,' said Mr Wyck firmly, 'and am prepared to promise to overlook their conduct. This,' he added, for the benefit of the major, 'is in order to assist in the detection of Conway's attacker, and for no other reason whatsoever.'

'Quite so, sir,' agreed the Superintendent. 'We can't afford to lose valuable evidence because the witnesses are afraid to come forward.'

'Oh, well! Oh, well!' said the major, waving the point aside. 'Now what was all this mud about Mrs Poundbury, and why weren't we told about it before?' His eyes gleamed hopefully.

'There is nothing to tell,' Mr Wyck replied. 'It was not anybody's business at the time except that of the two concerned, and, of course, Poundbury himself. There was no scandal attached to it. Mrs Poundbury was very sensible and, in any case, it occurred during the summer vacation and on board ship. It was nothing to do with the School, and I am sorry it ever came out.'

'Oh?'

'Yes.'

'But it left Poundbury pretty sore?'

'You heard what he said just now.'

'And you think he might have been the murderer?' The major spoke excitedly.

'I can think of nobody less likely,' replied Mr. Wyck, with his usual calmness.

'Well, we don't seem to have got very far,' said the chairman, 'and as the – the death was the only item on the agenda, I propose, unless Mr Wyck or Mrs Bradley has anything more to tell us, to declare the meeting closed.'

'I'd like to ask a question,' said the major. 'No offence, of course.'

'None,' said Mrs Bradley, perceiving that the question had been addressed principally to her.

'Right. Well, what I mean to say, what's your position with regard to – I mean, are you to be appointed officially by us, or what? Position ought to be made regular, you know, what!'

'My position has not, so far, been irregular,' Mrs Bradley

answered. 'I am here in the capacity of guest to Mr and Miss Loveday. Simply that, and nothing more.'

'Oh, well, that's all right, then. Just like to get these things straight. Meeting closed? Vote of thanks to the Chair? Right. . . .'

10. *Hecate at School House*

*

Who accuses me?

IBID. (*Act 2, Scene 10*)

SOME of the governors went home directly the gathering broke up, others remained to dine with the Headmaster. Mrs Bradley returned to Miss Loveday, but supper at the House was scarcely over when a message came from Mr Wyck. In response to it, Mrs Bradley was compelled to break the news to Miss Loveday that she was invited to shift quarters to the School House. This was much to the distress of Miss Loveday, who begged her to remain where she was.

'It would be unreasonable,' Mrs Bradley responded, 'to trespass further upon your hospitality.'

'Oh, I realize,' rejoined Miss Loveday, 'that you came merely to give Merrys an airing. Well, he is aired. We now know all about him. But we value you at par, and therefore, I say, remain.'

'I value you above rubies,' Mrs Bradley cordially responded. 'Nevertheless, I am bid to join the household of the Headmaster, an invitation which can hardly be disregarded.'

'Regard it by all means,' Miss Loveday replied in like tones, 'but remember that for you there is one corner in our Loveday House which is for ever Bradley.'

'I will indeed remember it,' said Mrs Bradley; 'you are too kind; much too kind. You should never cherish serpents in your bosom.' Having said this, it was with a certain sense of relief that she took leave of her eccentric hostess and moved over to the pleasant and commodious School House.

She had not been in the School House above a day and a quarter when she was asked to receive a deputation from Loveday's. This consisted of Merrys, Skene, and Takhobali.

'The thing is,' said Skene, who had been thrust into prominence partly by Merrys and partly by his own natural instincts, 'that the Tar-Baby thinks he ought to spill you something which perhaps you hadn't so far heard of.'

'Lights!' said Takhobali dramatically.

'Lights and soft music,' muttered Merrys.

'Lights?' said Mrs Bradley. 'It is full late in the day to mention lights. When and where? On the night of the death, do you mean? And over by the Roman Bath?'

Takhobali rolled his eyes.

'Do you know about the river lights?' he enquired.

'How can she know?' enquired Merrys. 'She wasn't there, was she, you ass? Tell her about them. It might be beastly important.' He looked at Mrs Bradley for confirmation of this view, and she at once supported him.

'I look forward to your revelations, Prince,' she said.

'There were lights. The Roman Bath, for Skene and Merrys. The river, however, for me,' Takhobali explained, waving his thin, long hands. 'I saw lights along the river. I told Merrys and Skene because I knew they had been out of the House one night, and I wanted to give them opportunity to forbid my telling you if they wished. But they say I should tell. It will assist, and I wish to make recompense for their kind help when I do not understand football game and wish to know. I saw the lights at about eleven o'clock. I was sick, and from the window of that place, I saw.'

'He's always sick after fish-pie. We had it for supper that night,' explained Merrys. 'Nobody takes much notice of lights over at the Roman Bath because Albert-Edward – Mr Loveday – is always doing weird things over there in connexion with the filters and the heating. But when the Tar-Baby mentioned he'd seen lights over by the river, we thought we'd bring him along. Apparently he's been in a flat spin ever since the murder, because he didn't know whom he ought to tell, or whether he ought to tell at all. He's been kicked so often he gets muddled about such things.'

'Ah, yes,' said the Tar-Baby, gleaming. 'I am not to tell tales or talk shop.'

Mrs Bradley went straight over to Miss Loveday.

'What were the lights at the Roman Bath on the night of the murder?' she enquired. Miss Loveday gazed in mild astonishment.

'They could have little bearing,' she replied. 'They were carried, I daresay, by my brother and myself. We go over occasionally to stoke the Roman furnace. We can scarcely wake our servants for such a task. The heating system is curiously unsatisfactory, although I would not care to have my brother hear me say so. The Bath is his main interest, as you know.'

'And you were there on the night of Mr Conway's death?'

'If anybody says so, yes. I suppose it was one of the boys who mentioned it? They should not have been up and about at such an hour.'

'And *you* did *not* mention it?'

'What bearing could it have?' Miss Loveday mildly enquired. 'Oh, I know that Gerald Conway was either wholly or partially drowned, but that's neither here nor there with respect to the matter under discussion.'

'So you have no objection to admitting that you and your brother were up and about that night?'

'No objection at all. Why should I have? My conscience is clear,' said Miss Loveday, closing the argument. Mrs Bradley sought the first opportunity of reopening it, but this time she attacked the weaker partner.

'What were you doing at your Roman Bath on the night of Mr Conway's death?' she enquired of Mr Loveday with considerable abruptness, going out to where he was embarrassing Cartaris by personally conducting and supervising a House football practice.

'Put your *head* down, boy!' yelled Mr Loveday; and then he replied vaguely, 'Doing? Oh, stoking the furnace, you know; the hypocaust. A tricky business. Just stoking, but it requires an expert hand, and is a disagreeable business because the roof is low. Slaves did the stoking for the Romans, as you are aware, but I cannot ask my servants to undertake it at night, although my knife-and-boot boy can see to it during the daytime, and usually does so.'

'How often do you go out at nights for the purpose?' Mrs Bradley enquired.

'Feet! *Feet!*' yelled Mr Loveday. 'Every now and then,' he added maddeningly.

'So that when the Superintendent of Police asked you what reason you had for setting your House in order,' said Mrs Bradley, paraphrasing a conversation which the Superintendent had rehearsed to her and of which she had been quick to see the point, 'your reason was really a very good one indeed?'

'How do you mean?' Mr Loveday enquired; but his body had stiffened, Mrs Bradley noticed.

'You yourself, not to mention your sister, had actually been out of the House and at the Roman Bath that night,' she gravely explained, 'and therefore you wanted to be sure that the police should not suspect you of having murdered Mr Conway.'

'Oh, nonsense!' said Mr Loveday, with unusual vigour. 'We could scarcely have known that somebody would attack and drown poor Conway on a night when we were out of the House! By putting my House in order, as I believe I termed it, I merely wished to be certain that none of my boys could be held blameworthy. It was a very great shock to me when I was told that Merrys and Skene had been absent from the House one night not long before the event.'

'By the event, you refer to – '

'Well kicked, boy!' cried Mr Loveday. 'Coincidences are bound to occur,' he added, turning again to Mrs Bradley, 'and it is coincidence, pure and simple, that our expedition that evening should anticipate Conway's death, but there is nothing very strange about it, surely? – particularly as Miss Loveday and I were in the habit of stoking the furnace.'

'I suppose not, if you put it that way,' Mrs Bradley agreed.

'Who composes the menus for the House suppers?' she demanded suddenly.

'My sister, of course, as my housekeeper. Or, rather, she keeps or delegates that privilege, as she chooses.'

'Does she often give the boys fish-pie?'

'They have it sometimes, except for Takhobali. He never eats it.'

'He did, on the night of the murder.'

'That was foolish of him, then,' said Mr Loveday. 'The boy knows perfectly well that it makes him bilious. Although why it should – *pass,* boy, *pass!* – I find it impossible to imagine. A simple, light, nourishing dish like – that's better, Forrester! Hand him off, man! – like fish-pie would not, one would fancy, upset anybody.'

'Some people are allergic to fish,' said Mrs Bradley. 'No doubt that is the case with Prince Takhobali. And I wonder who talked of eels to Mr Micklethwaite?'

'I suppose Takhobali saw the lights at the Roman Bath that night and thought the spot was haunted,' said Mr Loveday, turning thoughtfully away from his House practice and accompanying Mrs Bradley along the edge of Big Field towards the School House. 'And how do *you* react to our culinary miracles?' he enquired, almost in his sister's feminine idiom, but with an ironic note in his voice which rather surprised Mrs Bradley. She praised the cook's resourcefulness, remarked upon what a problem meals now provided for hapless housekeepers, and instanced her own French cook's difficulties and exasperations.

'Tell me', she said to Mrs Wyck, as they sat at dinner in the Headmaster's private dining-room – for Mrs Wyck dined only once a term with the School House boys – 'what you think of Mr and Miss Loveday.'

'What do I *think* of them? – as possible murderers, do you mean?' asked Mrs Wyck, who combined, as a Headmaster's wife had need to do, great simplicity and great perspicacity in unpredictable proportions. 'Well, I think they've been rather clever, so far, haven't they? – if they did it, I mean.

Of course, I don't really think they did, for a minute. But do let's talk about them as though they did do it. I'm so sick of policemen's questions that it will be a change to have a straightforward discussion without any questions at all.'

'But there will be heaps of questions,' said Mrs Bradley promptly. 'Heaps and heaps. And *I* shall ask most of them,' she added. 'First, tell me why you *don't* suspect the Lovedays.'

'I thought we'd agreed to suspect them. Oh, well, never mind. I don't think they're the sort of people to do anything *wrong*. Not anything as wrong as murder, anyway. I can't explain what I mean, but – well, just that.'

'I know exactly what you mean. And yet, you know, somebody killed Mr Conway.'

'Oh, good! We're going to suspect them, after all! But, you know, Gerald Conway had some very queer acquaintances, hadn't he? Some rather odd things have come out about him since his death. Don't you think it's much more likely – ?'

'Have some odd things come out? – Still, the police would look closely into all that sort of thing.'

'Yes, they have. They told Christopher so. Their own opinion is clear. They think somebody here did it. But, speaking seriously, I can't believe that. I keep going over everybody in my mind, and I can't fix upon a single person capable of such an act except – '

'Except?'

'I ought not to say it, even to you, but the only people I can think of are Brenda and Louis Kay.'

'Is his name really Louis? I was given to understand – '

'His name is Bennett Arturo Kay, and his wife calls him Benny, when she calls him anything. Anyway, I think they are the likeliest, because they've got the biggest motive, except for the Poundburys. Motive always counts most with the police, doesn't it? Of course, in real life, as I say, I don't believe *anybody* here did it, but if I were writing a detective story, or reading an account in the paper, I should plump

for the Kays. Louis was an enemy of Gerald Conway, and
with good reason, I believe.'

'And the Poundburys?'

'Oh, well, I like the Poundburys, and, between ourselves,
I don't really like the Kays at all. Besides, I think the balance
would have to be on the side of the Kays because, if what I
suspect is true, they *both* had a motive, whereas, in the case
of the Poundburys, only *he* would have had one. That's old
scandal, of course, and I ought not to repeat it, but I expect
everybody knows all about it by now. Even the police know,
which is rather dreadful, but I believe they are very discreet.'

'I know something about it myself, as the result of the
Governors' meeting,' said Mrs Bradley. 'But would you say
that Mrs Poundbury had no motive? She might have had
her own reasons for jealousy, particularly as his engagement
had been announced. But we're losing sight of the Lovedays.
Now what do you make of this?'

She recounted to Mrs Wyck the story of Takhobali and
the fish-pie.

'But why on earth did the silly boy eat the stuff if it always
makes him ill?' demanded Mrs Wyck. Mrs Bradley shrugged.

'That is one of the things I want to find out,' she said.
'But I don't want the boys to think it has any importance
beyond the importance they already know it has.' And she
told Mrs Wyck the story of the river lights on the night of
Conway's death. 'Then, you see,' she added, 'there is the
fact that the Lovedays were both out of the House on the
night of the murder.'

'That looks so bad that it must be a proof of their innocence, though,' said Mrs Wyck. 'What else is there against
them?'

'I was hoping that *you* could tell *me* that,' said Mrs
Bradley. 'Their behaviour since the murder has been what
one would expect. What I would like to know is how their
behaviour *since* the murder compares with their behaviour
before the murder. I cannot be more explicit, for it is only

since the murder that I have been privileged to make their acquaintance.'

'I don't think I can help. They seem just the same to me,' said Mrs Wyck. 'I know what you mean, though. You want to know of any actions which seemed innocent enough in themselves *at the time*, but now would look rather different if the Lovedays come under suspicion of having committed the crime.'

'I knew you would understand me,' said Mrs Bradley. 'Exactly that. Cannot you think of anything?'

'No, I can't. Besides, we are regarding this as a *planned* murder, aren't we? Do you really think it was? – seriously, I mean.'

'I really think it must have been. You see, there's not much doubt that if it had been done on the spur of the moment it would have been done differently.'

Mrs Wyck turned very pale, and Mrs Bradley apologized.

'The dog with the brick tied to its neck, you mean,' said Mrs Wyck, waving away Mrs Bradley's expressions of concern, and very rapidly pulling herself together. 'It does seem dreadful, and, as you say, probably planned; otherwise . . .'

'Miss Loveday referred to Mr Conway as a puppy,' Mrs Bradley went on. 'It was, perhaps, a revealing description. Our choice of words can disclose our secret thoughts in a way we do not always intend.'

'I see. You mean that her saying it that way provides, in itself, a clue,' said Mrs Wyck. 'I do see what you mean.'

Her tones were serious. Mrs Bradley nodded slowly and rhythmically.

'Mind you, there is no more reason, in a way, for suspecting Mr and Miss Loveday than for suspecting half a dozen other people,' she said, 'but they interest me very much. By the way, I wonder whether I might ask Mr Wyck an impertinent question?'

'Christopher would be prepared – more than prepared – to answer *any* question that would help to clear up this wretched business,' said Mrs Wyck, who had dropped com-

pletely her first assumption of lightheartedness and now
looked the worried woman which Mrs Bradley knew her to
be. 'He'll be down to dinner in a minute – yes, here he is,
with the sherry. Christopher, Mrs Bradley has something to
ask you. It has a bearing.'

Mr Wyck made no attempt to appear light-hearted. He
poured sherry from the decanter, handed the glasses round,
put his own glass on a small table, and dropped wearily into
an armchair.

'A man from Scotland Yard is coming early to-morrow,'
he said. 'I don't see what he can find out now. I'm sick to
my soul of the police!'

'I wonder whether I know the man they are sending?'
Mrs Bradley enquired.

'Detective-Inspector Gavin,' Mr Wyck replied.

'Good. He is engaged to my secretary. I am glad he is the
one to come,' said Mrs Bradley, without betraying the fact
that she had told the Chief Constable to ask for him. 'Now,
look here, Mr Wyck, what I want to ask you may have
some bearing on the case, and it is this: supposing there were
a vacancy for a Housemaster – suppose, for example, it had
been Mr Loveday, Mr Mayhew, Mr Reeder, or any other
Housemaster who had been killed, and not Mr Conway –
who would have received the appointment to the vacancy?'

'Well, it is a point I can only deal with unofficially, in a
way,' replied Mr Wyck, betraying no surprise at the question.
'Officially, the governors fill the vacant posts here, from my
own to that of the most junior member of the Staff. Unofficially, however, my own suggestions are almost invari-
ably adopted. In the case which you postulate, my own
choice would have fallen upon Kay. He is a sound fellow, a
capable and quiet disciplinarian, and, although he is not
particularly popular with the boys at present, I think time
would tend to adjust matters, since there is nothing in his
character, so far as I have been able to observe him, which
boys would persistently and inherently dislike. Conway
made a set at him, you know, and some sycophantic boys

have followed that very ill-advised lead. Of course, John Semple is the man I myself should prefer as a Housemaster, but he is too young at present, and, besides, the governors do like our Housemasters to be married.'

'They take no exception to Miss Loveday's acting as her brother's housekeeper, though?' Mrs Bradley asked. Mr Wyck glanced sharply at his wife, but she smiled slightly and shook her head.

'Well, it is curious that you should raise that point,' said Mr Wyck, apparently reassured by his wife's reactions, 'because there has been considerable discussion at recent meetings about the position of Miss Loveday in that House. It has been remarked upon that she seems to be in charge of it and that her brother occupies a secondary position. I have argued against this theory, of course, but I have encountered a certain amount of scepticism which, I am compelled to admit, is not unjustified. However, Loveday's is not an altogether satisfactory House, as the fact that those two boys, Merrys and Skene, were able to break out at night would seem to indicate.'

'So that Mr Conway, even after the announcement of his engagement to Miss Pearson, would not have been your choice of a Housemaster?'

'No,' answered Mr Wyck decisively.

'Would it be impertinent to ask your reasons?'

'I have two reasons. The first is that poor Conway was most improperly biased towards boys. A boy such as Issacher, for example, and a really brilliant but somewhat eccentric lad, such as Micklethwaite, would have stood no chance with him. I should hesitate to place Prince Takhobali in his House, or any other Eastern, near-Eastern, or Southern boy.'

Mrs Bradley, who had not before encountered these tactful adjectives, nodded solemnly.

'I see,' she said. 'Sound. Very sound, if I may say so.'

'My second reason,' pursued Mr Wyck, disregarding the compliment, which he had applied to himself years previously, 'is that a master who confuses the married state with a merely temporary liaison is not the man to place in charge of immature natures.'

'I agree entirely,' Mrs Bradley replied. 'And now I wonder whether you would connive at deceitfulness?'

'Certainly,' Mr Wyck replied without hesitation. 'The morals of the head of a school are always elastic. What do you want me to do?'

'I should like to be present at the School plays, and then I want you to pretend that I am going away a couple of days before the end of term; but I mean to sneak back here again without a soul except David Gavin and ourselves being the wiser. Is that possible?'

'It can and shall be done. This means that you have definite suspicions of someone here?'

'Yes, I'm afraid it does.'

'I see. A little more sherry?'

Mrs Bradley accepted gratefully.

11. *The Ladies, God Bless Them*

*

Insinuating Monster! So you think I know nothing of the Affair of
Miss Polly Peachum?

IBID. (*Act 2, Scene 9*)

'UNHAPPILY,' said Mrs Poundbury, 'we haven't a Hamlet
in the House. You will appreciate that it is so much simpler
to have at least the chief parts taken by boys in our own
House. The rehearsals, you know, and just that last little
ounce of whatever it is that puts the polish on the principals.
We should have done Hamlet, without a doubt, had we had
Issacher, who is quite the type, Gilbert says, and is, like
most Jewish boys, quite marvellously fluid on the stage, but
we haven't him. It really is unfortunate!'

Mrs Bradley remarked that to have a fluid Hamlet would
scarcely be just to Shakespeare, and at this Mrs Poundbury
relinquished serious platitudes for a girlish and attractive
giggle.

'I've heard Gilbert on the heartrending subject of "too,
too solid flesh",' she observed. 'The trials of a schoolmaster's wife! However, what we *are* putting on is something
much nearer to the hearts of our Philistine House. Gilbert
has produced three short plays. One is a play about murder.'

'Oh?' said Mrs Bradley. 'Won't that . . .?'

'Oh, Gilbert asked Mr Wyck, and Mr Wyck saw a couple
of rehearsals. He doesn't object at all. He thinks it will help
to rationalize the situation here. The boys show no signs of
it, but they must be pretty well strung up, like the rest of us.'

'Are the rest of you strung up?' asked Mrs Bradley; but
she did not say whether she agreed with Mr Wyck's applica-
tion of psychiatric principles to the minds of his boys. 'Well,
I shall look forward to it all very much,' she added, with
sincerity and no mental reservations. 'Now, tell me – are you

prepared to meet the young man from Scotland Yard?'

Mrs Poundbury looked surprised, and then she laughed and exclaimed, 'Who on earth am I, to take up the time of Scotland Yard?'

'You are a woman with a secret,' Mrs Bradley calmly replied, 'which secret may cost you very dear if you insist upon keeping it. Speak, Mrs Poundbury, speak; for, if you do not, I wash my hands of the consequences.'

'But I haven't any secret!' cried Mrs Poundbury. 'Not, at any rate, the kind of secret that could interest Scotland Yard.'

'Think again!' Mrs Bradley advised her. 'What did you do on the night of Mr Conway's death?'

'I?'

'You.'

'But I've told you – I've told the police – I've told everybody – I was asleep in my room, the room I share with Gilbert! And he was asleep there, too! At least, I don't know whether he was asleep, of course, but he was most certainly there. We've both got the same what-do-you-call it? – alibi. We can give it to one another. No one can contest that!'

'One might if a certain note of assignation were found,' said Mrs Bradley drily.

'Oh, but I – Oh, but!' said Mrs Poundbury, taken by a stratagem and struggling in the net of the fowler. 'Oh, damn and *blast!* How did you know?'

'I suppose you did have the common sense to burn it?' Mrs Bradley brutally enquired.

'No, I – no, I didn't,' said Mrs Poundbury, shedding all her artifices and insincerities, and looking, all at once, a terrified girl. 'I was so furious with poor Gerald for not turning up – of course, I realize now why he didn't – that I forgot all about the note until I heard – well, until I heard of his death. And then I couldn't find it! I've looked simply everywhere, but it's gone!'

'Your husband *wasn't* in the bedroom,' said Mrs Bradley,

even more drily than before. 'Do you believe that *he* killed
Mr Conway?'

'No, no! Of course I don't! Gilbert couldn't kill anybody.
He wouldn't hurt a fly. I *know* he wouldn't! I – I – ' She
broke off, and gazed in agony at Mrs Bradley's sharp black
eyes and alarmingly snake-like smile. 'Oh, do help me! Do
help me! You *must!*' she cried suddenly and wildly. 'It *must*
be somewhere! Where did I put it? Where *could* I have put
it? Oh dear!'

'You tell Scotland Yard all about it. That's the only help
I can give. And *find* the note. It must be somewhere,' said
Mrs Bradley, declining to help her at all. 'And your husband
can be violent. You yourself told me that.'

*

Mrs Kay received Mrs Bradley without any semblance of
cordiality whatsoever.

'I don't know what you expect me to tell you,' she said.
'I don't know where my husband went or what he did on
the night when Gerald was murdered, and as for boys –
well, if you knew as much about them as I do you would
realize that nine times out of ten their statements are all lies.
I wouldn't hang a dog on evidence supplied by boys!'

'I wouldn't hang a dog at all,' remarked Mrs Bradley,
turning thoughtfully towards the iron fence which separated
the Kays' cottage from the School drive. It had been over-
looked (probably for some good reason) by the Government
collectors of scrap metal during the war.

'The point is,' said Mrs Kay, following her in some haste,
'whether you want to hang my husband. I've been fairly
nasty to Benny, but he didn't do it, you know.'

'You were not at home at the time, Mrs Kay,' Mrs
Bradley pointed out, gently enough.

'No, but I know Benny. He's a coward, and that means
he isn't a murderer. If he were . . .'

'If he were?'

'Well, he'd have murdered *me*, and long enough ago, at

that,' said Mrs Kay, with a snort of wifely amusement.

'It is interesting that you should say that,' Mrs Bradley remarked. 'You don't think perhaps – but no! Murders are sometimes committed for love, but far more often for money.'

'Money!' said Mrs Kay, with another sardonic snort. 'There isn't much money in *this* job! If Benny had taken *my* advice, he would have thrown it up and gone into business long ago. He has plenty of brains, and could have held down a decent job, if only he'd given his mind to it, instead of sitting down and waiting for poor old Loveday's pair of shoes!'

'This holding down of jobs is extraordinary. It sounds as though sometimes the job can be stronger than the man. Is that so?' Mrs Bradley enquired.

Mrs Kay looked at her suspiciously.

'It's just an expression,' she said.

'But how strange an expression! "The labourer is worthy of his hire" is another expression, and, to my mind, a preferable one. What kind of job is it which must be held down? Why does it squirm to get away? And, in the name of vocations, if your husband prefers schoolmastering, *why* shouldn't he follow his bent?'

Mrs Kay did not answer. After a pause, in which distaste of and annoyance with her visitor were both plainly indicated, she said:

'All this chapel-going, too!'

'By the boys?'

'By the boys and the masters. That is what I meant. And by stupid old spinsters like Miss Loveday. I call it morbid. She attends *all* the services, and they are really only meant for the boys!'

'You call it morbid,' said Mrs Bradley, under her breath. 'I wonder why?' Mrs Kay regarded her with suspicion and deep dislike.

'Don't *you* call it morbid?' she demanded. 'These boys and men are brought up like monks. I don't believe in it.

There's bound to be trouble, and trouble, you see, has come.'

'And you think that with no chapel-going there would have been no murder?' asked Mrs Bradley, deeply interested, but not altogether in the subject under discussion.

'Oh, I don't say that! I simply meant . . . oh, I don't really know what I'm talking about! Look here, I'll be frank. I don't usually whine to people about my affairs, but I wouldn't mind having some advice. What would you do if . . .'

'If I'd received a note which took me out on a wild-goose chase . . . or a fool's errand?' said Mrs Bradley, saying the last two words so deliberately that Mrs Kay flushed with annoyance.

'Well, yes,' she said, swallowing her anger. 'That's just it. It came – or was supposed to come, from – '

'Of all people, Gilbert Poundbury,' said Mrs Bradley gleefully. 'Beautiful! Beautiful! Do you like jig-saw puzzles, I wonder, Mrs Kay?'

'No, I've no patience with the things!' said Mrs Kay, betraying by her tone, no less than by her words, first, that this was the literal truth, and, secondly, that her lack of patience applied equally to her visitor. 'They're only fit for children! I wouldn't waste time on them myself.'

'Yes, children *do* have patience,' said Mrs Bradley thoughtfully. 'They must have, mustn't they? – or they could never suffer grown-up people. Why do we call ourselves grown-up? We can only be so in the body, most of us. Has it ever struck you, Mrs Kay, that the majority of these so-called and self-styled grown-ups behave very, very much worse, more stupidly, more selfishly, than they would ever expect children to behave?'

'I've never thought about it,' said Mrs Kay, now very angry indeed, 'And if you're trying to be insulting . . .'

'I'm not only trying, I'm succeeding,' said Mrs Bradley smoothly. 'Never mind that, for the moment. What excuse did Gilbert Poundbury make for wanting to see you that night?'

'Since you're so well versed in my bad behaviour, you can probably guess!' said Mrs Kay, beginning to look thoroughly sulky as a protection against being asked any more questions.

'But there is just one thing I think you ought to make clear to Scotland Yard,' said Mrs Bradley, ignoring the façade and speaking to the terrified woman behind it. 'That is, if you want my advice.'

'Thank you! I don't think I do!' said Mrs Kay flatly. 'I suppose you mean I ought to explain that I *wasn't* away from this neighbourhood on the night of Gerald Conway's death? Thank you again! I'm not exactly going to stick my neck into a noose for Scotland Yard's benefit!'

'That is a serious decision to make. I advise you very strongly indeed to reconsider it,' said Mrs Bradley with finality.

Mrs Kay said suddenly, 'You can tell your monkey from Scotland Yard that I've been leading you up the garden.'

'You haven't, you know,' said Mrs Bradley, solemnly shaking her head. 'You think things over, and behave like a sensible woman. And just you give the police that note. It may be of first-rate importance.'

Mrs Kay turned and came back.

'Look here,' she said unwillingly. 'I don't want to get into trouble, but I haven't got any note. I learnt to burn the things long ago. Still, if you haven't done anything wrong, you can't be found guilty, can you?'

'Well, it is not a wise move to withhold evidence,' said Mrs Bradley.

'Well, look here, then,' said Mrs Kay, 'I trust you, although I don't like you. I'll tell you what happened, and you can tell your Scotland Yard nark what you like.'

'Nancy the Nark,' said Mrs Bradley amiably. Mrs Kay looked startled.

'You don't suspect *her?*' she demanded.

'Why? Do you?' Mrs Bradley retorted.

'Oh, I see. I said "nark" and you – and you just repeated

it.' Mrs Kay looked relieved, and laughed, and, the tension thus eased, as Mrs Bradley had intended that it should be, she continued, 'You see, Gerald and I – well, Benny isn't all that fun, and Gerald was an exciting sort of person in his way, and I hated being stuck down here with nothing but boys, boys, boys, and a few narky – I mean, bitter sort of women, all schoolmasters' wives and sisters and things – so, well – you can see how it was.'

'No, no,' said Mrs Bradley. 'You must explain clearly, if you are going to explain at all. This film dialogue is misleading.'

'Beast!' said Mrs Kay, bursting into tears. Mrs Bradley looked pleased. 'You're as bad as Gerald! That's the kind of beastly thing *he* would say! I hated him, and I hate you! I *hate* you! I hate you! I hate you!'

'Very interesting,' said Mrs Bradley. 'In other words, you did *not* receive a note making an appointment that evening, but you think that Mrs Poundbury did. Further to that, you really *were* away from home. You were *not* in this neighbourhood at the time of Mr Conway's death.'

Mrs Kay pulled herself together.

'I'm sorry,' she said apologetically, 'if I was a bit rude, but I was never educated like you and all these schoolmasters, and, to tell you the truth, the whole set-up gets me down. All I want is money and a good time. That's not much to ask for, at my age, is it?'

'According to present-day standards it is the minimum that any self-respecting person could desire,' said Mrs Bradley deliberately. 'What makes you so certain that your husband committed the murder, Mrs Kay?'

'I don't think Benny *did* do it,' replied Mrs Kay lugubriously. 'He's a poor sort of fish, but he wouldn't dirty his hands with murder. The trouble is, I know he was up to something that night, and he won't tell me what it was, and I feel almost worried to death. He tells nothing but lies, and until he comes out with the truth, I don't see how I can help him. I'd stick to him all right if he'd trust me, but Benny

doesn't trust anybody. Sometimes it makes me so mad I feel
I could kill him; and that's a nice thing to be saying, with
Gerald Conway lying dead and cold!'

This conversation left Mrs Bradley thoughtful. It would
have been so fatally easy for Kay and Poundbury to have
pooled their grievances that night, inflamed themselves and
one another to the point of murder, and then to have set
upon the unsuspecting Conway . . . supposing (and this was
the snag) that they knew where to find him.

There was another flaw in the theory that they were the
murderers, however. It was that these two would not have
used the Roman Bath; they would most certainly have used
the river; and the absence of any trace of river weed, or mud,
or sand in the clothing of the corpse would dispose of the
theory completely.

Mrs Bradley found herself longing for the resumed inquest,
so that the point could be cleared up finally. Meanwhile
there was not much doubt what the two wives thought about
matters.

Mrs Bradley was almost certain that Mr Poundbury had
been out of the House that night, or for part of it. She was
almost certain, too, that the note of assignation had been
sent to him and not to his wife. The absent-minded Poundbury must have left it lying about for Mrs Poundbury to
find. She had read it, and drawn her own terrible conclusions.

But Mrs Bradley found herself modifying her own conclusions as she considered the information she had obtained
from the two wives. She found herself wishing for some
concrete evidence which would at least show which persons
had had access to Mr Kay's garden on the night of the murder.

It was a bit of bad luck, she reflected, that so many people
had trampled on Mr Kay's flower-beds before the police
arrived. Mr Semple and Kay himself had both gone up to
the body, so had Mr Wyck, and so had the doctor, and
what might have been the most valuable of clues had been
lost for ever.

12. *The Case is Clearer*

*

Come, Filch, you shall go with me into my own Room, and tell me the
whole Story.

IBID. (*Act 1, Scene 6*)

If you can forgive me, Sir, I will make a fair Confession, for to be sure he
hath been a most barbarous Villain to me.

IBID. (*Act 3, Scene 1*)

ISSACHER, whose parents were orthodox Jews, did not
attend Chapel. Mrs Bradley arranged, therefore, with his
Housemaster, to interview him whilst the rest of the School
was out of the way.

Issacher had been apprised of this arrangement and ap-
proved of it. He shared a study with two other boys, and
invited Mrs Bradley in as he would have invited her into his
home. He removed a pair of football boots, a sawn-off shot-
gun, two books, and a box-file from the seat of the most
comfortable chair in the room and asked her to sit down.
Then he faced her, smiling hospitably.

'It is about your connexion with the two boys who broke
out of the House during the week before Mr Conway's
death,' she said.

'Ah, that,' said Issacher. 'We must talk fast. The others
will soon be out of chapel. I had no connexion with those
boys whatsoever, and therefore, as a matter of fact, my
knowledge is second-hand; but it is reliable. All my information is reliable.'

Mrs Bradley pursed her beaky little mouth and nodded
slowly. So reliable did she know Issacher's information to
be ('Issy knows everything' was an article of faith in his
House) that she was prepared to believe that what he said
required the minimum of corroborative evidence.

'So?' she prompted him.

'So when Merrys and Skene broke out and then told Eaves

and Meyrick (in their dorm, you know) that a murder might
be committed, and then the next thing was that a mur –
that Mr Conway was found like that, I investigated and
found that their story was funny. Peculiar, I mean. It
jumped to the eye that they could get Spiv – Mr Kay –
arrested or not, as they liked, but it would mean landing
themselves with the sack if they were not pretty careful.'

'How did Mr Kay come to be known by his soubriquet?'
asked Mrs Bradley, flying off at a tangent.

'Oh, that!' said Issacher, his dark eyes just a little wary. 'I
lampooned him.'

'And the name caught on?'

'Louis the Spiv? Yes. I got it from Conway, of course.'

'Did you dislike Mr Kay?'

'Oh, no. But the fellows had begun to call *me* Spivvy, so I
thought it time to pass the buck.'

'Then you know nothing about the time of the murder?'

'Nothing at all, and I can't guess. I suppose the police
know?'

'Oh, yes, the medical evidence . . .'

'Within the usual limits, I expect? My father's a doctor.
But, you know,' he went on, waving his pianist's hands, 'if
you'll pardon me, and if I were you – ' He lowered his voice
and dropped his eyes. 'If I were you,' he repeated quietly,
'I'd give up the whole thing. It will only make a stink, and,
honestly, it isn't worth it for a beast like Mr Conway.'

'You disliked him?'

'Can't you imagine? – "our not altogether unimaginative
opponent, Herr Hitler" – and then a lot of filthy stuff about
the Jews. And then he'd pretend to forget my name and call
me "Friend Barabbas – I beg his pardon, Issacher." And
then he'd talk a lot of tripe about the Wandering Jew when
he caught me not attending to his lesson. Oh, I don't know
who killed the swine, but I pray they get away with it!' His
voice rose high. Mrs Bradley went away, very thoughtful.
Her next interview was with the intellectual Micklethwaite,
whom she sent for out of a Divinity lesson.

Micklethwaite attempted to impress her.

'I still say that St Paul had no conception of the Athenian mentality,' said he. 'Judging from the account given in the *Acts*, he underrated the intelligence of the Greeks of the first century, over-estimated the appeal of the Gospels, and obviously had never heard of the Mysteries.'

'Have you been to Eleusis?' Mrs Bradley politely enquired.

'No, and I don't want to go. I intend to keep the places I revere safely within my Garden of the Hesperides,' replied the annoying and unorthodox child, adroitly blocking the question.

'It is interesting that you should have come straight out of a Divinity lesson,' said Mrs Bradley, restraining herself from hitting him over the head and, instead, leading the way to the School library, where, at that hour of the day, no one was likely to disturb them. 'It was about the Divinity Prize that I wanted to speak to you.'

'Oh, that!' said Micklethwaite. He was a well-made, sandy-haired, very tidy youth, with a fine brow and a short, plump, sensual mouth. 'That was to do with Mr Conway. What can you expect of a man who prefers Canaletto to Turner?'

'Less, obviously, than you can expect of a youth who knows one from the other,' replied Mrs Bradley. 'But re-count to me, Mr Micklethwaite, the full history of the award of the Divinity Prize of last year.'

'Nothing to tell,' said Micklethwaite, shrugging his curiously wide, slim shoulders. 'I suppose Conway *thought* I cribbed. I didn't, and I didn't want the prize. I shall say no more about it.' Neither did he.

'A *Judo* expert? Hm!' thought Mrs Bradley. She returned to consult Miss Loveday.

'I know nothing much of Micklethwaite, save that he once made a rather interesting statement to me,' said Miss Love-day solemnly. 'He once told me that the Prophet Samuel was responsible for all the misdeeds of King Saul. Could that be possible?'

'Psychologically quite possible,' Mrs Bradley briskly

replied. 'Is that the statement to which you refer?'

'Oh, no,' Miss Loveday responded. 'It was not that at all. I am not at all biased, and all my religious convictions are open to be disputed by clever boys. There is nothing more instructive than argument which is conceived in a scholarly spirit and carried on in a gentlemanly manner. No. He once told me that he hated cruelty; this after I had seen him throw a little non-swimming boy over his head into deep, deep water.'

'A *Judo* expert. Hm!' thought Mrs Bradley again. She went to her room in Mr Loveday's House and re-read her notes. Then she went in search of Mrs Poundbury, whom she found in the kitchen garden behind her husband's House – it was the pride of Mrs Poundbury that she rarely had to buy fruit, herbs, or vegetables for her husband's boys – helping the maid to gather Brussels sprouts.

She straightened up at Mrs Bradley's approach and smiled like an angel. She was, as Mrs Bradley again appreciated, an exceptionally beautiful young woman. Moreover, her anxieties seemed to have been resolved.

'Good morning,' she said. 'You're not going to be any luckier than last time if you've come to pump me about Gilbert. Won't you come into the house?'

'No. I'll pick Brussels sprouts,' said Mrs Bradley. 'They seem to be very fine ones.' She set to work.

'That will be enough, I think,' said Mrs Poundbury, at the end of twenty minutes. 'The boys like them, but they take a long time to prepare. I usually help with them during the afternoon. We give them to the boys at six o'clock.'

'Your husband does notice, I suppose, whether the boys have anything to eat or not?' Mrs Bradley enquired, as her hostess led the way to the House.

'I hardly think so,' Mrs Poundbury replied. 'Gilbert lives in the fourth dimension. By the way, I do hope you didn't carry away any – well – strange ideas last time? I like Gilbert, and – '

'You mean you are in love with him?'

'Oh, yes.' Mrs Poundbury smiled. 'There are some things that he doesn't muddle, you know.'

'Ah,' said Mrs Bradley, who had known from the moment they met that Mrs Poundbury was no longer associating in her own mind the eccentric Mr Poundbury and the fact of murder. 'Quite so. But you've made him very angry once or twice.'

'Twice,' Mrs Poundbury agreed. 'Once when Gerald Conway suggested that he and I should run away together, and once when I told him that I thought Socrates was a silly old man.'

'And did you take Mr Conway seriously?' Mrs Bradley enquired. Mrs Poundbury laughed outright, and Mrs Bradley liked her the better for it.

'Oh, yes, in a way,' she said. 'But really it was all ridiculous. When I told Gilbert, he punched Gerald in the stomach, and made him feel very ill; and then he punched him in the stomach again, and, when he fell down, Gilbert kicked him. When I remonstrated, Gilbert said, "Oh, did I kick him? Well, once is no good!" And he kicked him several times more. So I didn't want to run away with Gerald after that. And, of course, Gerald had his real girl and definitely wanted to get married.'

Mrs Bradley was delighted with this account of the relationship between Mr Conway and the Poundburys, and said so.

'It's so nice of you,' said Mrs Poundbury, wide-eyed with innocence. 'Gilbert is interested in violence. He says that without violence the world would have ceased to turn on its axis. His view is that effort is a moral, not a physical, attribute. He wrote a little treatise about it in connexion with football.'

'Did you read the treatise?'

'Oh, yes. I understood some of it, but not all. I don't really believe in violence because it seems to me to be uncontrollable. Everything worth while must be subject to some sort of law, I feel. Do you agree?'

She looked even more innocent than before, and Mrs Bradley knew quite well why she had been told about the fight and about the treatise. 'You see,' Mrs Poundbury was saying, in effect, 'Gilbert didn't need to murder Gerald Conway. He had already revenged himself on him, and had rationalized his emotions about him.' She respected Mrs Poundbury for this attitude, and changed the conversation.

'What kind of boy is Micklethwaite?' she suddenly enquired.

'He is an unbearable boy,' Mrs Poundbury replied, betraying no surprise at the sudden change of subject. 'Of course, he is not in our House.'

'I wondered whether he was likely to commit murder.'

'Oh, I should think he might. Do you suspect him of it?' Mrs Poundbury enquired.

'He is at the back of my mind,' Mrs Bradley answered. 'But, then, so are several other people.'

'Do tell me.'

'I should prefer *you* to tell *me*.'

'Oh, well, there's Gilbert, of course, as you keep on hinting,' said Mrs Poundbury, disingenuously, 'and Mr Loveday, Miss Loveday, Mr and Mrs Kay, John Semple, and poor old Mr Pearson, I suppose, since Marion became engaged to Gerald Conway. Daddy Pearson couldn't stand him, you know. Then, of course, there are always the boys! Issacher would have a grievance, no doubt, and Takhobali perhaps . . .'

'Takhobali? Ah, yes, what do you know of him?' Mrs Bradley enquired.

'Well, he is rather an interesting boy. He is West African, and rather uninhibited from a European point of view, although I expect he observes all sorts of *tabu* of his own.'

'I will continue to make his acquaintance,' Mrs Bradley promised. 'Is there anyone else you can think of?'

Mrs Poundbury considered the question carefully, and then replied, with an irritating affectation of honesty: 'Well, of course, there's always me. Poor Gerald was quite a nuisance at times, you know. I'm not at all sorry to be rid of him. Blackmail of a sort, too. Not money, of course, or anything like that, but just that little bit of extra pressure on me to go his way because, if I didn't, Mr Wyck would be informed of a few little things which wouldn't prejudice him in my favour and which might have cost Gilbert his House.'

'Oho!' said Mrs Bradley. 'So the land lay that way? I wonder whether you would care to drive through the village with me? There are some things over which I think you might be able to help me. What do you say?'

'I'd love to come. I've nothing more to do now we've picked the Brussels sprouts, and I never bother much about lunch because Gilbert lunches in Big School with the boys. I won't be more than five minutes.'

To Mrs Bradley's great astonishment she was quite as good as her word, and reappeared in four minutes' time ready for the drive. Together she and Mrs Bradley walked over to where Mrs Bradley's car was garaged, and soon they were heading for the School gate and the road to the village.

'Are we going shopping?' Mrs Poundbury presently enquired.

'No. We are going to the cottage which Mr Kay may have visited on the night of Mr Conway's death,' Mrs Bradley replied. 'I think the sight of the cottage may inspire you to make some valuable observations.'

'What makes you think I should know the cottage?' Mrs Poundbury enquired.

'Oh, it is a theory of mine that you may know it,' said Mrs Bradley vaguely. 'Anyway, here we are.'

'But this isn't the . . .'

'Ah,' said Mrs Bradley, 'you are right. This is not the cottage. It shows me that you know the right one when we come to it.'

'I may as well admit that I do,' said Mrs Poundbury, 'but I know nothing of the old woman who lives in it. Gerald always went in by himself.'

'What for?'

'Oh, herbs and things. He was rather interested in the old woman's remedies, I believe.'

'But not in her love potions, charms, and black magic?'

'Goodness, I shouldn't think so. Why?'

'Did he ever get you to try any of her concoctions?'

'No,' said Mrs Poundbury, with decision, 'he did not! And I never met the old woman.'

Mrs Bradley was so certain that this was a lie that she did not attempt to press the question or to get Mrs Poundbury to enlarge upon her answer. She drove on to Mrs Harries's cottage, and stopped the car.

'Are we getting out?' Mrs Poundbury enquired. She sounded nervous.

'*I* am,' Mrs Bradley replied. 'You, of course, will please yourself what you do.'

Mrs Poundbury got out, and followed Mrs Bradley up the path to the door. Mrs Bradley turned the handle and walked in, announcing her presence, as usual, on a loud and tuneful note. There was no reply, so she walked across the small front room to the kitchen. There was still no sign of Mrs Harries, so she went out through the kitchen to the long and narrow back garden.

The elderly witch was sweeping together the dead leaves which had fallen from the hazels.

'Bonfires?' enquired Mrs Bradley. The crone looked towards the direction from which the voice came.

'Ah, it's you,' she said. 'You're standing on Tom Tiddler's Ground. Did you know?'

'Yes,' Mrs Bradley replied. 'I did know, and I am trusting to you to get me out of it. How often did Gerald Conway come here?'

'Conway?' said the witch. 'A deep and resounding delivery, a conceited presence, a bull of a man, a bully of a man, a woman's man, a despicable fool of a man, a drowned man, his own worst enemy?'

'I feel that you have summed him up well. How often did he come?'

'Hereabouts and thereabouts, five times in a month, seven times in a year. Now he lies dead, and none so poor to do him reverence.'

'He didn't come five times in a month,' said Mrs Poundbury from behind Mrs Bradley's shoulder. The blind woman started.

'Strange,' she muttered. 'I did not know that anybody else was there. Who are you?'

'Never mind,' said Mrs Poundbury. 'I am nobody you would know.'

'You were born in the dark,' said the sibyl. It was Mrs Poundbury's turn to look startled and anxious. She did not leave it at that, but turned and fled from the presence of the witch.

'Born in the dark and now lives in the dark,' said Mrs Harries. 'I suppose my potions were for her? Did she come here with *him?*'

'It is possible,' said Mrs Bradley guardedly, feeling that it was not yet clear whether Mrs Poundbury and Mrs Harries had met before. She went a little nearer to Mrs Harries and said in low tones, 'I wonder whether it is of any use to ask how many times you let a room in this cottage of yours?'

'I shall answer you, although it is none of your business,' replied the witch. 'You have heard the answer once, and I will repeat it. I let the cottage five times in a week. That was during the summer. In August. Yes, back in August. I was paid well.'

'Ah, yes, I see. But you were gone each time before your tenants came in? You never spoke to the woman who came here with Mr Conway?'

'Never. It was in the contract.'

'And have you retained the contract?'

The old crone looked suddenly crafty. She shook her head.

'I know better than to keep evidence for which I might pay heavily,' she said. Mrs Bradley had a sudden idea which she did not disclose to her hostess. The latter lived up to this title by fishing in the pocket of the coarse apron she was

wearing and producing an onion. 'Take it,' she said. 'I have
said the runes over it. It will smell like a pomander from the
moment you take it from my hand.'

Mrs Bradley was the least suggestible of women. She took
the onion and sniffed at it delicately. An aroma, very faint
but undoubtedly characteristic, of clove pinks, came from it.
The crone chuckled and mumbled. Mrs Bradley took another
sniff at the onion, and there was no doubt about the scent.
She closed her eyes, concentrated mentally on the smell of
onion, and achieved the result she intended. The onion,
unlike Ben Jonson's rosy wreath, again smelt only of itself.
She put it back gently into the old woman's hand. The
witch grimaced and then nodded.

'We be of one blood, thou and I,' said Mrs Bradley. She
went out to the country road, very thoughtful, and joined
Mrs Poundbury, who was now seated in the car.

'Well?' demanded Mrs Poundbury.

'No, it wasn't you,' said Mrs Bradley. 'At least, I hardly
think so. You knew the cottage but I don't think you've
ever been inside it before. And if it wasn't you . . .' She did
not finish the sentence. There was no need.

'Ah!' said Mrs Poundbury, enlightened. 'She's an uncanny old thing,' she went on. 'I *was* born in the dark, you
know. The electric light failed as I decided to embark upon
a separate existence. But how could she *possibly* have known?'

Mrs Bradley did not attempt to answer this rhetorical
question.

13. *The Prince of Darkness*

*

'Twas to her I was oblig'd for my Education.

IBID. (*Act 1, Scene 2*)

'IT would be interesting to know,' said Mrs Bradley to the local inspector of police, 'whether Mr Loveday's keys have ever been missing.'

'He *says* they haven't, but he seems a vague sort of gentleman to me,' the inspector replied.

'What does *Miss* Loveday say?'

'She says she wouldn't put anything past the boys. But, of course, it's not boys we're after, whatever the Superintendent may say.'

'What does the Superintendent say?' asked Mrs Bradley, who had not heard the conversation between the Superintendent and Mr Wyck on the subject of boys and their possible misdoings.

'He says we've got to remember that Home Office affair, but that's all poppycock, if you'll pardon the expression, being one not often used by ladies. Young gentlemen like these at Spey don't go about murdering their schoolmasters. But what does seem to me the point about this business is that more than one person was concerned in it. A gang of boys and a pretty clever leader is the Super's idea, and he makes a proper sort of case for it. Of course, I suppose it *could* have been that, but only theoretical, like, if you understand me. What do *you* think about it being some of these boys, ma'am?'

Mrs Bradley ran her mind with agile ease over Scrupe and Micklethwaite, and then over Prince Takhobali. She also considered the temperamental and knowledgeable Issacher. She shook her head.

'Unlikely,' she said briefly. 'Most unlikely. But, of course, not quite impossible.'

'You've said it, ma'am. Unlikely, but, of course, not quite impossible. Began as a lark, most likely, and then it went a bit too far. Very high-spirited and a bit revengeful and determined, some of these young gentlemen, ma'am. You'd be surprised.'

Mrs Bradley did not contradict this last statement, although she knew it to be untrue. She would not have been surprised by anything which either boys or their seniors would do. She left the inspector and wandered off to watch a practice game of Rugby football on the upper field. She arrived in time to see a couple of ebony knees and two thin, almost delicate hands and a shining black face set round a wide, appreciative smile, collect a loosely-slung pass and streak for the line like a water-snake.

'A promising player,' she observed to a large, slouching, slightly scowling youth who was also watching the game.

The youth raised his tasselled cap and smiled politely.

'Yes, he's not bad,' he replied. 'He's a bit light and small for Big Game at present, but I should certainly consider playing him in the First Fifteen next season if I were here, which I shan't be. Only trouble is, he bites.'

'Literally?' Mrs Bradley enquired. The youth nodded, and answered gloomily:

'Doesn't mean to, I suppose. Gets excited, and the next thing you know is that he's literally chewing pieces out of anybody he has to tackle in the game. He's being thrashed out of it, of course, but it makes things awkward at present.'

'I believe he is Prince Takhobali?' Mrs Bradley enquired.

'Yes. Nice enough kid, too. Just goes getting carried away by his emotions.'

'I wonder whether you would care for me to take him over and treat him?' Mrs Bradley enquired. Cranleigh – for it was that great man in person – stared, smiled, straightened up, scratched his jaw (looking suddenly younger) and said:

'Do you mean you could stop him biting?'

'Oh, yes,' Mrs Bradley replied. Cranleigh studied her, and made up his mind.

'If you could do that,' he said, 'I'm not sure I wouldn't play him against Fieldbury.'

Mrs Bradley had heard of Fieldbury. It was a very famous school, a great deal larger than Spey.

'Are they strong this year?' she enquired.

'Very strong,' Cranleigh responded, 'and we've never beaten them yet. Our only chance would be to play a scrum-half they didn't know. They're banking on our playing Tickner. If I played young Tar-Baby instead, and put Tickner out for this one match . . .' He stopped. 'I'm boring you,' he concluded. But Mrs Bradley was very far from being bored.

'Do I know Mr Tickner?' she enquired.

'I don't see why you should. He's a bit of a wart,' said the captain of football candidly. 'He's not a bad half-back, but the trouble is that he only left Fieldbury at the beginning of this half. He played regularly for their Second Fifteen all last winter, and, of course, their First know all there is to know about his game. So, if I could depend upon Tar-Baby's goings-on . . .'

'You can,' said Mrs Bradley with a superb self-confidence which Cranleigh, himself not utterly lacking in *amour propre*, was swift to appreciate. 'Send him to the School sanatorium immediately this game is over.'

'The san?' said Cranleigh. 'Right. He won't want to come, but I'll jolly well see that he's there. *Pass*, you silly owl!' he suddenly yelled, resuming his study of the game. Mrs Bradley walked back to Mr Loveday's House to inform Miss Loveday that Takhobali would be late for his tea, and then she walked over to the sanatorium to borrow a room from the sanatorium matron. The matron, who was the terror of every Housemaster and by whom even Mr Wyck was secretly overawed, gave way at once to Mrs Bradley, for Mrs Bradley held the sacred status of a Doctor o

Medicine besides that of being a grandmother in her own right. The matron, in short, gave Mrs Bradley a choice of four excellent rooms, and placed her staff at Mrs Bradley's orders.

Mrs Bradley selected the pleasantest of the four rooms, ordered a fire to be lighted, demanded hot buttered tea-cake, China tea, and a couple more cushions, impounded the matron's personal vase of late chrysanthemums, and generally contrived to electrify the matron's maid into wondering whether the last trump was about to be sounded.

Takhobali turned up shining from his changing-room bath, damp-haired and beautifully dressed, and blinked in astonishment at the sight of the cosy room.

'Sit down, Prince,' said Mrs Bradley, briskly. Takhobali, with a terrified grin and a gesture which Mrs Bradley recognized as the one used in his Protectorate for keeping off evil spirits, sat on the edge of a chair, but very soon, what with the lassitude which resulted after his game, the delicious food, the crackling fire, and the general air of ease which gradually overtook him, he relaxed, Mrs Bradley was relieved to note, and was soon conversing blithely on casual matters cunningly introduced by his hostess.

'And now,' she said, 'I expect you feel thoroughly sleepy. Put your feet up, close your eyes, and I'll get the tea cleared away. No, I don't want any help, thank you.'

'Now, why,' asked the Tar-Baby, curling himself up like a lithe and sleek young leopard, 'why am I brought to this place?'

'For treatment,' said Mrs Bradley.

'But I have no injuries. I am not sick.'

'No. But you are a *biter*,' said Mrs Bradley distinctly. 'And until you cease to be one, you will not be put into the School Fifteen. Am I right?'

'Oh – yes,' said Takhobali, raising his head and giving a broad smile. 'I *do* bite. I do not mean to. It is all for love.'

'I understand that so well,' Mrs Bradley agreed. 'All the same, you must agree, I think, that it would be better for you not to do it any more. If you really wish me to cure you, I can do so.'

'Cranleigh has tried. He beats me. It is so good of him. But always I forget, and his trouble goes all to nothing,' said the Tar-Baby, with frank and delightful regret. 'I am so tiresome.'

'You haven't co-operated with him, that's all. You have said to yourself, He will cure me; you have not said, I will cure myself once and for all. Shall we say that here and now? . . . Close your eyes; relax; breathe a little more deeply . . . and slowly . . . and deeply . . . and slowly . . .'

So natural and uninhibited was the Prince that she soon had him under light hypnotic control, and then she droned into him in her beautiful and sympathetic tones the fact that he would never again bite an opponent during a game of football. She pictured the game for him, she described his own emotions, and then she put a complete and absolute veto on the one particular way in which he was not to express them.

'You can play him against a girls' school now, if you like, Mr Cranleigh. He still won't bite them, however much he loves them!' she said, later, to the embarrassed but grateful captain of football. 'I think you may include him against Fieldbury if you wish, and very good luck with your match.'

This slight incident was regarded by the School as belonging to the cauldrons of witchcraft, for, to the delirious astonishment of everybody, Spey beat Fieldbury for the first time in living memory.

The first bit of luck for Spey came almost at once, for the Tar-Baby collected a wildly-slung pass and lobbed it neatly to Murray, who was just behind his left shoulder. Murray, who was unmarked at the moment, tore for the line, and, the full-back getting across, Murray let the Tar-Baby have the ball a bare ten yards from the line. Takhobali touched down, and the god-like Cartaris, taking the kick, made no mistake about it.

Fieldbury replied half-way through the second half,

during a battle of Titans, with a try which, to the almost indecent joy of Spey, was not converted, and then Cranleigh, from his position as centre three-quarter, took an inspired drop at goal from almost the middle of the field and, to the dumb and then the tumultuous amazement of the School, brought it off. After that Spey fought until the whistle to keep Fieldbury off the Spey line.

Takhobali played like a demon throughout the game, but, as the beaming Cranleigh observed later to Mrs Bradley, like a muzzled demon. Cranleigh, in fact, to demonstrate his gratitude for Mrs Bradley's endeavours, capped the Tar-Baby after the game, an unprecedented occurrence at Spey, but one which found warm favour with the multitude, for, as one of Mr Loveday's ecstatic boys announced to his fellow-members of the Junior Day Room that evening, whatever you said about the Tar-Baby, he might be as black as a boot and as rich as old Ford, but he had not an ounce of side and never would have.

The Tar-Baby had himself photographed as soon as he could, wearing the fantastic head-gear of the First Fifteen. It accorded very oddly with his broad, noble, African face, but that mattered little. He himself was delighted with the effect, and he presented an equally delighted Mrs Bradley with a copy of the photograph, signed, 'From your Tar-Baby which has much thanks.'

'It is for *me* to thank *you*, Prince,' Mrs Bradley gravely and graciously replied. 'You have saved my reputation.' The prince looked puzzled.

'I think you are not young enough to have one,' he remarked simply. 'But you have rewarded me for my lights, I believe.'

Mrs Bradley had not forgotten the lights, it was true. She took the earliest opportunity of mentioning them to Detective-Inspector David Gavin of the Criminal Investigation Department when that handsome young Highlander descended upon Spey on the following morning.

'Um,' said Gavin, who had been supplied with all the

evidence the local police had collected and now had a formidable list of suspects at the back of his lively and imaginative mind. 'There wasn't any weed or mud or what-not on the clothes or in the innards of the body except the mud it had collected from being dumped on to that garden. Tell me something about all these people.'

He produced a list. It was headed by the name of the Headmaster and under that were the names of Marion Pearson, Mr Pearson, Mr and Mrs Poundbury, Mr and Mrs Kay, Mr and Miss Loveday, and John Semple.

'You should add one or two more names,' said Mrs Bradley. 'Put Issacher, Takhobali, Micklethwaite, Merrys, Skene, and Lecky Harries.'

'But aren't some of those boys at the School?' demanded Gavin. 'I've already argued with the Super about that. He thinks boys may have done it, but I'm pretty sure that's impossible. Public schoolboys don't murder the Staff.'

'I agree, in principle,' said Mrs Bradley, 'but Mr Conway appears to have been something of an anti-Semite and that may mean that he suffered from other aberrations such as colour-prejudice.'

'Say on,' said Gavin. 'I'm listening. But you don't really think boys did this. I can tell you don't.'

'No, I don't, but we must go to work methodically.'

Gavin glanced at her suspiciously. She had pulled his leg before.

14. *Enter Priapus Minor*

*

Poor Lad! How little does he know as yet of the Old Baily!
IBID. (*Act 1, Scene 6*)

A TACTFUL inquiry on the part of the local police into Gerald Conway's financial affairs had disclosed that whatever his murderer's motive might have been, it had not been greed for money. Conway had banked in the town nearest to the School, and had had no income except his salary. This had been paid into his account at half-termly intervals by the governors, and Conway had spent almost all of it, the money remaining to his credit at the time of his death being the sum of sixty-one pounds, seventeen shillings, and fivepence.

'Well, that disposes of that,' said Gavin, disclosing the facts to Mrs Bradley. 'Can't quite see what he thought he was going to marry on, but perhaps his future father-in-law was prepared to come down handsome. Let's go and visit him, and see.'

Mr Pearson, the woodwork master, lived on the further side of the village in an architect-designed, delightful, modern house with a sun-lounge, a garden pool with a fountain, and all the amenities which money could provide, for Mr Pearson had other sources of income besides his salary. The details of these other sources – all innocent and praiseworthy enough – came out during the course of conversation, for, like many people whose chief vehicle of self-expression lies in working with their hands, the woodwork master was a simple-minded purveyor, and a voracious recipient, of gossip. The adjective 'old' in front of his name was misleading. He was fifty-two, and powerfully built.

'Never liked the chap,' was his verdict on Conway, 'but admired his guts and cheek. I got to know him first when he asked me to help him over a fancy dress. Two years ago, it would have been. I was interested in his idea, and I took more trouble, in a way, than the thing was worth. Still, when we'd finished it, it wasn't bad, although I say it.'

'Where was it made?' Gavin asked. He did not want to know, but the turn the conversation had taken promised well.

'Here, mostly, although we finished it up at the School. I made some stilts for him, too, at about the same time. I never saw him in the full kit, and I don't know what he did with the outfit after he'd worn it. It was supposed to be for the Chelsea Arts Club Ball. Cost? Oh, I don't know, quite. I think we did the whole thing for about two pounds ten. I didn't charge him beyond the cost of the materials. I was interested, you know. It was good fun making the thing.'

'Now another sort of question,' said Gavin.

'You needn't bother,' said the woodwork master, with a one-sided smile. 'I was very glad to hear of Conway's death. My daughter Marion, you know. Yes, girls are rather silly. Actually, I'm quite fond of my daughter, and I believe that people, even young people, should plan their lives as they think best, but Conway was a bit of a bounder. Still, my girl decided to get engaged to him. Yes, Conway asked my consent, and got it. Sorry I've no more information, but kids don't confide in their parents, and quite right, too.

'The champagne party? Oh, well, you know how it is. Everybody knew I didn't like the fellow, so I thought it best to put a good face on things, for Marion's sake. I suppose I overdid the congratulatory side of the business, but when you dislike people you're apt to lose your sense of proportion.

'Marion? Well, naturally, she was rather upset at his death, but she'll get over it. She's a sensible girl. Takes after me, I think. Yes, you can see her if you like. No, I've no objection to your questioning her. She's twenty-five, and quite capable, I hope, of telling you to mind your own business. Who else knew I'd made the mask and the rest of the outfit? Why, nobody, so far as I know, except Marion who helped quite a bit. That's how they got to know each other, really, Conway and Marion. I was rather sorry, in the end, that I'd let her help with the thing. You see, I'd heard a fair amount of gossip about him by then, one way and another. I retailed it afterwards to Marion, hoping to choke her off, but you know what girls are like. The bigger the rascal the more exciting the lover, to their minds, I suppose. When I found what was happening I tried to persuade her to snap out of it, but it was no good, of course. Rogue elephants have nothing on girls who think they know their own minds. So I gave in gracefully, don't you know, and announced the engagement myself and threw this champagne party in the Masters' Common Room at School. It went quite well, I think, except for Jack Semple, who, I fancy, was hoping that Marion would have picked him instead of Conway. Still, possibly, as I say, I overdid it.'

'What about Kay?' asked Gavin.

'Oh, Kay doesn't drink,' said Mr Pearson, 'and anyway he wouldn't care two hoots whether Marion was engaged or not.'

'Not if a married Mr Conway stood the chance of the next House?' asked Mrs Bradley.

'Good Lord!' said Mr Pearson. 'Fancy your thinking of that! I suppose that *would* make a difference! And, of course, Kay hated Conway like poison. Never a civil word for the chap. I've often thought Kay would slug him in the Common Room. I say, that *does* add up! Poor old Kay! He isn't much of a hero, though. I shouldn't think he did it, you know.'

'What do *you* think?' Gavin enquired of Mrs Bradley when they had left Mr Pearson.

'I think it might be a good idea to see Marion Pearson,' she replied, 'particularly as her father does not appear to have any objection to your doing so. But I don't know that I'd see her just yet. Her father will have warned her.'

'Good idea,' said Gavin. 'I thought of it, too. Not that I can see what she can tell us. Of course, she was engaged to the fellow, but she hardly comes on to the list of suspects, does she?'

'We may know whether she does or not when we have heard what she has to say.'

They returned to Mr Pearson's house two days later, but had to wait until Marion returned from the village. Mrs Bradley thought she looked tired. She was very pale and her eyes were dark-circled from loss of sleep.

'No, I don't mind talking about Gerald,' she said, in reply to Gavin's first question. 'It was a shock when I heard what had happened, but now it's all over, it's as though I'd hardly known him.'

Mrs Bradley looked perturbed, but Gavin said he could understand what the girl meant. He asked how long the couple had been engaged.

'Oh, only six weeks, the actual engagement,' Marion told him, 'but we'd had an understanding for about ten months, only Daddy didn't know. He didn't like Gerald much, and I found out why.'

'Yes?' said Gavin encouragingly.

'Well, I expect you know what kind of man Gerald was, but I wasn't born yesterday, even if I do call my father Daddy. I simply told Gerald that once he was a married man and a Housemaster he'd have to behave himself, whether he liked it or not.'

'A Housemaster?' said Gavin. The girl nodded.

'I've always wanted to be a Housemaster's wife,' she said placidly, 'ever since I was six and proposed to Mr Loveday. That was nineteen years ago, but I've never forgotten it, and neither has Mr Loveday. He still teases me about it when I see him, and when the Lovedays come here to tea he always mentions it. He's an absolute pet. All he cares about in the world is his Roman Bath, and I think that's ever so sweet of him.'

Gavin laughed.

'And what did Miss Loveday have to say to your proposal to her brother?' he asked.

'Oh, Miss Loveday is as much of an old duck as Mr Loveday. I think they're both terribly quaint, don't you? – and

they take ever so much trouble over looking after their boys.
The Loveday boys are notably well fed. I often tell Miss
Loveday that when I'm a Housemaster's wife she'll have to
show me all the ropes. She's promised, too, and says she'll
lend me all her diet sheets and things.'

'Which House?' asked Gavin, who was keenly interested
in the turn the conversation had taken, but who realized
that it would be desirable to treat the subject lightly. 'Which
House did you suppose you might be going to have?'

'Oh, Mr Mayhew's,' replied the girl without hesitation.
'He's always talking about starting a prep school, you
know, and he's got the money to do it. Mrs Mayhew is rather
delicate, though, and the air here suits her, otherwise I
think they'd have gone before. They would start the prep
school in this neighbourhood if they could, and send their
boys to Spey, but there isn't a suitable place for miles around.
It would mean building, and there isn't a hope of that at
present. Gerald and I had counted on waiting – well,
perhaps five years. I shouldn't have minded that at all. We
could just about have managed on Gerald's salary and the
money Mother left me when she died. I believe, really,' she
added, simply, 'I'm more sorry about the House than about
Gerald.'

'You don't know, of course,' said Gavin, slowly, 'of any
bad enemies he had?'

'Gerald? You mean bad enough to kill him? I go over
and over in my mind all the poeple who could possibly have
borne him a grudge. You must have to feel awful about anybody to do a thing like that. I mean, murder is final, isn't
it? I can only think of one thing that would bring *me* to kill
anyone, and that would be if Daddy's life was in danger, or
if someone could bring him into some dreadful disgrace.'

'Or misery?' Gavin suggested.

'No, not misery. I think people have to put up with
misery, don't you? But I can't think of anyone who had
reason enough to kill Gerald. I mean, I know his manners
were often appalling and I know he had a very bitter tongue

when he liked, and I know he had this reputation of being a sort of little Don Juan, but I can't imagine anyone taking any of it as seriously as all that. Can you?' She tried to look as ingenuous as her words.

'Well, people vary so much,' said Gavin. 'Where level-headed citizens like you and me would either laugh it off or sock him in the jaw, others, less level-headed, might possibly see cause for bumping him off. That's all I can make of it. By the way, I suppose you were here, at home, when it happened?'

'No, I wasn't,' said the girl, quickly. 'I was staying in London with my aunt. I should have come back on the Monday, but auntie particularly asked me to stay for a dinner party she was giving the next week-end.'

'Yes, I see,' said Gavin. 'Well, now, Miss Pearson, one more question. You've probably seen a good bit of the School and its life, and you may be acquainted with some of the boys. Will you tell me? – I've asked some of the masters, but, as you can imagine, they're a prejudiced lot where their boys are concerned, so I'm wondering whether you can help me.'

'In what way?' she enquired; and he watched her face change.

'Will you tell me of any boy who might conceivably have had sufficient grudge against Mr Conway to have killed him – or helped to kill him?'

Gavin, watching her, saw the struggle going on in her mind.

'Well,' she said, 'I suppose I'll have to tell, although I promised secrecy. But it's too important for me to think of that.' Gavin still watched her, and waited. 'It's Scrupe, you know,' she went on. 'You know Scrupe, I suppose? He's one of Mr Mayhew's boys, and – of course it sounds ridiculous – it *is* ridiculous – but he's in love with me. I found him in Gerald's cottage. I had a key which Gerald had given me when we got engaged – well, actually, a few weeks before that – and I'd gone along there to get some letters I'd written to Gerald. Our engagement hadn't been made public, and I didn't much want people to know about it after he had – died in that way.'

'By "Gerald's cottage," I suppose you mean the room he rented from old Mrs Harries?' interpolated Mrs Bradley. For the first time, Marion looked scared.

'Well, yes,' she admitted. She turned to Gavin, as though to a sympathetic presence. 'Daddy didn't like Gerald, so I had to meet him somewhere by mutual arrangement. I couldn't go to his room at the School, naturally, and I couldn't very often have him here. So he found this way.'

'Did you know,' asked Mrs Bradley, 'that somebody else had previously met him at Mrs Harries's cottage?'

'Oh, yes,' Marion replied, readily. 'It was Mrs Poundbury. He was a very silly boy. He tried to get rid of her by giving her old Mrs Harries's anti-love potions.' She laughed heartily, and then looked enquiringly from one to the other of her hearers. 'You don't think that's funny?' she enquired.

'Not very, you know,' said Gavin apologetically. 'In fact' – he hesitated a moment – 'in fact, I rather think that you are well out of a very dirty business. Well, good-bye, Miss Pearson. If you think of anything else we ought to know, I'm sure you'll come and tell us.'

'You don't like Miss Pearson very much,' said Mrs Bradley when, for the second time, they had left the house.

'I like her so little,' said Gavin deliberately, 'that, if she had the physical strength, I'd suspect her of murdering Conway herself. I said *she's* well out of it, but I'm not sure I'd have cared to be in Conway's shoes, either. Chelsea Arts Club Ball? Wonder whether there's anything at the London end which would help us?'

This seemed to Mrs Bradley doubtful. Conway's London life, so far as Gavin had been able to make out in his previous researches, could have been summed up as Love Among the Intelligentsia. In a Bohemian and rootless society he had flourished like the green bay tree. His easy conquests and even easier retreats had left no more than a

tolerant memory of themselves, for no such fluttering of the
dovecots had attended his amoral and amorous adventures
in London as had caused so much havoc in the monastic
seclusion of Spey.

He had not been much liked by the beards and berets of
the colony, but then, as they explained, waving paint and
nicotine-stained fingers, they had never got to know him
very well. He came and he went. For instance, said they,
they had never realized that he was, among other things, a
Schoolmaster; on the other hand, they had never enquired,
of course. Live and let live was their motto.

'Glad you can live up to half of it, anyhow,' thought
Gavin; and went on to interview the ladies of the little
colony. These spoke well of Conway. He was inclined to be
sadistic in his love-making; all were agreed upon that. But
he was healthy, strong, vigorous, wilful, and amusing. They
had been sorry to hear that he was dead. Some jealous
husband, they surmised, had gone outside the canons of
good taste and had done for him, once and for all. Good and
proper, they added, their tones congratulating the jealous
but manful husband.

'I should like to have painted Gerald dead,' said one lady,
dreamily. 'He must have looked like Itylus.'

'Icarus,' said her friend.

'Yes, I meant Icarus.'

'He hadn't exactly grown wings, had he?' said Gavin,
grinning. 'And he was dressed, when he was found, in
flannel bags and a sports jacket. Still, beauty is in the eye of
the beholder, and, no doubt,' he added gallantly, 'at the end
of her paint-brush, too. Did anyone ever paint him, by the
way? Alive, I mean.'

'Oh, yes,' was the immediate response from the first of the
two. 'We *all* painted him, of course, at different times. He
was terribly paintogenic.'

It was at this point that Gavin had one of those irrational
hunches which are the gift of the gods to deserving, intelligent, open-minded policemen.

'Was he ever painted in fancy dress?' he enquired.

'Oh, yes, of course. He made a divine Bacchus, and most of us at one time or another did him as Hamlet, too.'

'Laertes,' said the friend who had corrected her before.

'Oh, well, Laertes, then. It comes to the same thing.'

Her friend, who had experienced a normal education before she had received the urge to paint, smiled at Gavin and did not reply. He did not reply to the smile.

'And, of course, there was that thing Camelot Eager did of him,' said the first girl, doubtfully, 'but it wasn't Gerald, if you know what I mean. What with that horrible mask, and the stilts and things, it could have been simply anybody. Still, there's no doubt that Gerald was a great success at the Chelsea Arts Ball. The rest of us just crept under his huge legs, and all that sort of thing. He was on stilts, you see.'

'Ah!' said Gavin, on a note of deep Scottish reverence. 'Was he really? And did he bring anybody with him?'

'*Did* he!' replied the girl in a tone which blended annoyance with unwilling and rueful self-depreciation. 'I'll say he did!'

She proceeded to give a portrait-in-words of Mrs Poundbury. Gavin was delighted. 'And how long ago did you say this was?' he demanded. The answer dashed his hopes.

'Oh, it was the one they had in the year before last.'

'Too far back,' he thought despondently. 'It doesn't get us any further.' He had reported the information to Mrs Bradley, however, and before he returned to London to make further enquiries she suggested that he might try to get hold of the pictures of Conway which his friends had painted.

He came back to Spey with two portraits.

'Interesting, but not helpful, I fancy,' he said. 'Now what about this boy Scrupe and Marion Pearson?'

'There was nothing much *in* the letters,' said Marion, at this next interview.

'I know. We read 'em,' said Gavin. 'The signature didn't

mcan anything to us at the time, although we supposed we should have to contact this Marion sometime or other. But the letters, if you don't mind my saying so, were so innocent, and sort of prattle-y, that we weren't particularly interested in the writer, especially as the letters were undated and there was no hint of – forgive me! – passion and all that. We thought, as a matter of fact, that they might have come from a cousin of his, or someone.'

'Yes, I expect they were pretty ordinary,' said their author. 'Lucky for me, I suppose.'

'More about Scrupe, please,' said Gavin. 'He's one of the boys you particularly liked, I gather – apart from his embarrassing fondness, I mean. He's rather a clever boy, isn't he?'

'Yes, he's a most entertaining, attractive boy. I found he'd broken into the cottage and I caught him with a mask in his hands. He didn't seem a bit surprised to see me. "Hullo, Marion, darling," he said. "What are you doing here? – and what the devil's this I've got hold of? Did Mr Pearson make it! It looks like his work. I say, I couldn't borrow it, I suppose? I'm going to a fancy dress dance at my aunt's this Christmas and my aunt's been chivvying mc to write and tell her what sort of costume I want. This would be a smasher, wouldn't it? How do you think I'd look with my manly torso all painted an irresistible deep chocolate colour, and with a garland of pussy's-tails round my slim and connubial middle?" '

'And what did you say to that?' enquired Gavin, fitting this portrait of Scrupe into the frame already supplied by Mrs Bradley, and reflecting, in his crude, masculine way, that six with an ashplant would do the youth very little harm.

'I pointed out that everything in the cottage belonged neither to him nor to me, and that, in any case, he had no business to be there. Then Scrupe very cheekily asked me what *I* was doing there, then. "And letting yourself in with a key, too, as large as life," he finished up.'

'But how did the young devil know that the mask was there?' demanded Gavin.

'I don't believe he did. I believe he was just snooping round. I accused him of it, in fact, and he just put his head on one side and said, "That's all very well, you know, precious, but I adhere to my previous question. If I'm snooping so are you. Now, why?" I was idiot enough to get angry at that, and I told him pretty sharply to mind his own business. "If you were a gentleman," I said, "you'd go away at once. My private affairs are nothing to do with you." He just grinned like a monkey at that, and – well, I had to tell him. At least, I thought I had to. "I am engaged to Mr Conway, if you want to know," I said, "and I'm here to take back my letters." He sobered down at that. I've never seen such a sudden change in anybody. He is really a very nice boy. "I say, old thing," he said, "you *are* a fool! You'd better get out of that, you know. I don't want to speak ill of my mentors and preceptors, but Conway is a tick." I boxed his ears, hard, but he just shook his head, like a horse shaking off a fly, and said, "Your guilty and disgraceful secret is safe with me; is mine with you if I just borrow this head?" Then he climbed through the window and ran away.'

'With or without the head?'

'Without. I suppose he must have come back for it later when I'd gone home.'

'And you think that the news of your engagement was such a shock that this boy laid for Mr Conway?' demanded Gavin. Marion shook her head.

'I've been answering your question, that's all,' she said. 'You asked me what I knew about Scrupe.'

'The devil I did!' thought Gavin.

'And another thing,' he added to Mrs Bradley. 'Now that I know the girl was away from home that night, I shall have to see whether Pearson's got any sort of alibi for the time of the murder.'

'I should tackle Scrupe first,' said Mrs Bradley, 'and leave Mr Pearson's alibi to simmer.'

Gavin took this advice on the principle that a nod was as good as a wink to a blind horse.

'Now, Scrupe,' he said, having obtained Mr Wyck's permission to talk to the boy and having disposed of Mr Mayhew's objections to this course, 'I'm going to ask you some questions which it may seem well to you that you should refuse to answer.'

'Not at all, sir,' said Scrupe, squinting modestly downwards.

'Well, we'll see,' said Gavin good-humouredly. 'Sit down.'

'I never sit in the presence of authority, sir.'

'Perhaps, in the presence of authority, you are usually in an almost recumbent position?'

Scrupe hitched his trouser knees gracefully and sat down. 'At your service, sir.'

'Right. What made you go to old Mrs Harries's cottage?'

'When would that have been, sir?'

'Why, did you go more than once?'

'No, sir.'

'All right. Answer the question, then.'

'I am interested in the occult, sir.'

'Yes?'

'Yes, sir.'

'Would the occult, in your view, include reading other people's letters?'

'Certainly, sir. Why not?'

'You don't think it wrong to read other people's letters?'

'I thought we were discussing the occult, sir.'

'Well?'

'The occult is neither right nor wrong, sir. Shakespeare has a phrase – "but thinking makes it so." '

'I see. So you thought it was all right to read letters which Miss Pearson had written to Mr Conway?'

'No, of course not,' said Scrupe, speaking patiently. 'I'm not talking about those sort of letters. I met Miss Pearson there one day when I was really after something else. She told me she had come for some letters. I advised her not to marry Mr Conway. I escaped by way of a downstairs window.'

'I see,' said Gavin. He hesitated a moment, and then said, 'Look here, Scrupe, I don't suppose you'll believe me, but I would like to tell you that if you could add anything to all this, you'd be doing Miss Pearson no harm.'

Scrupe got up.

'If I think of anything, I'll let you know,' he said grandly.

'No, no,' said Gavin. 'Don't go yet. You know, I suppose, that I have every reason to suspect that Mr and Miss Pearson are responsible for the death of Mr Conway?'

'You're bluffing,' said Scrupe.

'Have it your own way. You must please yourself what you believe. What was all this about borrowing a fancy dress?'

'I was commissioned to borrow it for the School plays, sir.'

'By whom?'

'By Mr Poundbury. I told him I thought I could lay hands on a suitable costume.'

'The one belonging to Mr Conway?'

'Yes, sir. Marion – Miss Pearson – had told me of the one her father helped to make.'

'And did Mr Conway – I mean, was he prepared to lend it?'

'I didn't like to ask him, sir. On the other hand, Mr Poundbury is a very enthusiastic sort of man, so I thought – '

'Oh, rot!' said Gavin. 'You saw the mask by accident when you visited the cottage and – '

'Yes, sir.'

'And that's all I could get out of him,' said Gavin, retailing the conversation. 'I wish *you'd* have a go at him.'

Mrs Bradley shook her head.

'Where fools rush in, angels fear to tread,' she unkindly observed.

15. *And Puppy-Dogs' Tails*

*

But now, since you have nothing better to do, ev'n go to your Book and
learn your Catechism.

IBID. (*Act 1, Scene 6*)

THE School Concert was one of the great occasions of the
year. From three o'clock the parents began to turn up.
Lessons were cancelled from half-past twelve onwards, and
the School veiled itself in its best. By half-past three Big
School had begun to fill up. Parents did not sit with their
boys. These formed a solid phalanx at the back, except for
the School prefects (who acted as stewards to the visitors),
and the House prefects (who were responsible for the order-
liness of their Houses). The masters, gowned and remote,
occupied the second and third rows. Directly in front of
them, on either side of Mr Wyck (whose throne-like chair
was in the middle of the first row), sat such members of the
governing body as had chosen to grace the occasion with
their presence. Directly behind the Staff sat the twittering
and egoistic parents.

*

Ingpen, of Mr Poundbury's House, had, on the day of the
plays, a very adventurous time. Spey depended upon no
preparatory school in particular for its regular intake, and
when, under Mr Wyck's predecessor, the numbers had
fallen slightly below the complete accommodation of the
School, the governing body had decided to instal a small
preparatory department of its own for boys of eight to
thirteen.

These children were allotted in strict rotation to the
Houses, so that each Housemaster received his fair share of
them. Wealthy Housemasters, such as Mr Mayhew, thought
them a complete nuisance. Indigent ones, such as Mr

Poundbury, charged them some extras and were very glad
to have them.

There were strict rules governing their upbringing. They
were in charge of a special prefect in each House whose duty
it was to make certain that they were not bullied, imposed
upon, or spoilt by the older boys. They went to bed a good
deal earlier than the rest of the House, and had special
dormitories allotted to them. They had their own Day
Room, which was not in the House at all, but in an annexe
of Big School, so that they were nominally, during parts of
the day, in Mr Wyck's own charge.

They were in great request at certain times and seasons.
The treble voices in the School choir were bound, for obvious reasons, to be chosen from their number. One of them
usually coxed the School boat. As children, dwarfs, *Mid-
summer Night's Dream* fairies, girls, and so forth, they were
much in request for the School plays. Mr Poundbury, in
fact, made even more use of them than this, for he made
them pay a Dramatic Society fee and charged them heavily
for the hire or purchase of their costumes, two impositions
from which his older actors were free. The governing body,
as a matter of actual fact, financed all such School activities,
but Mr Poundbury felt that the pleasure experienced by the
little boys, and the pride taken in their dramatic prowess by
their mothers, justified him in these otherwise doubtful
sources of private profit.

On the day of the School plays, Ingpen, nephew of the
woodwork master and a robust and comely child of nine
and a half, awoke at the sound of the rising bell, and, re-
membering what day it was, jumped out of bed excitedly,
slid on his bedside rug underneath which the housemaid
had smeared and rubbed up a forbidden household polish,
and cracked his head rather hard against the wall towards
which, as Fate would have it, he had taken a toss.

Ingpen, who was a plucky enough creature, got up rather
shakily, explored, with delicate finger and wincing eyes and
mouth, that part of his cranium which had struck the wall,

said, 'You silly fools, it's not funny,' to the rest of the
dormitory, and was suddenly very sick in the middle of the
dormitory floor.

The catcalls, whoops, realistic imitations, and general
pandemonium caused by this performance brought along
Timms, Mr Poundbury's unfortunate Preep-Weep, as such
dry-nurses were called at Spey, for question and answer.

'Now what?' shouted Timms, successfully dealing with
the din.

'Please, Timms, Ingpen catted. Look.'

Timms, who had a queasy stomach before breakfast, unwisely accepted this invitation.

'*Lord!*' he said, in disgust. 'Here, you, Tomalin, go and
tell matron. What's the *matter* with you?' he added wrath-
fully to Ingpen. 'Have you been eating in dorm, you filthy
little beast?'

'Please, Timms, he slipped on his Prigga and hit his head,'
volunteered a pale child whose bed was next that of
Ingpen.

'Lord!' said Timms, more mildly this time, however.
'You'd better sit down, you little fathead. What on earth do
you want to slip on mats for?'

'I don't know, Timms,' replied Ingpen; and astonished
and alarmed his interlocutor by sitting on the bed, falling
sideways, and, apparently, going to sleep. Matron, fortunately, arrived at this moment, scanned the mess on the floor
with noteworthy lack of interest, pointed it out to the maid
who had followed her up with sand, sawdust, disinfectant,
and such other appurtenances as the situation demanded,
and then hurried all the children out of the room with their
clothing under their arms. She commanded Timms to lift
up Ingpen and bring him into the Senior Day Room, which,
at that hour of the morning, was empty.

There they walked him up and down a bit, and the School
doctor, for whom Mrs Poundbury, summoned at matron's
request, had immediately telephoned, examined the bump
on Ingpen's head. The doctor did not think the concussion

was serious, but advised that Ingpen should be kept quiet
and caused to 'go steady' for a bit.

'A bit?' said Mrs Poundbury. 'What does that mean,
doctor? He's in one of the School plays this afternoon! He'll
go crazy if he isn't allowed to go on!'

The doctor was a sensible man. He did not think that the
child was seriously hurt. He studied Ingpen.

'A big part?' he enquired.

'Oh, yes, sir, please, sir, *no*, sir!' gasped Ingpen, who
believed that the play could not possibly be put on without
him.

'Well, you keep very quiet until this afternoon, then, or
I'll take you out of the whole show,' said the doctor.

Ingpen was enormously relieved. His mother, father, and
sister were all invited to the play, and his Uncle Henry and
his Cousin Marion were on the premises already. It would
have broken his heart to fail them. On the other hand – he
studied the luminous hands of his watch in the darkened
room when everybody had gone and he was left tucked up
under a rug on Mrs Poundbury's drawing-room sofa – at
least five hours, and perhaps more, must elapse before he
could rejoin his fellow-men; hours and hours and hours
when he would have nothing to do, no one to talk to, no
lessons, no anything.

It has been remarked upon more than once by those who
are knowledgeable and experienced in such matters, that
young children genuinely enjoy school work. It is only in
early adolescence that the irksome, irritating, and unnecessary nature of the tasks allotted by our mentors and preceptors becomes obvious. At nine and a half, young Ingpen
enjoyed his lessons. He honestly and ingenuously believed
that it would be much more dull without than with them.
Odd as it might seem to the rest of Spey, the preparatory-
school section even mildly liked the staff who taught them,
and offended these less from set intention than from sheer
puppy exuberance or as the result of legitimate experiment.

At the end of twenty minutes' peace and boredom, Ingpen

was almost desperate. He was meditating a quiet sneak out on the excuse, if he were encountered, of needing to visit the privy, when a maid carrying a breakfast tray followed Mrs Poundbury into the room.

'Well, Bill,' she said – following her casual habit of addressing all boys under twelve by this cognomen – 'how goes it?'

'Oh, I'm *quite* all right,' declared Ingpen. 'Please mayn't I go over to School?'

'Better not. Have some breakfast with me. Would you like me to send for Marion? She came over with your uncle to his woodwork class to show the boys how to upholster the chairs they're making.'

'No, thanks. Just talk to me, please.'

Thus passed a pleasant half hour, but then Mrs Poundbury had to go away. She consented, however, as there was no sunshine, to leave the curtains partly open so that Ingpen could see the garden.

'You must keep very quiet, or the doctor won't let you go on in the play,' she said. 'Does your head ache much?'

'It doesn't ache *at all*,' said Ingpen, not quite truthfully. But he did not renew his entreaty to be allowed to go over to School.

Another half hour went very slowly by . . . and then another half hour. It would be a long time yet, reflected Ingpen miserably, even to mid-morning break. He loved mid-morning break, with its shrill hooliganism, its glass of milk and its biscuits. Then a dreadful thought came to his mind. Perhaps he was not to have a mid-morning break! Perhaps they would forget all about him! He grew restless and felt suddenly very hungry. There was nothing to do; there was nothing to eat; there was nothing to learn; there was – Ah!

He put back the rug and swung his feet to the ground. His head still hurt, but it was nothing more than a tight, bruised sort of feeling. He stood up, began to feel better, walked over to the bookcase and scanned the backs of the books. You

could learn *something*, even from titles, he decided. He would
not *touch* anything, of course, but surely Mrs Poundbury
would not mind a man *looking* at her books?

Most of the titles were beneath notice; novels of a type
which he did not like at that age, and never did like afterwards. These filled one and a half shelves; some of Mr
Poundbury's more scholarly reading filled two and a half;
then – and Ingpen caught his breath – *then* came a whole
shelf of detective stories. Ingpen read title after title . . . then
he stretched out a small, still babyishly plump hand.

The note fell on the floor unheeded at the moment by the
child. He carried the book to his sofa and tucked it under the
rug. Then, with the depravity common to his years, he
returned to the bookcase and artistically adjusted the
position of the rest of the books on the shelf so that no gap
was immediately to be noticed. Then he spotted the note,
and realized at once that it must have dropped out of the
book which he had borrowed.

He did not open the folded paper. It did not interest him,
for one thing. He merely took it over to the sofa and used it
as a bookmark. This was necessary, for twice, whilst he was
gobbling the story, somebody came in and he was obliged to
push the book under the rug until he was alone again.

Lunch was at one. He had it where he was. From twenty
minutes to two until two o'clock the preparatory schoolboys
were obliged to sit quietly in their Day Room, under strict
supervision, and read, before they went on with the lessons
which intervened between this free time and their football,
gymnastics, or boxing.

Ingpen read harder than anybody. Mrs Poundbury,
coming to fetch him to be costumed and made up for the
play, found him red-eyed, flushed, and not at all rested and
refreshed. So worried did she feel – for she was a tender-
hearted woman where the smallest boys were concerned –
that she sent a maid for Mrs Bradley to ask whether she
would be kind enough to give an eye to the patient.

Mrs Bradley turned up within ten minutes. She looked at

the patient, touched the bruise on his head with gentle, exploratory, yellow fingers, and then, before the child could divine her intentions, she had whipped the rug back with her free hand and disclosed the incriminating book.

'Oo!' said the jackdaw, nonplussed. 'I'm sorry! I ought to have asked, but there wasn't quite anyone to ask, and *really* I haven't hurt it! I've been most *fright*fully careful, *really* I have!'

But neither the old nor the young woman was taking the slightest notice of him, for the bookmark had fallen to the floor.

'Good heavens! *There* it is!' said Mrs Poundbury, hastily snatching it up.

'You had better give that to me or to Detective-Inspector Gavin,' said Mrs Bradley at once. She turned to the round-eyed child on the sofa. 'And now, young man, I think perhaps a drink of milk and soda, and your promise to lie here, quite still, whilst I myself go on reading this most delightful story aloud, would be the best way of ensuring that you play your part this afternoon. How long can you give him, Mrs Poundbury?'

'Oh, as long as you like – that is, if I make him up last. We don't begin the plays until four, and the School has tea in the first interval. He doesn't come on until the third play – do you, Bill? – oh, dear, must I really give the note to Scotland Yard?' She found difficulty in pulling herself together, it was clear.

Mrs Bradley grimaced and nodded.

'Unless you'd prefer to give it to me,' she repeated, 'you must show it to the police.'

'Oh, no!' said Mrs Poundbury hastily. 'No, I couldn't do that!'

Mrs Bradley gave a faint cackle, reminiscent of the far-off calling of rooks. 'Don't be foolish,' she said. 'You don't want to get into trouble.' She then picked up the detective story and settled herself beside the child.

16. 'A Night at an Inn'

*

The Muses, contrary to all other Ladies, pay no Distinction to Dress.

IBID. (*Introduction*)

AT the School Concert the Housemasters' wives had almost nothing to do. For the most part they sat among the parents and were not easily distinguishable, for several were parents themselves, chiefly, oddly ,enough, of girls. Mr Wyck, himself the father of two daughters, maintained that this was due to a compensatory clause in the otherwise tooth and nail contract between Nature and Humanity.

The Housemasters' wives, therefore, at School functions, were rather less in stature than the boys' parents, and were scarcely in evidence.

Mrs Kay and Mrs Poundbury were not in evidence at all. Mrs Kay was helping to superintend the preparations for the visitors' teas, and Mrs Poundbury, in the role of assistant stage manager, was behind the scenes helping her husband with the make-up.

There was the usual loud hum of conversation from the audience, and then, just as Mr Wyck was looking at his watch – for the time was ten minutes past four – the curtain rose on what was to be the most talked-of entertainment which had ever been given at Spey.

The first of the three one-act plays which formed the bill on this particular occasion was *Campbell of Kilmhor* with a Scottish boy named Innes in the name part and Skene in the small part of his secretary. This magnificent play was a great success. The women's parts were played by the Headmaster's daughters. The idea of following it with a long interval was a good one, for the other two plays chosen by Mr Poundbury were of very different type. One was Lord Dunsany's *A Night at an Inn* – the murder play referred to by Mr Poundbury and greatly liked by the boys; the other was Pinero's domestic farce *Playgoers*, not less popular because all the women's parts were played by boys.

'Well, how goes the silly old coconut?' asked Mrs Poundbury, smearing make-up all over Ingpen's face in preparation for his appearance as the kitchen maid in the last of these three plays. 'No, open up, Bill! Don't screw your eyes and nose up like that! You'll come out looking like the clown in a circus if you do! Now, when I've done you, you can watch the *Night at an Inn* from the wings. You'd like that, wouldn't you?' This, she thought, would be the best way of keeping him quiet.

The curtain went up for the second play on an eerie effect of black and white trellis-work lighted with sickly lime-colour. The play began well. All the actors were well cast, and the part of Smithers, the terrified Cockney, was noticeably well taken by a mightily-disguised Issacher, the best actor in the School. Three-quarters of the way through, indeed, the audience were leaning forward in their seats, as the almost incoherent Smithers came back to the stage after he had been sent to the back of the inn to get some water. He was supposed, during his absence from the stage, to have seen something which filled him with fear. The audience was strangely stirred; they were half-way in atavistic worship between wild applause and complete silence, as the boy spoke his lines.

Mrs Bradley leaned forward, too, for in Issacher's shrill accents she heard something which the audience did not hear. She heard the boyish squeak of definite and hysterical terror. This was not acting; this was genuine, unreasoning panic crouched behind the screen of the script.

She had chosen a seat at the end of a row. She got up and made her way quietly through a doorway and so to the back of the stage. Suddenly she heard from the stage, as the curtain suddenly came down, a yell of enlightening horror.

'But I *did* see it, you silly fool! I *saw* it! I *saw* it! I *saw* it, I tell you!'

At the side of the stage she found a half-fainting Issacher, supported by Mr Poundbury, and a very little boy in tears, for Ingpen had seen something else. Mrs Bradley hustled him into the dressing-room and closed the door.

'Now,' she said, 'what did you see?'

But before the sobbing child could get out a word, there was a tremendous commotion at the door, and Mr Poundbury burst in, dragging Issacher, very green about the gills, and followed by several Sixth-Form boys from his own House.

'Not in here!' he said to these followers, pushing Issacher into a chair. 'Sit down, boy. Away, boys, away!'

'What has happened, Mr Poundbury?' Mrs Bradley enquired.

'I don't know,' answered Mr Poundbury, beginning to recover himself. 'It's something to do with this lad, but I can get nothing much out of him.'

'An accident?' Mrs Bradley enquired.

'I don't really know. Anyway, the curtain's been rung down, and Mr Wyck is out in front telling lies to the audience. Now, boy, now! Pull yourself together!'

Mrs Bradley was entertained by the crude statement describing Mr Wyck's activities.

'You had better leave Mr Issacher to me,' she said. 'Haven't you another play to put on?'

'Yes, yes! But the boys can manage,' said Mr Poundbury, giving Issacher an unnecessary thump on the chest. 'Up, boy, up! The paper must go to bed to-day, you know, and the show must go on!'

Mrs Bradley seized him in a scientific grip and propelled him towards the door.

'Get the *Playgoers* on,' she said, 'and then you can come back here.'

Mr Poundbury wandered stagewards once more. Mrs Bradley returned to the dressing-room and seated herself in front of the two boys.

Little Ingpen glanced fearfully at the door; then, at a nod

from Issacher, whose colour was beginning to come back, he went over to the door and turned the key.

'Gosh!' said Issacher, wiping grease-paint from his face with the sleeve of his shirt and then regarding the resulting stains with detachment. 'Don't give me side, but what did *you* make of it, sprat?'

Ingpen was about to tell him when the handle of the door was vigorously rattled and the voice of the call-boy was heard.

'Third play, Ingpen wanted! Third play, Ingpen wanted!' he chanted loudly and continuously. Ingpen rushed to the door and flung it open. Outside with the call-boy was a grim-faced Mr Poundbury.

'Come along, come along, boy!' he said. 'You can't keep the whole stage waiting!'

Ingpen gulped, and then ran past him. Gratefully he joined a huddle of boys in the wings.

'Good heavens! You look as if you'd seen a ghost!' said Scrupe, who lived near Ingpen at home.

'I've seen a murder, Francis,' said Ingpen.

'Then for God's sake forget it,' said Scrupe. 'And mind you give me the proper cue this time, or I'll murder you!'

'And now, Mr Issacher,' said Mrs Bradley, 'what will the harvest be?'

*

The third play, acted by thoroughly excited boys, brought the house down. A ponderous Fourth-form boy named, happily for himself, Cooke, was particularly outstanding as the cook, Scrupe, as a simpering parlourmaid, was also excellent. The young Ingpen, as the kitchenmaid, brought tears to his mother's eyes, and the Captain of Football, as the lachrymose useful-maid, astonished even the Headmaster.

The last-named sought out Mrs Bradley directly the entertainment was over.

'Mrs Poundbury is badly hurt. We do not know yet what occurred. I have sent for Issacher,' he said. 'Do you think,

by any chance, that the lad could have attacked Mrs.
Poundbury whilst he was off-stage during the second play?
All the circumstances were so extraordinary that . . .'

'I think there can be little doubt that Mr Conway's
murderer attacked Mrs Poundbury,' said Mrs Bradley composedly, 'and I do not suspect Issacher of having killed Mr
Conway. I wonder whether Mrs Poundbury was foolish
enough to tell someone about the missing note that turned
up so unexpectedly to-day? I should hardly think she would
mention it, though. Perhaps the little boy Ingpen told somebody about it. And yet . . .' She looked perplexed. The
Headmaster looked thoroughly worried.

'Is there likely to be another attempt?' he asked. Mrs.
Bradley shook her head.

'Who can tell? It depends upon how much nerve the
murderer has, and whether Mrs Poundbury recognized him,'
she said.

Mrs Poundbury had been found at the foot of a short
flight of stone steps leading from the east end of the dressing-
room corridor to the open air. Her skull was fractured, but
she had a reasonable chance of recovery.

However, the nature of her accident or the details of the
murderous attack – whichever it should turn out to be –
could not be gathered until she recovered consciousness.
Mrs Bradley had made her own views clear. The note had
gone, and Mrs Poundbury, in Mrs Bradley's experienced
view, was far too intelligent to have destroyed it. It had not
been shown to Detective-Inspector Gavin, for Mrs Bradley
had asked him point-blank about it as soon as she knew of
Mrs Poundbury's injuries.

'I've seen no note,' he said. 'Pity she didn't hand it over
to you. It would have saved her this knock on the head. She
never got that from falling down steps, did she?'

'No, she did not,' Mrs Bradley replied; for she had made a
point of examining Mrs Poundbury. 'The contusions from
the fall are clear enough, and the knock on the head was not
one of them.'

'I wonder how soon we'll be able to get her to talk to us?'

'Not for two or three days.'

'Too bad. Still, it can't be helped. I wonder what the youngsters can tell us?'

'A good deal that is strange, but not much that's helpful,' prophesied Mrs Bradley. 'We must let them get over the shock before we question them further, I fancy.'

'A bit garbled, are they?'

'Their stories are curious and interesting. You are having Mrs Poundbury closely guarded, I presume?'

'Yes. Nobody will get at her now. But I doubt whether she'll be able to name her assailant, and, if the note has gone, and the attacker has got what he wants, she's probably safe enough, as long as the thug can be sure she didn't recognize him.'

'Whom do you suspect?' enquired Gavin.

'Mr Pearson is the obvious suspect, of course. It leaps to the eye,' said Mrs Bradley. 'However, there are other possibilities. We must investigate them one by one. All the same, I have made cautious enquiries, and Mr Pearson left his seat at the concert before the performance began, and did not return until the second interval.'

'Rather a long time to be out. I should think he'd have an alibi, you know.'

'Well, we shall see,' said Mrs Bradley.

17. 'A Peep Behind the Scenes'

*

By these Questions something seems to have ruffled you. Are any of us
suspected?

IBID (*Act 2, Scene 2*)

'WELL,' said Issacher, when he had been told by Detective-
Inspector Gavin to sit down, 'you saw our play. You know
the plot of it. We three sailors and our leader, the Toff, are
supposed to have taken the ruby eye from a Hindu god in a
temple. The three priests of the temple follow us to England.
We rent a disused pub, lie in wait for them there, and murder
them one by one. We know there are only three of these
priests, so, when it's all over, we celebrate. Then the nervous
one – that's me – is sent out to get some water to put on top
of the whisky. I am supposed to see the image itself which
has come all the way from India to avenge the three priests
and get back the ruby eye. Then we are all called out, one
by one.'

'Very well and concisely stated,' said Mrs Bradley, as
Issacher paused. 'And then . . .?'

'And then,' said Issacher, 'there were two of them, you
know – two idols. I looked for Salisbury, who was taking the
part of *our* idol, and there he was, and then I saw behind him
sort of lurking in the shadows, the *other* idol. Of course I see
now it was somebody playing the fool, but at the time I was
scared out of my life. This other idol – well, Salisbury looked
as beastly as we could manage – a huge green mask and
popping-out eyes and a great, lolling, red tongue – but this
other idol, well, it was *tall*, you know, and it had eyes that
blinked at you. I just bolted back on to the stage and babbled.
I don't know what I said. Then young Ingpen began
yelling, I believe, and Mr Poundbury drew down the curtain,
and hustled us all off the stage on the O.P. side, and then we
heard that Mrs Poundbury had fallen and hurt her head. I

wondered if she'd seen it, too, and perhaps fainted or something. It was enough to make anybody faint.'

'And that is all you can tell us?' asked Gavin, writing it down.

'That's all. I didn't see anything more. Don't *you* think,' he added, turning to Mrs Bradley, 'that perhaps Mrs Poundbury saw it, too, and ran away, and fainted, and that's how she came to tumble down the steps?'

'An intelligent suggestion,' said Mrs Bradley, before Gavin could speak. 'Thank you, Mr Issacher.'

'Now, I want you to be very careful how you answer this,' said Gavin, looking evenly at the boy. 'Did this second idol remind you of anybody you know? Thinking it over now, in cold blood, I mean.'

'No. I didn't look at it long enough. Besides, it was tall – above human height, I mean.'

'What did you think when you saw it?'

'I – well, it sounds pretty feeble, but – ' He hesitated, and then rushed at it. 'It's sheer punk, I know, but I suppose I thought it was the – well, the *real* idol, you know, and that somehow we'd conjured it up. It sounds awful rot now, but when I'm in a part I really feel like the person I'm meant to be, and Smithers didn't expect to find the idol outside the back door of the pub, so I used to try and forget that Salisbury was out there. Well, then, when I saw this other thing – *behind* Salisbury – ' He looked anxiously at Mrs Bradley.

'Yes?'

'Well, it was rather, sort of, well, it must have been a very *prepared* sort of joke, if you know what I mean.'

'Mr Issacher,' said Mrs Bradley suddenly, 'have you ever seen a mask such as is used by Tibetan devil-dancers?'

'Oh, yes, and it wasn't like that. That's what Salisbury's mask was like. Mr Pearson, the woodwork master, young Ingpen's uncle, made it for us.'

Mrs Bradley said no more, and, at a nod from Gavin, the boy went out. Mr Wyck, who was present, by invitation of the detective-inspector, whilst the interrogation was being carried out, rang a bell, and in came little Ingpen. The child looked pale and tired. Mrs Bradley deduced correctly that the bump on his head was hurting him, and that it was past his bedtime. She also realized that he dreaded the thought of going to bed that night.

'Ah, Ingpen,' said Mr Wyck, 'your matron thinks you had better have a quiet room and one companion to-night, owing to the bump on your head. You will be sleeping' – he paused impressively – 'next door to *me*.'

'Oh, sir! Oh, *thank* you, sir!' exclaimed Ingpen, who, so far, had had no cause to fear grown-up people, and who was, as a matter of fact, enormously relieved and not at all taken aback at the thought of spending the night in the proximity of the Headmaster.

'You must be *quiet* and go to *sleep*,' pronounced Mr Wyck, 'and you may choose your own companion provided that he also is *quiet* and goes to *sleep*. I will make arrangements for you to be taken to your House and back. Now, before you go, is there anything you would like to tell us, my boy?'

'Please, sir,' said Ingpen, 'where did it go?'

'Where did what go?' Mr Wyck enquired.

'The – the *thing*,' said Ingpen. 'I was watching the stage, and Issacher went into the wings, and I heard him shout out, and then he ran back on to the stage, and I thought how well he was doing his part, and then I got suddenly horribly frightened, and I turned my head and *there it was!* And I ran on to the stage . . .'

'Yes, yes, my boy,' said Mr Wyck, reassuringly. 'We know all about that very stupid joke. Think nothing further about it. I suppose you don't know who it was?'

He sent the child, under escort, to Mr Poundbury's House for his pyjamas and to choose his stable companion, and he also sent for Mr Poundbury, who arrived hot, bothered, and full of disjointed exclamations and vague questions.

'Mr Poundbury,' said Gavin calmly, regarding the witness with suspicion, 'your wife was seriously injured during the presentation of the second play. Can you tell us anything about it?'

'Of course!' Mr Poundbury looked surprised. 'I'm always telling her she ought to wear her glasses. You know what it is. All the steps seem to swim into one. Extremely disconcerting, especially as she *will* rush about.'

'And that is your explanation of the accident?'

'Of course it is. How soon can I go in to see her?'

'The day after to-morrow, probably,' said Mrs Bradley. 'And now, Mr Poundbury, to your own share in the mystery: describe to us, if you please, the head and mechanics which you devised for the Hindu idol.'

'I did not devise anything. The boys did that themselves. I believe that the head was made in the workshop. The boys themselves could tell you. It was a copy of a Tibetan devil-mask, I believe. It was modelled in clay, then made over with *papier-maché* and muslin, then they cut out the clay – you know the method, I expect?'

'Yes, I have made puppets that way,' said Mr Wyck, rather to the surprise of his audience. 'But what about this second idol, Poundbury? You know about that, I suppose?'

'I heard a garbled account from some of the boys, but my anxiety, as you will appreciate, was for my wife.'

'But you rang down the curtain,' said Gavin.

'Yes, I operated it myself, as a matter of fact. Issacher was hysterical. I cannot imagine why. Surely a mere practical joke . . .'

'It was this particular practical joke which ruined your play,' said Mr Wyck.

'Suppose,' said Mrs Bradley, gently, observing the effect of this last statement upon the witness, 'that you give us your own version of what happened, Mr Poundbury. Where were you during that first long interval, for instance?'

'Oh, talking to people – the parents like to speak to the producer – and part of the time I would have been behind the scenes, no doubt, making certain that the make-up was as it should be, and hurrying the boys who had been in the first play and were wanted for the second or third one. . . .'

'Ah!' said Gavin, who had been taking notes and who now looked up from his writing. 'And which boys were those, Mr Poundbury?'

'I can't possibly remember. Let me see, now. Yes . . . there would be Issacher, Boltwood, and Skene . . . they were in *Campbell of Kilmohr.*'

'Elucidate,' demanded Mrs Bradley.

'Issacher was Captain Sandeman in the first play, and Smithers, the nervous Cockney sailor, in the second play. Boltwood was Dugald Stewart in the first play and the master of the house in the third play. Skene was the secretary, Mackenzie, in the first play, and the housemaid in the third play.'

'The third play, surely, need not concern us,' suggested Mr Wyck.

'Well, that brings us back to this boy Issacher,' said Gavin, 'who is, as I can see for myself, an excitable, foreign sort of type.'

'He is Jewish,' explained Mr Poundbury. 'He is an artistic boy – very musical. A gifted boy in many ways. He is often inclined to be hysterical. He is most conscious of his race and very proud of it. Not an easy boy. Not an easy boy at all. But, of course, the best actor in the School. I wish he were in my House.'

'Do you think he would attack people?' demanded Gavin. Mr Poundbury looked at Mr Wyck.

'I don't say he would *not*, given sufficient provocation,' said Mr Wyck promptly. 'But that could be said of most unbalanced persons, and Issacher is, in some respects, unbalanced.'

'He would not, at any rate, have attacked my wife,' said Mr Poundbury, perceiving the drift of the question. 'The boy was fond of her. She had helped him a great deal over his interpretation of his various parts in the plays, and also with his make-up and costumes. I cannot think that he would so far forget himself, even in his terror, as to attack her. Besides, this suggestion that she was attacked is new to me, and I find it particularly repugnant.'

'Really?' said Mr Wyck.

'It might not have been an attack, of course,' said Gavin slowly. 'A boy half-mad with fright might knock a slight woman down as he rushed past her. Issacher is a stoutly-built boy. He would weigh considerably more, I imagine, than Mrs Poundbury. As soon as we can get her to speak to us, we shall, of course, know more about it. The circumstances seem to have been confused.'

'It seems to me,' said Mr Wyck, 'that we shall get very little further in the matter, either with or without Mrs Poundbury, until we discover who played the practical joke I refer to this second and larger idol, whose existence I should not believe in if the tiny boy Ingpen were not a witness to it. From Issacher's description of the thing he saw, it was so large that it could scarcely have escaped unseen from the building, and, for my own satisfaction, I propose to find out who played such a stupid trick. It is very dangerous to frighten boys so badly. I am not so much concerned about Issacher, since he is older, and has a deeply morbid side to his character, but I am perturbed, and very deeply perturbed, at the thought of the possible effect of such an experience on a tiny boy of the age of Ingpen. It may well leave a permanent impression on such a young child's mind.'

Mrs Bradley agreed, but neither she nor Gavin was inclined to regard the appearance of the second and more horrible idol as a practical joke, for there was no doubt whatever that Mrs Poundbury had been attacked, and there was no doubt that the note had disappeared.

Gavin, in conclave with Mrs Bradley, stated an ugly but obvious fact.

'It's pretty clear,' said he, 'that the second idol, far from being a joke, was the murderer's disguise, and, judging from what has happened, not a bad one. I wonder whether any of the other kids who were in the plays saw anything?'

But it turned out that nobody had set eyes on the second

idol except the two boys, Issacher and Ingpen, who had been interviewed already. The other actors in that play were, all but one, on the stage, so that except for young Ingpen, who had had permission to watch from the wings, there were no back-stage or off-stage witnesses, except the boy who had taken the part of the first idol, and he had seen nothing at all.

'What about your stage-hands?' Mrs Bradley enquired. But the stage-hands, all members of Mr Poundbury's House, had nothing to tell.

'When we've set the scene and put the props ready, we go into the body of the hall until we're wanted again,' was the sum of their story. 'Mr Poundbury won't have people hanging about behind the scenes.'

'Who manages the curtain, then?' Mrs Bradley enquired. It appeared that one Billington was responsible for the curtain, but that he went by the script, and returned from the auditorium to his charge at a rehearsed point in the play or scene, ready to lower the curtain when this was necessary. Mr Poundbury himself, of course, had manipulated it during the disturbance.

'What about the prompter?' asked Gavin.

'We don't prompt, sir, from the wings,' replied Billington. 'If anybody fluffs, one of the other people on the stage says the lines. They are all responsible for all the dialogue.'

Mrs Bradley thought this an ideal scheme, and it forged an important little link in the rather slender chain of evidence because it seemed to narrow down the identity of Mrs Poundbury's assailant. There could only be a limited number of people who knew that normally there would be nobody much about whilst a scene was being acted. It narrowed it further to somebody who also knew something about the timing of each play and the order of the programme.

Gavin, at this point, plumped for Mr Poundbury. 'It all hangs together,' he pointed out. 'Nobody meeting him backstage would think twice about it. He had a pretty strong motive for getting rid of Conway, and he may also have intended to kill his wife sooner or later.'

Mrs Bradley admitted the force of this reasoning, and tackled Mr Poundbury again.

'Who, besides yourself, your wife, and the boys concerned, could have known the order in which the three plays were to be produced, and who else could have known how long each one took to perform?' she demanded straightly.

'Oh, the programmes were printed on the School press about a fortnight ago,' Mr Poundbury replied, apparently without a moment's thought. Mrs Bradley noted down this answer.

'So that, roughly speaking, anybody connected with the School . . .' she began.

'Could have known all there was to know? Yes, I suppose so. And, of course, the governors could have known,' said Mr Poundbury. 'Their programmes were sent off as soon as they were ready. Then, we have one or two visiting masters, and a young woman who takes the smallest preparatory boys for dancing. Each of them received a programme well in advance of the performance.'

'Who are the visiting masters?' Mrs Bradley enquired of Mr Wyck. She did not press the first and much more important question of the time each play took in the performing.

'A man named Pearson comes twice a week for wood- and metalwork; another, named Stenson, comes once a week for advanced art; a third, named Boulton, comes once a week for fencing and single-stick, and then there is a Mrs Wilkie for the youngest boys' dancing class. Oh, and Pearson's daughter Marion sometimes lends the School secretary a hand.'

'Ah!' said Mrs Bradley with satisfaction, whilst Gavin snorted with frustration. 'The ripples spread widely, I see.' There was nothing more to be done, it seemed, until Mrs Poundbury regained consciousness and was sufficiently recovered to be questioned.

'Unless,' said Gavin, when Mrs Bradley propounded this view, 'we could find out whether that grotesque get-up which scared those two boys so much came from Mother Harries's cottage. I shall get to work on that at once. It's quite likely it was the fancy dress belonging to Conway which Scrupe wanted to borrow.'

'We might question the boy Salisbury again,' suggested Mrs Bradley. 'It is as well to leave no stone unturned.'

'He said he knew nothing,' Gavin pointed out. 'Still, kids always say that.'

Salisbury was wary. He was a thin-faced, obviously intelligent boy, and he side-stepped the Headmaster's questions by repeating, 'I'm sorry, I don't know, sir,' to almost everything he was asked. Mr Wyck then came to the point.

'Now, boy,' said he, 'what arrangement had you come to with the second idol?'

'Please, sir,' said Salisbury, 'I had nothing to do with Mrs Poundbury's accident, sir.'

This sounded promising, and, Mr Wyck pursued the point.

'Very well, boy. I accept that. But that is not what I asked you to tell me. Now, what do you know of the second idol?'

'Well, sir,' said Salisbury, 'I did have a letter, but I don't know who sent it. All it said was . . .'

'Have you the letter in your possession?'

'No, sir. I tore it up.'

'Why?'

'Well, Mr Poundbury saw me reading it, sir, and made me, sir.'

'Aha!' said Gavin, with a smile at Mrs Bradley.

'You were reading it at the wrong time, I suppose. Well, what did the note have to say?' asked Mr Wyck.

'It said, "You're not the only pebble on the beach, and, if you see me, don't be surprised. I can make a better job of your part any day than you will, silly twerp." That's all, sir.'

'Were those the exact words, boy?'

'Sir, yes, sir.'

'And you saw nothing of this practical joker?'

'No, sir, really I didn't. As a matter of fact, sir, I had forgotten about the note, and I was looking on to the stage all the time.'

'Very well, Salisbury. You may go.'

'Please, sir . . .'

'Yes, boy?'

'Please, sir, I heard about the head of the other idol. I think it may have been something out of the Lucastra Museum, sir. They have several Tibetan devil masks there, and, from what I've heard from Issacher, it sounds a bit like one of them, sir.'

'I am obliged to you, boy,' said Mr Wyck, but in such sepulchral tones that the lad was glad to escape.

'The head of the second idol did not come from the Lucastra Museum,' said Gavin. 'We have already made enquiries there.'

'Quite so,' said Mr Wyck, who had made independent inquiries himself. 'I am quite convinced it did not. I wonder, though, what made Issacher mention the museum? I thought that he was in a state of unreasoning terror when he saw the second idol.'

'Not unreasoning, apparently,' said Mrs Bradley. 'What is the Lucastra Museum?'

'It is a semi-private collection of Eastern and prehistoric treasures. It is housed in a mansion about eight miles away, and is open to the public on Thursdays. It takes its name from the wife of the owner of the collection, Lady Lucastra Sunningdale. We take the Third Form boys to see the collection every year. Everybody in the School above the Third Form will have seen it, therefore.'

'I should like to see it myself,' said Mrs Bradley. 'Is it open on Thursdays all the year round?'

'Yes, all the year round.'

'Then I shall go this next Thursday, when the School has

broken up for the holidays. And I want to see Issacher again.'

Issacher was sent for and admitted to the Headmaster's drawing-room. He, like Salisbury, was sworn to secrecy concerning the questions he was about to be asked, and was informed by Gavin that he would be guilty of obstructing the police in the performance of their duty if he so much as dropped a hint to anybody of anything which was said at the interview. Issacher smiled in a superior way, but promised readily enough.

'And now,' said Mrs Bradley, 'I would like to ask you one question, Mr Issacher. You thought that perhaps the mask used by the second idol might have come from the Lucastra Museum. Now, if you could think of something so – if I may state my point in this way without offence – so rational at such a time, why were you also so much alarmed by what you saw?'

'I've been thinking things over,' replied Issacher calmly. 'I *was* scared at the time, but since then I find that I have a mental picture of what I saw, and I have examined it at my leisure.'

'Don't pose, boy,' said Mr Wyck kindly. 'And you had better remember that this is not what you told us before.'

'The point is,' continued Issacher, taking the first part of this advice and adopting a natural tone, 'the figure I saw was so frightfully *tall*.'

'Ah!' said Mrs Bradley. 'You mentioned this tallness before. Was the figure more than six feet high, do you mean?'

'Oh Lord, yes,' Issacher replied. 'I should think it was ten feet high at least. It was *definitely* more than normal height, and I don't think, sir,' he added, turning confidently to Mr Wyck, 'that ten feet would be an exaggeration.'

'Now, Issacher,' said Gavin, 'we want you to tell us who it was. You say you've thought the matter over, and that means that you've come to some conclusions.'

'Yes, but I'm not going to tell you what they are,' said Issacher flatly. 'I can't prove anything, and it's not right to ask me to guess.'

'Very well, my boy,' said Mr Wyck.

'Is that all, sir?'

'Yes, that's all,' said Mrs Bradley. 'I see that it was the height of the figure even more than its ugliness which impressed you.'

'It looked a devilish thing,' said Issacher. 'Good night, sir.'

'That boy doesn't like me,' said Mrs Bradley placidly, 'but we have found out one thing of great importance. Now to find out another.'

'What is that?' Mr Wyck enquired.

'Where that mask is hidden, and what were the means used to make up those added feet of height. If it was stilts, I would say that the case is completed.'

18. *Hoodoo, Voodoo, and Just Plain Nastiness*

*

We are treated too by them with Contempt, as if our Profession were not reputable.

IBID. (*Act 2, Scene 10*)

'PLEASE, sir,' said Scrupe, 'could I speak to you for a minute?'

'Of course, boy,' said Mr Wyck; for Scrupe had been announced and admitted by the butler to the Headmaster's private lodging. 'You had better come into the library.'

He emerged, towing Scrupe, at the end of a quarter of an hour, turned the boy over to Mrs Bradley for a repetition of his story, rang up Gavin, who was quartered at the village inn, and sent his butler to summon Ingpen.

'Now, Mr Scrupe,' said Mrs Bradley, favouring the boy with a leer.

' "And welcomes little fishes in with gently smiling jaws," ' muttered Scrupe defensively.

'Quite so,' the saurian replied. 'So now, Mr Scrupe, to your evidence.'

'It isn't my evidence; that's the trouble,' said Scrupe, without a trace of his usual bravado. 'It's something young Ingpen told me behind the stage. He said he'd seen a murder. Well, he hadn't, of course, because Mrs Poundbury isn't dead, but I've been thinking things over, and I wondered whether perhaps I ought to mention what he said.'

'Quite right, boy,' said Mr Wyck, who had returned from issuing his summons to the Detective-Inspector. 'Ingpen will be here in a moment. I trust that he will have recovered from his fright and will be able to tell us something helpful. There can be no doubt that there is a highly dangerous lunatic abroad. Mr Conway may have given offence to a personal enemy, but who in his senses would wish to attack Mrs Poundbury?'

Mrs Bradley could think of more than one person, but she said nothing. Ingpen arrived in a fluster which was not relieved when Mr Wyck, who was determined to extort any information which the child might possess, stood him in front of the large writing-table in the library, seated himself in his swivel chair, opened a large note-book, and said:

'Now, then.'

'Please, sir,' bleated Ingpen, 'I didn't mean to do it.'

'Do what, little boy?'

'Please, sir, call Miss Loveday Nancy.'

'Ah,' said Mr Wyck; and there followed a dreadful silence. 'Ah, we must never speak disrespectfully of women, little boy, never, never, *never*. Do we understand that now?'

'Oh, please, sir, yes, sir!' gulped Ingpen, while two tears of fright rolled down his babyish face.

'Then we will say no more,' said Mr Wyck. 'You may sit down.' The child sat down beside Mrs Bradley, who reminded him of a grandmother who spoilt him whenever he went to stay with her. 'Tell me,' continued Mr Wyck casually, 'what happened to frighten you so much at the School Concert.'

'It was – it was the tall idol,' said Ingpen, glancing at Scrupe for support.

'No, the other thing,' pursued Mr Wyck. 'The other thing that frightened you. Something else you saw.'

'I saw the idol knock Mrs Poundbury down the steps, sir, please, sir.'

'Are you quite sure of what you saw?'

'Sir, yes, sir.'

'I thought you had been allowed to stand in the wings to watch the play? Wasn't that what you told us last time?'

'Yes, sir. Please, sir, I *had* to be by the steps.'

'Why?'

'I hadn't got a handkerchief, sir, and I thought that if I took a short cut down the steps and out past the furnace-room I could get across to the House and back, sir, before I was wanted.'

'But you knew quite well that those steps and the furnace-room are out of bounds!'

'Yes, sir, please, sir. I thought it was better not to be late for when I was wanted, sir.'

'You are a naughty little boy,' said Mr Wyck. 'Tell me exactly what you did and what you saw.'

'I saw the idol. I wasn't scared much because I knew there was going to be an idol in the second play, and I thought it would look – very nasty. Then I saw Mrs Poundbury in front of me, and I thought I mustn't hurry because she would send me back to the wings, and I *had* to have a handkerchief. So I just kept behind her – '

'Remained behind her.'

'Yes, sir. I just remained behind her and then I saw the idol and I thought it was Salisbury up on stilts, and then I knew it couldn't be, because it hit Mrs Poundbury on the head, and she fell down the steps and the idol went after her and I rushed back to the wings, and saw Salisbury and then I saw Mr Poundbury and I told him where Mrs Poundbury was, and then it was all a muddle, and I told Fran – Scrupe there had been a murder.'

'I suppose,' said Mr Wyck slowly, 'that you've no idea who this tall idol could be?'

The child looked troubled and then his mouth set. He shook his head.

'Very well,' said Mr Wyck. 'And, remember, we do *not* take a lady's name lightly!'

'Oh, *no*, sir!' said Ingpen, on a gasp of thankfulness at being dismissed. Mr Wyck, still seated at his writing-table, tapped thoughtfully on it with his pencil, and suddenly called him back. 'Have you a good memory?' he demanded.

'Yes, sir. I think so, sir.'

'Tell me what was going on on the stage when you decided to go and get a handkerchief.'

'It was where they start drinking, sir, after they've knifed the three priests. I waited until I'd seen what I thought would be the most thrilling part, and then I – please, sir, I *had* to have a handkerchief by then – '

'I understand, and will overlook your naughtiness *this* time. Now you may go. Scrupe,' he added, as soon as the child had disappeared, 'what can you add to this story?'

'Nothing, sir, really, sir. He told me about it after he got back to the dressing-room.'

'Go and ring up Issacher and Salisbury and ask them to come here. Give them no hints. I can hear what you say from the hall,' said Mr Wyck. At this moment Gavin arrived, and was given a report of Ingpen's story. 'And I have a fancy that the little lad has an idea, if no more, of the identity of Mrs Poundbury's assailant,' Mr Wyck observed.

The stories told by Issacher and Salisbury did not vary from their previous evidence.

'I don't understand it,' said Gavin, when the two boys and Scrupe had gone. 'The idea seems to have been to attack Mrs Poundbury. Why return to the wings to frighten the boys?'

'To create a certain amount of uproar and confusion,' said Mrs Bradley. 'For some reason, this was necessary to his purpose. I think perhaps it was to enable him to establish some sort of alibi, although exactly *how* it helped him we don't yet know. It may have been sufficient for his purpose just to get the curtain rung down a few minutes before the appointed time.'

*

Before the School was cleared of boys and masters the discovery was made of the second idol's head, and that in what one would call the most accidental manner. The discovery was made by Mr Loveday. He had gone, accompanied by his knife-and-boot-boy, to make certain that the latter had effectively damped down the hypocaust furnace before School broke up, and there was the idol's head, or so he told Mr Wyck, leering at him from the top of a heap of coke.

'It serves me right,' said Mr Loveday, whose mind frequently took an unforeseen track, 'for using a modern fuel. The Romans knew nothing of coke.'

He had taken the head in his own hands and so presented it to Mr Wyck. Mrs Bradley was not on view. She spent most of the day and took all her meals in the little upstairs study which Mrs Wyck allotted to her. She would have liked to be present when Mr Loveday brought along the idol's head, but she was dependent upon what Mr Wyck could tell her of the interview. According to Mr Wyck the meeting had produced a conversation which he reconstructed (verbatim, he thought) for Mrs Bradley's benefit.

'Ah, good afternoon, Headmaster.'

'Good afternoon, Loveday. Good heavens! You haven't found it?'

'Well,' said Mr Loveday, pleased at the Headmaster's tone. 'It does begin to look a little like it. We shall need to display it to the boys who saw it, I imagine.'

'But where did you find it?'

'Of all places,' Mr Loveday replied gaily, 'in my furnace-hole – the Roman Bath, you know.'

'Really! But the – but that had already been searched.'

'Anyhow, there it was, and I have my knife-and-boot-boy for witness.'

'Oh, really!' said Mr Wyck, laughing. 'I see no need of a witness for your statement, my dear fellow. Of course, had it not been for the dastardly attack on Mrs Poundbury, an assault which appears to have been committed by this person who wore the mask, the affair could be dealt with differently. As it is, I must at once get in touch with the police, and hand your fact over to them.'

This he did, and Gavin came immediately. His first response was to ask for Issacher and little Ingpen again. Both were reassured and were informed that they were helping the police. Then the conditions under which they had seen the horror were reproduced. The School Hall was reduced to darkness, the stage lighting went on, and the idol's head, on top of the bamboo safety hook borrowed from the School bath, was placed in the wings where Issacher said he had seen it. Then Ingpen was shown the head. Both boys declared, independently, that it was the one they had seen at the School Concert.

Mrs Bradley carried out her plan of affecting to leave Spey a few days before the end of term, and she went so far as to go to London after she had made her farewells. She came back immediately, however, and smuggled herself into the Headmaster's House under cover of a particularly black December night.

Mr Wyck, she thought, seemed distrait, and Mrs Wyck's almost over-warm welcome was a sign of overwrought nerves. It soon came out that a governor's meeting had been fixed for the first day of the Christmas vacation, and that some searching questions would be asked to which Mr Wyck would be unable to make any reply which would be even remotely satisfactory either to himself or to the governing body.

'I shall attend that meeting,' said Mrs Bradley, 'and you had better refer the questioners to me. What line do you expect the governors to take?'

Mr Wyck looked astounded, but Mrs Wyck said quickly:

'General school discipline, of course. It's a sitter for Christopher's opponents. Some of the governors, Beatrice, as you already know, are very jealous and reactionary. They don't like Christopher's reforms and they think he is much too gentle and moderate. They would be glad to give him a setting down about the discipline. They couldn't do much about Gerald Conway's death, as it is not possible to prove that it even occurred on School premises, but this business of Carola Poundbury will be so much meat and drink to the brutes! They'll be bound to point out that all the evidence we've been able to accumulate points to an attack on her by one of the boys. And, also, of course,' she added, with the naïve candour which Mrs Bradley found so helpful, 'if any of the other nonsense comes out, we're sunk, and Christopher will resign.'

'But Christopher can scarcely be held responsible for the fact that Mr Conway was the cat among the pigeons,' Mrs Bradley observed, correctly interpreting 'the nonsense' and regarding the gloomy Mr Wyck with compassion, 'particularly since he was not pleased at Mr Conway's appointment.'

'Pleased!' snorted Mr Wyck. 'I was against it from the first, and I told the governors so. An 18B man has no place, in my opinion, in a school of any type, but particularly he has no place in a school where boys are resident and are largely divorced from outside interests and preoccupations. Nevertheless, as Grace says, if the scandal he seems to have caused should really come out, I should have no option but to resign. I thought it was coming out at the last meeting. It would all sound much worse now.'

'By the way,' said Mrs Bradley, without contesting this, 'there is a small, a very small, feature of the case which preys on my mind to a rather uncomfortable extent. Did you ever hear of the lampoon which was launched, some little time ago, at Mr Kay?'

'Oh, you mean *Louis the Spiv*,' said Mrs Wyck. 'Yes, we did hear it. Carola Poundbury told it me. Why?'

'Well,' said Mrs Bradley, 'Issacher claims authorship.'

'He *would!*' exclaimed Mrs Wyck. 'I detest that boy! He's a rat!'

'Your views interest me. Am I to understand, then, that the author is neither anonymous nor Issacher?'

'The doggerel in question,' said Mr Wyck, with a faint smile, 'was composed and disseminated by Micklethwaite, of the Fourth Classical.'

'All his own work, do you suppose?' Mrs Bradley enquired.

'You mean the sophisticated wit would indicate a mature mentality?' asked Mr Wyck, laughing outright. 'The boy, as a matter of fact,' he added at once, 'is not without gifts. Some of his more sober and reputable efforts have appeared in the School magazine.' He went out of the room and returned with a portfolio. 'I've kept a copy of each number,' he continued. He sorted through the magazines and soon came upon the one he wanted. 'This is his best effort, up to date. I think it, really, rather good.'

'A sonnet?' Mrs Bradley exclaimed. 'He flies high!' She read the poem slowly through. *'If one of us should die and that one me* – addressed to his mother, I see.'

'She is a widow,' said Mr Wyck, 'and he is the only child. His father was killed at El Alamein.'

'Hm!' said Mrs Bradley. *'She breaks our beauty-bond who grieves; More than a prince's pall have I, Who lie beneath the lovely leaves.'* She handed back the magazine and repeated softly: *'Louis the Spiv, Had not the right to live; Like every other skunk, He stunk.* Rather a morbid preoccupation with death, wouldn't you say?'

'Good heavens, no!' cried Mr Wyck violently. 'That's the worst of you psychiatrists. Even a joke indicates morbid preoccupations to you!'

'It often does indicate morbid preoccupations,' said Mrs Bradley mildly, 'particularly if it is a practical joke.'

'I do not regard what is called a practical joke *as* a joke,' said Mr Wyck. 'It is often cruelty very thinly disguised, and it is always stupid. Take this last example we have had – '

'Yes, I wanted to,' said Mrs Bradley, meekly.

'Detective-Inspector Gavin is hoping to be able to take a statement from Mrs Poundbury to-morrow,' said Mrs Wyck. 'I am hoping that she will be able to tell exactly what happened and when.'

'I will prophesy,' said Mrs Bradley, 'that she will only be able to tell us *when* it happened. She will not, in my opinion, have the slightest idea of the identity of her assailant, or, if she has, she will not confide it to us.'

This melancholy prophecy proved true. Mrs Bradley remained in strict seclusion all next day, and at four in the afternoon Gavin came over to the School House to report that, according to Mrs Poundbury, she had been struck on the head from behind just as she was going down to the

property cupboard for the pail which was required in the
last play and which had been forgotten. She had gone herself
because all her stage-hands were at that time in the auditorium, and her husband, who acted as stage manager, was
not available, either, because he had been making up the
lad Cooke a little more heavily than Mrs Poundbury had
already made him up.

'So that's that. And she didn't see the second idol,' said
Gavin. 'In other words, we've lost a couple of days waiting
for a statement which doesn't get us any further forward.'

'It gets us further forward if by any chance Mr Poundbury
was *not* engaged in making up Cooke,' said Mr Wyck. 'I
suggest that we see Cooke at once.'

'How many of the Housemasters live in their Houses during the vacations?' asked Mrs Bradley, most obviously
changing the subject.

'None of them. My wife and I will be here for part of the
time, but nobody else except the servants.'

'Doesn't look as though it will help to see this boy Cooke,'
said Gavin, thoughtfully. 'The chances are, he's like Issacher,
and won't give Poundbury away.'

'I agree that it is highly immoral to allow boys to perjure
themselves,' said Mr Wyck. But on the last morning of term
Mr Poundbury asked for an interview.

'Oh, dear!' said Mr Wyck resignedly. 'I suppose Poundbury has forgotten to send to the bank for his boys' journey
money.'

'That has happened before,' said Mrs Wyck, when Mr
Poundbury's messenger had returned to Mr Poundbury with
the tidings that the Headmaster would see him at once.
'Since then, Christopher has always kept a sum in small
notes and silver ready at the end of term.'

But Mr Poundbury had nothing to say about journey
money. He came in great agitation to confess to serious
crime. He was closeted with Mr Wyck for about twenty
minutes, and then Mrs Bradley saw him ambling, with
curiously uneven, uncertain, and uncoordinated steps across

the Headmaster's lawn; he was staggering from side to side with a lolling kind of movement, as though his legs had no connexion with his body except for the irresponsible liaison afforded by his trousers.

She turned to Mrs Wyck and was about to speak when Mr Wyck came into the room. His expression was that of a person who has received incredible and dreadful tidings.

'Poundbury,' he announced, 'is responsible. I never really believed it, but there it is.'

'What?' his wife enquired. 'Has there been an accident?'

'There has been no accident,' Mr Wyck replied. 'All that I can think is that the man must be off his head.'

'Why, what has he done or left undone?' Mrs Wyck asked at once.

'He confesses that it was he who struck down his wife at the top of those steps,' said Mr Wyck. 'And, of course, that makes it clear to me that he, and he alone, is responsible for poor Conway's death.'

'Did he also confess to having taken the note?' asked Mrs Bradley. Mr Wyck shook his head.

'He did not mention a note. All he said was that the sight of her made him sick, and that, before he realized what he was doing, he had hit her on the head. He adds that immediately he had done it he ran back to the dressing-room to finish making-up Cooke.'

'Did he say what he hit her with?' was Gavin's first question.

'I did not think to ask. He was greatly agitated, naturally, and said that he had confessed so that nobody else should be blamed. He also said that his wife had forgiven him.'

'I'd better see him myself,' said Gavin. He came away from the interview convinced that the confession was bogus. 'I don't know what he thinks he's up to,' he remarked, 'but his whole story is a fabrication from beginning to end. He wants me to believe that he knows nothing about the second idol beyond what he was told at the time, that he hit his wife over the head with a tack hammer he had been using to repair a bit of the scenery, and that he quite forgot he'd done it until about two days ago. Does any of that make sense?'

'The first and last statements,' said Mrs Bradley, 'but not the middle one. He may not have known about the idol unless he *was* the idol, and, as he would have been under great emotional stress, he may have suffered since from temporary amnesia. It is the tack hammer which makes nonsense. According to the School doctor, and according to my own examination of the injury, Mrs Poundbury was struck by something with a much broader end than a tack hammer; something more like an Indian club or a fairly heavy bottle.'

'We haven't found anything yet,' said Gavin. 'I suppose whoever used the weapon managed to get rid of it at once. I hope we find it soon, though, for the sake of the fingerprints, if any. I had better see this boy Cooke.'

Cooke declared that Mr Poundbury had not left him in the middle of making him up. Moreover, on breaking-up morning, Mr Loveday came excitedly to the Headmaster, bearing an Indian club.

'Discovered in my furnace-hole,' he announced proudly. 'As the last object found there was the idol's head, I presume that this must be the weapon which struck down Mrs Poundbury.'

Gavin, ruefully surveying the exhibit, swore quietly to himself. Then, suddenly, his sombre gaze brightened. Mr Loveday had certainly imposed his fingerprints on any others which the club might bear, but there might still be a chance of showing that it was not only the weapon which had struck down Mrs Poundbury, but that with which Conway had been stunned.

*

Before this theory could be proved, Mrs Bradley went to visit Mrs Harries.

'Item,' said she, 'one toad. Item: one stolen cockerel.'

The blind witch, fastening brilliant eyes on her, nodded.

'He wanted paddock,' she mumbled.

'Who did?'

'Paddock lighted on your bed.'

'He did. Why?'

'Then he stole the cockerel. He said it would make bigger magic than mine. But I put the three curses on him, and paddock came home again. There he is, just behind you.'

Mrs Bradley turned round. There was a toad malignantly squatting in the middle of the bare stone floor. Mrs Bradley stooped and picked him up. He was real, she was glad to discover. He sat on her cold yellow hand, his throat pulsating and his heavy-lidded eyes as wise as Solomon's. Mrs Bradley touched the top of his head. Then she carried him into the garden and placed him very gently on a flower-bed.

When she returned to the kitchen a black cockerel was dangling head downwards from the door-handle. It had not been there when she went out, and she had not heard the old woman move.

She stroked the cockerel's feathers. They seemed soaking wet. She took away her hand. It was dry. Old Mother Harries chuckled grimly. Mrs Bradley took down the bird and laid it upon the kitchen table. She examined it very carefully. The cockerel had a bruised head and had been strangled. She looked up.

'How did you know?' she demanded. Mother Harries walked to the table, picked up the bird without fumbling, carried it over to the door and hung it up again.

'These things are told me,' she said. 'I know not how they come. He is dead. He had the potion of me. The other one had the wax and the sheep's heart and the black-headed pins. What are men to me? I am too old for love. Yet love is blind. Leave me. You know who he is. He will not escape you. There is love and there is love and there is love. His is love in the middle degree.'

'Yes, I know,' Mrs Bradley answered. She decided to try an experiment of her own. She took down the cockerel once more and laid it in the middle of the floor where the toad

had been. 'Oh, look!' she suddenly cried. To her relief, the
witch started back with a shriek of fear.

'By Lilith, daughter of Samael, be gone from me! Be
gone! Go, screech owl! Go, contour in the form of an ass!
Go, Lamia! Go, Queen of Devils! Go, go!'

Mrs Bradley grinned evilly.

'Evil word has banished evil sight. The cock has his head
again, the paddock is to the garden gone, the dead man lies
down speechless,' she pronounced with becoming solemnity.
The old woman sank trembling into a chair.

'Who are you?' she demanded. 'Who is it that can make
me see what none should see? Who told you that I told him
what to do?'

19. *Nymph Errant*

*

Away, Hussy. Hang your Husband, and be dutiful.

IBID. (*Act 1, Scene 10*)

THE meeting of the governors produced no immediate re-percussions. Mrs Bradley and Detective-Inspector Gavin were both present, and the former was the chief speaker and kept the governing body in their places by what Mr Wyck referred to later as 'the iron hand of the expert witness'. Mr Poundbury's unfortunate and ill-timed confession was not mentioned by anybody, and neither was Mr Loveday's dis-covery of the Indian club, for this object was suspect. Gavin, in fact, stated flatly to the Headmaster that he considered Mr Loveday over-zealous.

'I don't say he manufactures evidence to give himself a kick out of this case, but he certainly does make a pest of himself,' he said. Mr Wyck was too loyal a Headmaster to concur verbally in this opinion of a member of his Staff, but his sympathies were with Gavin. 'Oh, well,' the latter con-cluded, 'now for Mrs Poundbury '

As soon as the meeting of the governors was over and they had been fed and cossetted by Mrs Wyck, and had been seen off by Mr Wyck, Mrs Bradley had gone to see Mrs Pound-bury. She got rid of the nurse, looked at the patient's tem-perature chart, and then got down to business, for it had been agreed that she should question Mrs Poundbury first, and Gavin's more formal interview should come after-wards.

Mrs Poundbury's story was that she did not know who had struck her down, and that she had not seen the second idol. Mrs Bradley appeared to accept these statements, and returned to the subject of the note.

'Oh, that wretched note! I'm sick to death of it!' said the

invalid. 'Why must you drag it up again?' Mrs Bradley did not trouble to answer this question.

'You say you had it in your possession up to the time you were attacked?' she said. Mrs Poundbury was emphatically certain that she had. 'Think carefully, then,' said Mrs Bradley. 'Who else, except for myself and little Ingpen, could have known that it had been found, and that you had it?'

'No one but Gilbert. I told him about it and showed it to him.'

'What did he say?'

'He was rather angry. He said that I ought not to have taken any notice of it when I received it, or else that I ought to have shown it to him then. He said that I could think myself lucky that I had not been charged with Gerald's death.'

'He knew that you had kept the assignation?'

'Yes, he did know that – well, I *think* he knew.'

'From whom did the note purport to come?'

'From Gerald, but it was typed and not signed. I knew it was from him, though, because he had put our secret mark on it.'

'Yes?'

'It was a tiny design which you can make on the type-writer by using an open bracket, two colons and a closed bracket, like this (::). It means *I hold you in my heart*. I used to put it in my letters to him, too. All this, of course, was before we broke it off, but when I saw this sign on the note, I knew where it came from.'

'I see,' said Mrs Bradley. 'And you kept the appointment when and where?' Something in her tone caused the patient to say quickly:

'Don't you believe what I'm saying?'

'Finish saying it, and I will answer that question,' Mrs Bradley replied.

'Oh, well, you see – ' She watched, fascinated, as Mrs Bradley drew out a small note-book and began to flick back the pages.

'Yes?' said Mrs Bradley, unscrewing the top of her pen.

'Well,' said Mrs Poundbury, 'you remember taking me to the cottage – Gilbert's – no, I mean, Gerald's cottage?'

'After we had picked the Brussels sprouts? – I do.'

'And you remember you tried to trick me by pulling up outside the wrong cottage?'

'Yes.'

'And the trick came off,' said Mrs Poundbury, without bitterness. 'Well, I met – I mean, I expected to meet Gerald there that night. Of course, he wasn't there.'

'No, he wasn't there. At what time did you arrive?'

'I – well, let me see! Oh, at about ten, I should think.'

'How did you get in?'

'I had a key. Each of us had a key – Gerald and I, I mean. We each had one. Oh, dear!'

'Where is your key now?'

'I threw it away as soon as I knew of Gerald's death.'

'Where?'

'I – I don't remember.'

'Mrs Poundbury, you've had a nasty knock on the head and I don't want to say anything which might distress you, but this I do say: tell me the truth. Believe me, you have nothing to lose, and your husband, whom I believe you love, may have everything to gain.'

'I am the best judge of that,' said Mrs Poundbury. 'But, if you want to find the key, you had better look in the river. Exactly where I threw it in I have not the faintest idea. I was terribly upset by Gerald's death, and I was terribly afraid that Gilbert might have done it, so my first thought was to – '

'Are you sure that the key is not in your husband's possession?'

Mrs Poundbury looked thoroughly alarmed by this question, and there was a pause whilst she thought it over.

'I – I am sure Gilbert hasn't a key,' she feebly replied.

'I am sure you are right,' Mrs Bradley cordially agreed.

'All right, Mrs Poundbury. By the way, you do realize, don't you, that far from shielding your husband by telling me that you kept the appointment, you are exposing him to very great danger?'

Mrs Poundbury lay back and closed her eyes.

'You ought not to come here and bully me,' she said feebly.

'My dear girl!' said Mrs Bradley sadly. 'I know perfectly well who committed the murder. If you really love your husband, do not expose him to suspicion.'

Upon this sinister note they parted, and, Gavin also having failed to impress her with the danger of manufacturing information, she was given a few hours to get back to normal and improve upon her story before he resumed the interview.

'While I'm giving her the time to cook up some more lies, I think I'll have a go at Kay again,' he said. 'He's still at his cottage. He and his wife have nowhere to go for Christmas, I understand, so they're staying put, and are having an old aunt, or someone, to stay.'

*

Mr Kay was no more delighted to see the police than he had been the first time he encountered them. Grudgingly he invited Gavin in, and, even more grudgingly, offered him a chair.

'I'll sit at the table, if I may,' said Gavin, easily and pleasantly. 'I can write better there.'

'I'm not going to make a statement,' said Kay flatly, 'so you can begin by writing that.'

'There's no question of a statement,' said Gavin. 'I just want a little help from you, that's all.'

Mr Kay, with a very rude remark, implied that the police could go elsewhere for help.

'Look here,' said Gavin, 'I know how you feel, of course, but I've got my job to do and my job is to clear up this business of Mr Conway's death. If you won't answer any more questions, you won't, and you'll be within your rights, but I don't mind telling you that you're still pretty high on the list of suspects. We know you hated Conway and we know why. We know you were out of your cottage that night, and we know where you were and approximately when, and we know all about old Mother Harries and her spells. So what about it?'

'So what about what?' said Kay offensively. 'I'll tell you what I told the other nosey parkers. You can get to hell out of here, and do your dirty job yourself. You'll get no help of any kind from me. If you think I killed that poisonous swine, well, go ahead and prove it. But you'll have your work cut out. As for the witch, I was doing folk-lore research, as you know.'

'Did your wife keep an assignation with Conway that night?' asked Gavin, without moving from where he sat. Kay half-rose, but then sat down again. To Gavin's surprise he pulled out, filled, and lighted a pipe before he answered the question. Then he said composedly:

'How the hell should I know? She doesn't go shouting that sort of thing all over the place. People don't. She keeps her own counsel, the same as I keep mine. And to save your breath and the strain on your intellect, I might as well anticipate your next question: I don't know where Brenda went or what she did, because *she* was away from home on holiday, and *I'd* gone out to see a man about a dog. Does that satisfy you?'

'Of course it doesn't,' said Gavin. 'Look here, Kay, be a sensible chap and come across with what you know. Give me the dope, and stop hedging. You know I'm not accusing you of having murdered Conway.'

'Aren't you?' said Mr Kay bitterly. 'You're the only person who isn't then, I should say. No, it isn't any good, Mr Nark. I'm not saying anything at all unless you charge me. And then I'm saying it all in front of my lawyer. I don't like ruddy little blasted policemen, especially when they're so obviously English and clean-limbed, and particularly especially when they talk with a bloody Oxford and Cambridge B.B.C. accent. See?'

'I see,' said Gavin, unperturbed. He took out his own pipe. 'Well, now, every drop of blood in my veins is good Scots on both sides for four generations. I was educated at Loretto and at Edinburgh University. My complexion isn't particularly ruddy, and, compared with you, you undersized, miserable runt, I'm not exactly little. So what?'

But Kay refused to continue the argument. That he was perturbed, however, was shown by his next action, for he thrust down the glowing tobacco in his pipe with each of the fingers and then the ball of the thumb of his right hand. He winced with pain as he did it, for every thrust was slow and hard, as though he were thrusting down something evil. When he had finished he laid the pipe on the edge of the metal ashtray which lay between him and Gavin on the table, and surveyed his scorched and blackened finger-tips with a certain amount of melancholy pride.

'So much for your precious finger-print system,' he said. '*These* won't help you much.' He put each burnt finger into his mouth and licked it. Then he smiled triumphantly at Gavin.

'Don't worry,' said Gavin coolly. 'We've got all the records of your prints that we're likely to want, my lad, and now you can dree your ain weird, which is my Oxford-Cambridge for stew in your own juice. I've given you your chance and you've mucked it. Have it your own way. Neither sailors nor policemen really care, you know.'

Kay, slumped in his chair, made no answer.

20. *A Scrum for a Line-Out*

*

But, hark you, my Lad. Don't tell me a Lye; for you know I hate a Liar.

IBID. (*Act 1, Scene 6*)

THE inquest on Gerald Conway was resumed during the Christmas vacation, and, to their great annoyance, several of the masters were called upon to attend. Mr Loveday, Mr Semple, Mr Wyck, Mr Kay, and Mr Poundbury were all there. Also among the witnesses were Miss Loveday, Mrs Poundbury, and Mrs Kay.

So far as the police were concerned, no fact of importance emerged, and the verdict, one of wilful murder by person or persons unknown, caused no surprise and not much gossip.

'Well, there we are,' said Gavin. 'I would say that so far there's not a shred of evidence. Let's have a round-up of the possibles and see whom we can eliminate once and for all. Now first of all there's Kay. He had a motive, but it doesn't seem any more likely that he did the job than that Poundbury or even old Loveday did. Put with them the Jewish boy Issacher and you've got four suspects whose temperaments would be the deciding factor. Of course, if we could show a possibility of collusion, or even an accessory either before or after the fact, it would help a good deal, but we can't.'

'Then there is Mr Semple,' Mrs Bradley pointed out. 'He was robbed of his *amorada* by Mr Conway.'

Gavin looked doubtful.

'I don't see Semple committing murder,' he said. 'As a matter of fact, that goes for Loveday, too. Still, what I think isn't evidence. No, as I see it, we're back to Pearson, as you suggested before. I suspect him because of the idol's head. He's the only person who would have known about it, I should say. I know! We'll ask that rather poisonous pal of

Conway – Sugg – whether *he* knew anything about it. If he didn't it is fairly certain that the others didn't either.'

'The boy Scrupe knew about it,' Mrs Bradley felt compelled to point out.

*

The new term commenced half-way through January. The weather was at its worst. Deep snow-drifts had piled up against the hedges, and Big Field had become a battleground not of football but of snow-fights, House against House, School House emerging victorious.

Gavin gave the new term and the seasonable weather a week; then he descended again upon Mr Wyck and the Staff with a list of people whom he wished to interview.

'Scrupe?' said Mr Wyck doubtfully, referring to the first name on the list. 'Yes, of course. But Scrupe is a peculiar boy.' Gavin promised to be careful and tactful, and this time Scrupe proved to be an ideal witness – honest, non-suggestible, non-gullible, and good-tempered. He denied absolutely and entirely that he had worn the head of the second idol at the School Concert.

'Consider,' he said, 'my schedule. I was in the first play as one of the soldiers. I was not in the second play, it's true. But I was in the third play in the character of the Odd Man. I shouldn't have had *time*, apart from anything else, to remove my first make-up, shove on the head and pursue Mrs Poundbury, and then get made-up for the third play. Chance is a fine thing, you know.'

'Didn't you take the head from Mr Conway's room in that cottage, then?' demanded Gavin, ignoring the impudent gambit.

'No, I didn't. I was a bit put off at finding Marion there. I didn't like it much, to tell you the truth.'

'No? Why not?' asked Gavin.

'Oh, various reasons,' said Scrupe, lightly. Gavin did not press the point; neither did he ask how Scrupe knew that Mr Conway rented a room from Mother Harries. Jealousy is not only strong as death; it has an enquiring and detective quality.

'Who, besides yourself, knew of the existence of this idol's head? Did you ever mention it to anybody?'

'No, I didn't, because I was going to pinch it if I could.'

'Coming back to the night of Mr Conway's death, what exactly were you up to then?' asked Gavin; but Scrupe was immovable upon this point.

'Innocently and ignorantly asleep,' he pronounced solemnly. 'Didn't know a thing about anything until the beastly rising bell next morning.'

'And you didn't take the head home for the holidays, either?'

'No. When I went next time it had gone. I suspected then that Marion had taken it, but, of course, I know what happened to it now. Anyway, I didn't brood much. It just seemed to me it would have been a good idea, that's all, to have it for fancy dress. I could have played up to it, too.'

'So there was no leakage there,' said Gavin to Mrs Bradley. His next victim was Mr Sugg. Here again he drew blank.

'But if the thing was made and worn two years ago, I wouldn't have known Conway then. I'm nearly new here,' pointed out Mr Sugg in a peevish voice.

'We had better tackle old Mrs Harries again,' said Gavin gloomily. 'We might as well find out whether Conway went there on the night he was murdered. Would *you* care to take her on? You'd get more out of her than I should.'

Mrs Bradley was not sure about this. What she did think was that she might interpret more successfully what she was told by the witch.

She came to Mother Harries's cottage at midday, fairly certain then of finding the crone at home.

'Ah,' said the old woman, as soon as she heard Mrs Bradley's step across the threshold. 'You have come for your book. Put your hand up the chimney. It is such a book as will burn the hand that grasps it.'

Mrs Bradley laughed, and the witch, putting an iron lid

on the witch-like pot she had been stirring (and which gave forth an appetizing smell of rabbit and onions), sat down on a small wooden box and motioned her visitor to a chair.

'I want to know,' said Mrs Bradley, 'whether you ever thought that your cottage was invaded by naughty boys.'

'Frequently,' the hag replied. 'Boys bring luck. Girls never. Their virginity is against them.'

'Are not boys virgin?'

'Oh, yes, but the power of the dog is there too. Boys are lucky. If ever I went to sea I would take a boy along with me.'

'Yes, that is an old superstition. What made boys come here?'

'One sought his love and another his lust.'

'Would you call the latter a *boy?*'

'It is no matter,' said old Mrs Harries. 'He is dead now. Drowned in the pool of his own darkness.'

'I know whom you mean. How long did he rent your room? And how many women did he bring to it?'

The witch shook her head.

'There was a golden voice and a silver voice and a voice of lead,' she answered. 'And the leaden voice was the marrying voice. Ah, but she meant to have him!'

'And the golden voice?'

'I think she was beautiful. They laughed together. He brought the mask and the stilts for her to see.'

'How do you know?'

'They were happy. They called me in and told me all about it.'

'And the silver voice?'

'She was the wife of my dark gentleman. They hid from him when he came to consult me one evening.'

'What did he do with the head of the cock?'

'How should I know? The cock crew and the spirits glided back to their graves. Called by Hecate! Called by Hecate!'

'Who stole the cock. Do you know?'

But the witch shied away from the subject of the cock. Gavin had already interviewed the angry farmer who had attempted to chastise Scrupe, and the man had grudgingly agreed that there was no evidence against the boy but that he had been a frequent and annoying visitor to the farmyard.

'My view is that Kay stole the cock to practise this black magic he was interested in,' Gavin had said to Mrs Bradley; but Mrs Bradley suspected that the actual theft had been carried out by a hireling.

*

'You are still with us, then?' Miss Loveday remarked, when next she encountered Mrs Bradley. 'I thought you had left for good just before the Christmas holiday.'

'I have been asked to treat Mr Poundbury, who seems to be indulging in a nervous breakdown,' replied Mrs Bradley, 'and I am still partly in attendance on Mrs Poundbury, whose recovery seems to be slow. I think she has had a bad shock.'

This leading gambit was pointedly ignored. 'She suffers from self-pity,' said Miss Loveday. 'And that is a bad sort of medicine. What she needs is an airing.'

'What kind of an airing?' Mrs Bradley enquired.

'Why, she needs to tell somebody how she came to be struck on the head. She knows very well who did it, and why,' said Miss Loveday positively. 'She should be made to unburden herself. Not for nothing was the Confessional invented. Leo the Isaurian knew that.'

'Did he?' said Mrs Bradley, somewhat puzzled by this last reference. 'We have tried to get from Mrs Poundbury how she came to meet with her accident, but she declares she does not know.'

'Shielding *him*, I suppose,' said Miss Loveday, with a virtuous, spinsterly snort. 'Thank heaven, there is only one man *I'm* foolish about, and that is my brother. Brothers, I find, are the only satisfactory members of their sex. They can drive the car, and climb step-ladders, and do not require one to waste time and strength in procreation.'

'The Poundburys have no children, though,' Mrs Bradley felt compelled to point out.

'Ah, but they cohabit,' proclaimed Miss Loveday. 'You can see it in their faces.'

This diverting and debatable assertion intrigued Mrs Bradley very much, but she wanted to get on with the business in hand; so she abandoned, although with great reluctance, the subject under discussion, and said that at any rate it had come to light that the mask used by the second idol had once been the property of Mr Conway, and that it had been made with the assistance of Mr Pearson.

'I don't like that man,' said Miss Loveday decidedly, referring, obviously, to Mr Pearson, as her next speech made clear. '*Widowers' Houses*, you know. It would not surprise *me* if Mr Pearson knew a great deal more about Gerald Conway than he has told you. I suppose he mentioned that that flighty miss of his had entangled herself?'

'Flighty?' said Mrs Bradley. 'I thought that Miss Pearson was rather hard-headed and sensible.'

'Oh, well, so she is,' Miss Loveday agreed, 'but some of our boys broke bounds at the beginning of the term, and were caught by Gerald Conway, and were forgiven by him. There must have been conditions attached to that forgiveness, don't you think?'

'Which boys were those?' asked Mrs Bradley; but Miss Loveday shook her head.

'No, no. I can be a gentleman myself when the spirit moves,' she said. 'Bygones are bygones with me.'

'But how did you come to know anything about it?' Mrs Bradley persisted.

'Lucius Apuleius knew of more than one witch,' was Miss Loveday's smug but enlightening rejoinder. She contrived to make this statement sound like the utterance of a minor prophet. 'That's all I know and all I need to know. But in case my reply should seem to be discourteous, I will tell you, in your private ear, when wind of Gerald Conway's goings-on first came to my notice, I realized at once his necessity for a strategic base. A close study of his migratory habits led me in the right direction, and I was soon in possession of the information I sought.'

'You love knowledge for its own sake?' Mrs Bradley enquired. Miss Loveday nodded vigorously.

'Exactly,' she said. 'For its own sake, and, of course, for a sense of the power it gives me. I love power. I would like to have absolute power. I should not misuse it.'

'All power corrupts,' began Mrs Bradley.

'And absolute power corrupts absolutely,' concluded Miss Loveday. 'Yes, I know. But if one did not realize that one was corrupt? Do you think the jiggery-pokes, the place-men, the pocketers of boroughs, the financial jugglers, the tax-dodgers, the pimps, trulls, trollops, and macaronis, *know* that they are corrupt?'

'Were the macaronis corrupt? I should have thought they were chiefly silly and perhaps a little stupid and cruel,' said Mrs Bradley, ignoring the major issue although she realized its intrinsic importance.

'Perhaps I should have said *murderers*,' Miss Loveday good-temperedly responded. 'Where, in your galaxy of wrong-doing (which is, by interpretation, wrong-thinking), do you place murder, I wonder?'

'Below rape, and above grand larceny,' Mrs Bradley promptly replied. 'Where do *you?*'

'*Real* murder is the most terrible of crimes,' pronounced Miss Loveday. 'But there is such a thing as essential elimination.'

'Under which heading comes the death of Mr Conway?'

'Oh, surely, under neither. Why should anybody desire to cut off in the prime of life so comparatively innocuous a youth?' Miss Loveday demanded. 'And yet, did he not rush, as it were, upon self-elimination?'

'Well, I can think of several people who were glad to see

the end of him,' said Mrs Bradley. 'Who do *you* think hit Mrs Poundbury over the head?' ·

'So we are back where we started,' said Miss Loveday, comfortably. 'Suppose you tell me the answer.'

'Mr Poundbury seems to have had but little opportunity; the murderer of Conway may have had the motive. Mrs Poundbury was carrying about with her a note her husband received the day before Conway's death. It has disappeared,' said Mrs Bradley, disobligingly.

'It contained a clue, you think, to the identity of the murderer?'

'Hardly that; but it might contain a clue to his typewriter.'

'The note was typewritten, then?'

'That much I could see, although I was not shown the contents, of course.'

'Foolish woman!' said Miss Loveday indignantly. 'I'll tell you what you ought to do. You ought to go and see Marion Pearson. She might know the kind of thing he used to write when he wished to make tryst with young women.'

'So she might,' Mrs Bradley agreed, without discussing Marion further.

'Talking of all that,' pursued Miss Loveday, suddenly tapping the window to attract the attention of a passing youth, 'it seems that because of their antics, both Kay and Semple have laid themselves open to being suspected of the murder. But then, of course, so have my brother and myself. The police have made that quite clear. So kind of them, really, because one knows exactly where one is, and can spend time on deceit and take pleasure in subterfuge.' She broke off to address the boy, who was politely awaiting her attention outside the window.

'Where's your House-badge?' she demanded, mouthing the words so that the youth could lip-read them. The boy pulled at the neck of his sweater and showed the badge attached to his shirt. Miss Loveday nodded, and the lad ran jogging away. 'They dislike their badges,' said Miss Loveday, turning again to Mrs Bradley. 'They make the boys conspicuous. But I like our lads to be conspicuous. It helps them to make their mark in the world later on. But to this affair of Gerald Conway. Thanks to the proceedings at the inquest, we now all know how the deed was done. Your policeman thinks my brother and I did it at the Roman Bath. You think Bennett Kay and Gilbert Poundbury did it. There is also nothing at present to exclude the thought that Brenda Kay and Carola Poundbury did it. It would not be beyond the scope, I take it, of two young and healthy women to have fallen upon the man and drowned him? Brenda Kay was presumed to have been from home at the time, and' – said Miss Loveday, with an expression of great cunning – 'I do happen to know that Carola Poundbury had her hair permanently waved on the following morning, because I could not get at her to tell her the news of the murder until four o'clock in the afternoon.'

'Interesting,' said Mrs Bradley. 'There is also one other combination of persons who might have had an interest in Conway's death.'

'You mean Marion Pearson and her father, but that's absurd,' declared Miss Loveday. 'Marion is well-balanced.'

'You said just now that she was flighty,' Mrs Bradley pointed out. Miss Loveday opened her mouth to speak, but shut it again without saying anything.

*

'And now, Mr Loveday,' said Mrs Bradley, waylaying the head of that House on his way to his Roman Bath, 'perhaps you will be good enough to confide to me the reason why Inspector Gavin should not arrest you for the murder of Mr Conway.'

'I can think of no reason,' replied Mr Loveday, 'except that I did not murder Mr Conway.'

'Are you sure?' Mrs Bradley enquired, falling into step beside him. 'Which fortunate boys bathe to-day?' she added, with less inconsequence than was apparent.

'Micklethwaite for services rendered, Merrys for excellent conduct, Skene to give him an airing, Parsons because he wishes to learn to swim, and Findlay to save us the trouble of supervising the others,' said Miss Loveday, joining her brother and Mrs Bradley, whom she had followed out on to the gravel.

'Mrs Bradley has just suggested that I ought to be arrested for the murder,' said Mr Loveday. 'What do you say to that, Annette?'

'I have heard of the gambit before,' proclaimed Miss Loveday. 'It is on the principle of the Kipling euphorism: the bleating of the lamb excites the tiger.'

'Would you say euphorism?' Mr Loveday demanded. His sister did not reply.

Mr Loveday admitted his boys to the Bath, and, very shortly, what with Micklethwaite tearing through the water like a shark, little Parsons shivering in the shallow end until the noble Findlay, arriving late, seized him and terrified him into swimming four short, panic-stricken strokes before he grabbed wildly at his mentor and was steered kindly to the side of the Bath, and Merrys and Skene outdoing one another in swimming under water, all were lost to the outside, terrestrial world.

'Surely Micklethwaite is an unusually accomplished swimmer?' said Mrs Bradley. Miss Loveday glanced at her sharply.

'I have often thought I would like to make a film out of the death of Gerald Conway,' she said. 'Imagine the setting: first one would get a general view of Spey, and then an enlarged picture of Loveday's House. From a dormitory window, like prowling cats, creep a couple of sinuous boys. They are nameless up to the present, but, as their originator and author, I shall decide to call them Merrys and Skene.'

'On the night of Mr Conway's death?' enquired Mrs Bradley.

'Certainly.'

Mrs Bradley, recollecting a piece of evidence which she

had tabulated some time previously, suddenly cackled. Miss Loveday, not put out by this, went on:

'They creep round to their Housemaster's private garden and impound his bicycle. They go off on it, and the roving eye of the film camera follows them over hill and dale, and picks them out a little more clearly at last at the gate of a lighted cottage. The lads are lost, and have called at the cottage for guidance.'

'Mr Conway's cottage, of course? Or, rather, the cottage in which he lived his secret life.'

'Yes, and Mr Conway is in residence.'

'But . . .'

'Allow me to continue. He is in residence, but he is no longer alive. Two persons are in the cottage with his dead body. The film does not indicate yet which persons they are. Their figures are thrown in silhouette on the blind. They are, however, John Semple and Bennett Kay.'

'You are basing this theory on the unassailable fact that Mr Semple and Mr Kay were the two who discovered the body,' said Mrs Bradley.

'Exactly so.'

'But on nothing else?'

'John Semple is fanatically devoted to the School. He would do anything to preserve its good name.'

'But surely it does not preserve that good name to have a master murdered!'

'A clever point,' Miss Loveday admitted, 'but it shows me that, with all your vaunted knowledge of the human mind, you do not understand young Semple. He is a fanatic, and my definition of a fanatic is that he must be a seemingly intelligent person with but one dominating thought, which thought, by feeding upon itself, eventually crowds out all other thoughts, so that the person becomes, in effect, mad.'

'Mr Semple certainly does not seem to me mad,' Mrs Bradley protested.

'That is because you see him with a narrow, medical eye. To me he is completely insane.'

'I will bear your opinion in mind. Do, please, go on with your film.'

'It attracts you?'

'It fascinates me. The body of Conway is in the lonely cottage. The two boys are knocking at the door.'

'Quite so. They flee at the sound of a well-known voice – the voice of Bennett Kay. That disposes of the boys. We see no more of them.'

'What a pity! I should have liked to follow them home.'

'The original script did, but the cutter removed the sequence to save time. Meanwhile, we are admitted to the cottage kitchen. The sink is full of water. The drowned man lies on the floor. We are left to draw our conclusions, while the shadows of his murderers, in the light of the kitchen candle, pass slowly, one after the other, over the recumbent victim.'

'A powerful sequence.'

'I think so. The shadows stoop and then straighten, and a bizarre procession walks into the pouring rain. We follow it to the School and to Bennett Kay's garden.'

'Rather a curious place to choose if he was one of the murderers?' Mrs Bradley felt bound to suggest. Miss Loveday waved the point aside.

'I can see how your mind is working,' she observed. 'You think my brother and I drowned that unspeakable puppy here in the Roman Bath. But you know very little of my brother if you think for a single instant that he would sully the apple of his eye with that gross and pampered mote, the body, alive or dead, of Gerald Conway.'

21. *The Hunt is Up*

Where was your Post last Night, my Boy?
IBID. (*Act 1, Scene 6*)

'AND that *is* the obstacle, of course, to the Roman Bath theory of the drowning,' said Mrs Bradley. 'Her striking metaphor carries extraordinary weight. Mr Loveday would never have polluted his Roman Bath by throwing Mr Conway into it.'

'That wouldn't apply to *Miss* Loveday, though,' said Mrs Wyck. 'That's what you're getting at, isn't it? I wonder why she hates poor John Semple?'

'I don't think she does. But I certainly think (as I have thought all along) that she is pretty certain of the identity of the murderer, and does not propose to share her knowledge with us. I have a theory, too, that her brother shares this secret. It might be much easier to force his confidence than hers.'

'Well, the next thing *I'm* going to do is to have another go at that chap Dobbs, Mr Loveday's knife-and-boot boy,' said Gavin. He sent immediately for the youth, who arrived under the escort of Miss Loveday herself.

'I hope,' said the latter, 'that there is no complaint against Dobbs. He is, in every respect, an excellent lad, keen, clean, and obliging, of sanguine temperament and innocuous habits. State your case.'

'We want to ask him who committed the murder,' said Mrs Bradley, before Gavin could speak.

'Do you know, Dobbs?' enquired Miss Loveday severely. 'If so, you should have spoken before. Much time, and a great deal of public money, have been wasted already over this apparently fruitless enquiry.'

''Ow should *I* know anything?' demanded Jack the

Ripper, alarmed into a display of pugnacity. 'If all these 'ere narks and coppers can't follow their noses better'n a poor bloke what's done no 'arm to nobody . . .'

'Your words are ill-advised and ill-selected, Dobbs,' said Miss Loveday, breaking in with vigour upon her man-servant's jeremiads. 'There is but one nark present, and she is resident at this seat of learning and discipline. Confine and annotate your nouns.'

'Beg pardon, madam,' responded Dobbs, looking sheepish. 'But I never knoo you knoo . . .'

'But little escapes these ears, these eyes, or this enquiring and pertinacious proboscis,' pronounced Miss Loveday. 'Give attention, Dobbs, to your mental superiors, the police.'

Upon this advice, she departed, accompanied by a sigh of relief from Gavin and sped by Mrs Bradley's eldritch and appreciative cackle.

'And now, Dobbs,' said Gavin, 'what were you doing on the night of the murder?'

'Being took bad,' replied the Ripper.

'How do you mean?'

'Fish pie,' said Dobbs. 'We doesn't often 'ave it down-stairs, but there was no 'elp for it that night. It was fish pie or go without. We 'ad even finished up the cheese ration, that goin' nowhere with Mr Loveday in the 'Ouse.'

'Doesn't Mr Loveday like fish pie, either?' asked Mrs Bradley.

'Nobody don't like fish pie if they can get meat,' said Jack the Ripper. 'But being as 'ow it was fish pie or nothink, well, fish pie 'e 'ad, and fish pie 'e wished 'e'd never 'ad, for I met 'im in 'is dressing-gown, bein' on me way to *a place*, and 'e looks green as grass. Green as grass 'e looks, and 'e shoves past me without a single bloomin' word.'

'At what time was this?' asked Gavin.

'I reckon it would 'ave been around two o'clock in the morning. I never felt me qualms come on before eleven, and after that I 'ad a rare old time of it, I don't think, trottin'

there and back, and there and back till I wonder I 'ad any
bloomin' inside left be'ind.'

'What else happened that night?'

'Nothing, so far as I'm aweer.'

'Are you sure you can remember nothing else?'

'Me mind was on other things than murder,' said Dobbs
with dignity. They were obliged to let him go.

'Point is, Loveday might have been green as grass with
fish pie, or green as grass after witnessing murder,' said
Gavin, gloomy with disappointment and frustration. 'You
know, Mrs B., I don't believe you're trying.'

'Time flies quickly enough,' said Mrs Bradley complacently. Her sharp black eyes and beaky little mouth gave
nothing away. 'We must try someone else, that's all.'

'Mr Loveday was in his dressing-gown,' said Gavin. 'Over
a bathing suit, do you suppose?'

Mrs Bradley cackled.

'Stranger things could be true,' she answered, 'but, if you
are canvassing my opinion, I am bound to tell you that I
think it most unlikely.'

'Well, I'm going to try to reconstruct the scene in the last
Common Room that Conway attended. It might give us a
line.'

*

'I am asking no questions,' said Mr Wyck, to his wife's
intense disappointment, 'except that I should be interested
to know what Gavin hopes to gain from this reconstruction
of a Common Room meeting.'

'He hopes to sow alarm and despondency,' Mrs Bradley
replied. 'The murderer has been singularly discreet and
sensible, but the Detective-Inspector believes that the attack
on Mrs Poundbury may have followed the murder because
she was in possession of a letter which might have proved
dangerous to the murderer.'

'And is that letter now destroyed?'

'It is reasonable to think so. There is not much doubt that
the murderer got it back.'

'Does Detective-Inspector Gavin want me to be present at this Common Room gathering?'

'That is as you wish. From his point of view, it would be much better if you stayed away.'

'Very well. My presence would undoubtedly depress some of the Staff. Whom will you get to play the part of Conway?'

'Oh, Mr Poundbury, of course. He is much the best actor, I fancy, and will give us all that he can remember of Mr Conway's exact words.'

'That means that you do not suspect him of being an accomplice to the murder?'

'Does it? It means, at the moment, that we are hoping that he will prove to have an excellent verbal memory and some slight gift of mimicry.'

'Ah,' said Mr Wyck, vaguely.

The Common Room, four hours later, presented a familiar appearance to its members, but was filled with an atmosphere alien to its traditions. It was a place of suspicion and fear. Its groups stood about, chiefly in the corners and around the hearth, and at the moment of Gavin's and Mrs Bradley's entry, Mr Reeder, who seemed the only person at ease, was suggesting that he hoped the business was not going to take long, because he had papers to mark and a move of chess to play against his postal opponent in Australia.

'I am sorry, gentlemen, to break into your leisure time,' said Gavin, advancing, 'but we have arrived at the point in our enquiry where a reconstruction of some conversations which may have taken place on the evening of Mr Conway's death may help us very considerably. I wonder whether you would be good enough to stand or sit about just as you were at that last Common Room which Mr Conway attended?'

'Right,' said Mr Reeder, taking charge. 'Let's begin at the beginning. Now, when *I* came in there was nobody here but Painter.'

'That is so,' said a dark man who was standing near the window. 'I was sitting at the table here, I think, correcting English essays. You came in . . .'

'And said: "Mind if I shut the window?" Then, when it was shut, I lit my pipe . . .'

'Neither of you two gentlemen is important to my plans,' said Gavin, 'and the rest of that conversation does not matter. Could we come to the point of Mr Conway's entry?'

'He came in with Johnson, Semple, and myself,' said Mr Sugg. 'By that time the Common Room was almost full. We were late because we'd sat at table after dinner discussing the Richmond and Blackheath match, which Conway and Johnson had been to see – '

'Yes, they went up to Town,' said Mr Poundbury, who had recovered, it seemed, from his breakdown and also from his confession. 'I think, myself, that it is too far to go in a short week-end, as one has to start back so early on the Sunday to get here before the small hours of Monday morning.'

'Yes,' said Mr Loveday, 'I quite agree. In fact, there, I always say, Housemasters, in spite of what some have chosen to consider as their privileges, are at a distinct disadvantage when it comes to week-end leave. Why, only last summer . . .'

He was firmly interrupted by Mr Poundbury, who said loudly;

'Yes, yes. We've had all that out before. Where do you want me to pick up Conway's dialogue, Detective-Inspector?'

Everybody looked astounded, for this was not the Poundbury they knew. Mr Reeder went so far as to enquire of Mrs Bradley in a stage whisper:

'What's all this? Have you been playing one of your tricks on him, as you did on young Takhobali?'

'No, no,' Mrs Bradley replied. 'His nerves have had a rest and a change, that's all.'

'If you're talking about my hitting my wife over the head, you're an old ass, Reeder,' said Mr Poundbury genially. 'Now, then, someone, give me my cue.'

'Very well,' said Mr Loveday, breaking the strange silence

which succeeded Mr Poundbury's remarks. 'Here it is, so far
as I can remember: "It's time we thought of some better
way of managing boys than by beating them and putting
them in Detention." Then I think I said something rather
insulting about poor Conway's form-room methods and he
retorted by mentioning Mr A. S. Neill, the progressive
schoolmaster whose life-work, as you probably know, has
revolutionized what we are pleased to call discipline. Nobody who has read his enlightened books . . .'

'Oh, no, Loveday! That was a much earlier conversation!'
cried Mr Semple. Mr Loveday looked annoyed and then
confused.

'Yes, yes,' he said feebly. 'Yes, so it was. Oh, dear!'

'What you said was something about wasting time in term
which ought to be devoted to the interests of the School.
You said – '

'My turn,' said Mr Poundbury. 'Here you are: "Go and
work it off somewhere else, Loveday, old dear. I can't help
it if your wretched puppies . . ." '

'Whelps,' amended Mr Johnson, grinning. 'And then
Loveday knocked the system of evening prep, as usual,
didn't you, Loveday, and – '

'And talked about "competent teaching" again. You
were damned rude, you know,' said Mr Reeder.

'Was I! I know he mentioned bats and moles,' said Mr
Loveday. 'Not that I bear the poor fellow any malice now,
of course, but he used to try me high. He talked about my
Roman Bath, too, in a most improper and, sometimes, a
most indelicate manner. You were all witnesses,' he added.
'I remember, on one occasion . . .'

'Yes, it must have been most provoking,' said Mrs
Bradley. 'Go on, Mr Poundbury.'

'Not until I get my cue,' said Mr Poundbury. 'Come on,
Loveday. You *must* remember what you said next.'

'I think I do. I *expect*,' said Mr Loveday, with a nervous
and propitiatory smile, 'that I mentioned my Roman Bath
once more.'

'*Mentioned* it! I should think you nearly drowned the fellow in it!' said Mr Reeder. 'Oh, Lord! Sorry! Tongue running away with me, as usual.'

'It certainly is,' said Mr Mayhew. 'And I should like to say, in this connexion, that I personally consider these proceedings to be farcical. We can gain nothing by this muck-raking . . .'

'Except some useful pointers to Conway's murderers,' said Gavin.

'Murderers!' The plural was passed from one master to another until it came to Mr Kay, who was standing in a very inconspicuous position just inside the doorway, almost hidden behind the massive and Olympian Mr Semple.

'*Of course* it was the work of more than one person!' said Mr Kay. 'Anybody but an idiot would have seen that from the beginning.'

'Hullo, Kay!' said Johnson. 'What are *you* doing here? You don't usually favour us with your company after dinner.'

'I've as much right in the Common Room as you have!' was Mr Kay's angry retort. 'Some of you clean-run English-men think everybody stinks except yourselves!'

'Gentlemen, please!' said the Bursar urgently.

'All right, I've got my cue, I think,' said Mr Poundbury. 'I'm afraid I can't repeat the whole speech verbatim: it amounted to a description of Loveday's House by Conway. He said Loveday's boys ran out and about at nights exactly as they pleased, stole his property – his bicycle I suppose was meant – and, as usual, said that his House were lazy, dirty, and slack, and finished up . . .'

'No, no!' cried Mr Loveday, in great agitation. 'I won't listen to that again! It cannot and must not be repeated. I cannot have my sister insulted!'

'But it wasn't his sister who was insulted. It was Loveday himself,' said Mr Semple. 'And, anyway, that was the former time again, wasn't it?'

Mr Loveday rushed out of the room. There was no sound

for a moment but the embarrassed shuffling of the younger masters' feet and Mr Reeder's dry cough.

'Go on, Mr Poundbury,' said Mrs Bradley.

'I think that was about all. After that, the conversation broke out generally.'

'And then?'

'Oh, well, Loveday didn't rush out, of course. There wasn't any worse row between them than usual. It was just that the conversation turned on to Scrupe and the cockerel–'

'Yes, *I* began that bit,' said Mr Reeder proudly, 'and Loveday said that he didn't believe in fisticuffs, and Conway took that up. And soon after that, Pearson walked in with his champagne and startled us all into a fit.'

'How did Conway take the champagne and compliments?' enquired Gavin.

'Well, that's the strange part,' said Mr Reeder, in his gossiping way. 'The chap seemed completely at sea. Didn't seem to know what the congratulations were about. However, he rallied himself, more or less. Old Pearson seemed a bit queer, though, I thought. Looked like a walking corpse trying to laugh at its own death, if you can follow me.'

'Interesting,' said Mrs Bradley, in mild understatement, when the Common Room meeting was reported to her.

'Oh, yes, there's no doubt about Pearson,' said Gavin seriously, 'except that I can't see why Mrs Poundbury had to be knocked on the head and the note taken from her.'

'We should have to see the note to know why she was knocked on the head,' said Mrs Bradley. 'And the note, of course, has been destroyed.'

'I'd like to know what was in it,' said Gavin wistfully.

'Well, arrest Mr Loveday, or some other innocent person, and see what happens,' suggested Mrs Bradley carelessly. Gavin looked at her.

'You've got an idea about the note, haven't you?' he said. 'What is it?'

'It is not about the note. I can guess what that was about.

I think the boy Micklethwaite knows more than he has told us, though, about the night of the murder.'

'Do you, by Jove!'

'Yes.'

'What would loosen his tongue? Any good springing it on him, and demanding that he tell us?'

'Would that have worked with you when you were fifteen or sixteen?'

'No, it wouldn't. I was shockproof. Most boys are.'

'Then we must bluff. Let us look at the facts of the death once more. The body was found at some distance from the water. The man had been drowned. He had also been knocked on the head. We have assumed – and the medical evidence at the inquest bears us out – that Conway was stunned – '

'Probably never even knew who hit him – '

'And then his unconscious body was dumped into water. By the other marks it seems likely that a heavy weight was tied round his neck to keep him under. Now what we have to look for and to find is a swimmer sufficiently accomplished to remain under water long enough to release the dead body from the weight and to bring the body and the weight severally to the surface.'

'Then comes the business of transporting the body to Kay's cottage garden, though,' said Gavin. 'We still don't know how that was done, and he was lying right on a flower-bed, you know.'

'I do know. I have turned the question over in my mind from the very beginning. What do you say to those stilts?'

'Eh?'

'The appurtenances used to give height to the second idol.'

'But I don't see . . .'

'Don't you? Given sufficient strength and resolution, it would be simple enough. Imagine a fireman's lift, the arms and legs of the body secured together, and the possession of ood thigh and abdominal muscles by the rescuer. With a little assistance, it would be quite possible, although, I agree, not easy, to step up on to the stilts. The absence of footprints, and the negligible imprints of the stilts on the gravel and the stretches of damp turf, predispose me to wonder whether this was the method used to transport the body.' She cackled, as though she dismissed this ingenious but unlikely argument.

'But the fellow who did all that – for Conway wasn't a light-weight, you know – must have been a trained fireman or a giant,' said Gavin seriously.

'He wasn't, I am sure. He was a big, athletic young man with a mission in life – two or three missions, in fact. It was probably the fact that he had more than one mission which caused him to help move the body of Mr Conway.'

'You're not talking about Semple?'

'Whom else?'

'Well, I'm damned!'

'No, no. I doubt that,' said Mrs Bradley, paraphrasing George Bernard Shaw. 'All the same, it is not Mr Semple that we want to see next, but the lad Micklethwaite, preferably in front of his Housemaster.'

'Micklethwaite?' said Mr Loveday, approached upon the matter. 'Surely you don't suspect the boy of being concerned in Conway's death?'

'In his death, no. As an innocent accessory after the fact, yes,' said Mrs Bradley. 'But, as I want you for an absolutely unbiased witness, I shall not prejudice you either for or against the boy.'

'One is always prejudiced in favour of one's boys. I'll see him at ten,' said Mr Loveday. He looked deeply perturbed. 'You did say *innocent?*'

'I said it and meant it,' said Mrs Bradley firmly. 'The boy had nothing to do with the death. I am quite convinced of that. Neither had he any wish or incentive to assist the murderer. Can you, and will you, possess your soul in patience? We are almost at the end of the matter.'

'I will undertake to put the whole thing out of my mind,'

said Mr Loveday. 'It is an exercise to which, as Housemaster, I am not entirely unaccustomed.'

'There goes a worried man,' said Mrs Bradley complacently. 'Now to arrange our little tableau. I think a uniformed constable is indicated. Will you telephone for one to come along? And I think it would be only fair to take Mr Wyck into our confidence.'

'You might do worse than take *me* into *yours*,' said Gavin, grinning.

*

As it happened, Mr Wyck was not, after all, in a position to attend the interview with Micklethwaite at ten. At ten minutes to the hour, he received a visit from Mr Semple who came bearing a telegram and wearing a grave expression.

'Your father? I am so sorry, my dear fellow,' said Mr Wyck. 'I had no idea he was so ill. Nor did I realize that he was living in Ireland. Go at once to him, of course.'

'I – if it *is* the end, I shall have to stay for the funeral, sir.'

'Of course, of course, my boy. Do not dream of distressing yourself about returning! I will just make some arrangements about your work . . .' He called up the School secretary on the House telephone, and the three of them were soon busily engaged in reconstructing the School time-table. This took some twenty-five minutes, and, after leave-taking, Mr Semple went out by the Headmaster's french doors – rather to Mr Wyck's surprise at that time of the year – and the Headmaster suddenly remembered Gavin, Mrs Bradley, and Micklethwaite.

Micklethwaite had been sent for out of class. He arrived to find his Housemaster in the presence of a police constable.

'Micklethwaite, my boy,' said Mr Loveday, 'not a word. You know you promised me.'

'Well, sir,' said Micklethwaite. He hesitated, and then seemed to make up his mind. 'Very well, sir. I expect the police are only bluffing.' So stalemate was established until Mr Wyck came in.

'Look here, Micklethwaite,' said Gavin, hoping for an ally in the Headmaster, 'I want you to understand that I'm not asking you to give anybody away. You may take it for granted that I've got my facts. I only want them confirmed. All right?'

'Certainly, sir,' replied the intelligent boy. 'You know all the answers, but I'm to supply them first.'

'Now, don't be impudent or clever, boy,' said Mr Wyck. 'You are to be given a chance to explain some very mysterious actions. Take the chance that is offered you, and regard this as by far the most serious occasion of your life.'

'Pardon me, sir,' protested Micklethwaite. 'I think you forget my Confirmation.'

Mr Wyck, with pardonable irritation, reached over and caught him a sound box on the ear.

'I warn you, boy, that you test my patience,' he said kindly. Micklethwaite apparently interpreted this statement correctly, for he lowered his eyes and murmured, 'Yes, sir,' as meekly as the words could be said.

'Well, now,' said Gavin, 'it appears that you are an accessory after the fact of murder. Will you enlarge on that point for me? Just a simple account will do. In fact, the simpler it is the better, so long as it's strictly truthful.'

'I abominate lying,' said Micklethwaite, with an apologetic glance at his Housemaster, 'and, besides, it seems that the time has come. The fact is that on the night of Mr Conway's death I was roused by Mr Loveday and was taken over to the Roman Bath. Mr Conway was lying at the bottom of the water, at the deep end. He had two great bags on his back. I found out afterwards that they contained huge lumps of rock – from the boulders on the moor, I should imagine.

'Miss Loveday was at the Bath side. She said, "Micklethwaite, we are afraid Mr Conway has done something terrible to himself." I said, "It looks like it, Miss Loveday.

Ought you to be here? Can't Mr Loveday and I cope?"

'She said, "My brother is most upset." Well, Mr Loveday did look most horribly green, sir, didn't you? She went on to say: "Do you think that, as Mr Loveday and I are not very accomplished divers, you could release Mr Conway from what appear to be weights upon his shoulders?"

'I didn't like the idea much, but, of course, I went down and cut the bags from the – from Mr Conway with a knife Miss Loveday had given me. I got the body to the steps after several tries, and Mr Loveday helped me to get it out. It took some doing, and Mr Loveday was pretty well whacked at the end, weren't you sir? We laid it on the edge of the Bath. Then I had to go in again for the bags. I thought at first I shouldn't manage them, and by the time I'd got the second one up I was feeling pretty well done.

'Then Mr Loveday told me to go back to bed, and he would speak to me again in the morning. But he didn't speak to me in the morning, did you, sir? – and by lunchtime we'd all heard about the murder, and how the body had been found outside Mr Kay's cottage. So I went to Mr Loveday, and he told me I must have dreamt the whole thing. He brought in Miss Loveday, and she said that it was of no use for Mr Loveday to try to protect me like that: it was better to acknowledge the truth.

' "The trouble is," she said, "that it appears to have been murder, not suicide, and the murderer, by some means unknown to the police at present, must have broken into the Roman Bath after we all left it last night."

'I asked her whether she had told the police this, and she said she had not, but that she intended to do so at the first opportunity. I asked where I came in, and she took ten separate shillings from her silver teapot, and said, "You come in for this, my dear, brave lad, and I trust that you didn't take cold."

'I asked what I had to do to earn the money – not that it was all that much, but the whole thing struck me as being very fishy, if I may say so without offending Mr Loveday.

She said I had to do nothing, as it was payment for services already rendered. I asked her flat out whether I had to keep my mouth shut, and she said, "Not at all, my dear Micklethwaite, but I should wait until you are questioned by the police. It is sometimes considered injudicious to rush to them immediately with a story. We do not yet know the identity of the murderer, and a too talkative youth might find himself in great danger," and – and I think that's all, sir.'

'I can't think why you didn't come to me with this tale instead of keeping it to yourself all this time, though,' said Gavin, busily writing.

'When I thought it over, I knew I ought to, but I funked because I was afraid you might think I'd had something to do with the murder,' answered Micklethwaite limpidly. Gavin scowled at him and Mr Wyck drummed on the table.

'Did you ever think that Mr and Miss Loveday might have been concerned in it?' asked Gavin.

'Good heavens, no, of course not!'

'Weren't you surprised to find them over there at that time of night?'

'Oh, no. They go over often to stoke up the furnaces and see that the whole thing is working. We all know that. Nobody takes any notice.'

'You were sick later on that night, weren't you?'

'No, but going back I ran into a fellow who *was* sick, and I had to think up an excuse for being up and about.'

'How did Mr Loveday manage to wake you up without disturbing the other boys in your dormitory?'

'I don't sleep in a dormitory. I have special permission to have a camp bed in my study, so that I can work in the early mornings. I got my parents to stipulate for this. I do my best work between five and seven a.m.'

'Good Lord!' said Gavin, awed at last. 'Is he quite right in the head?' he demanded of Mr Wyck when the lad had gone.

'He is rather a talented boy,' said Mr Wyck, with his usual mildness, 'and, of course, he has told the story because he believes that Mr and Miss Loveday are innocent.'

'Oh, so do I,' Gavin answered. 'They've been criminally foolish, though.'

22. *Hare and Hounds*

If I am hang'd, it shall be for ridding the World of an errant Rascal.

IBID. (*Act 2, Scene 10*)

'I SUPPOSE the Lovedays are simple sort of people really,' continued Gavin, 'and if they thought they had a suicide on their hands, it was natural to try to get rid of him. It was very annoying of Mr Wyck to allow Mr Semple to go to Ireland, though.'

'Yes, once he really gets away it may be very hard work to find him,' said Mrs Bradley.

Gavin gloomily agreed.

'Although I doubt whether we could prove he was the one who dumped the body for them,' he added. 'Of course, Loveday did "find" the mask and the Indian club for us, so I suppose he's got cold feet all right. Something may break pretty soon.'

'I think it will,' said Mrs Bradley cheerfully, 'particularly as Miss Loveday has just informed me that she intends to join her boys in a paper-chase this afternoon.'

'Good Lord! Miss Loveday actually joins in?'

'Do you really join in?' Mrs Bradley enquired, as Miss Loveday came into the room.

'For the first mile and a half,' Miss Loveday replied. 'After that, I turn round and trot home again. My brother does not join us. He leaves the whole thing to Cartaris. I believe that Issacher makes a book on the result. It is deplorable that boys bet, but it is impossible to prevent their doing so. Mr Wyck does not like it, but there it is.'

'I suppose Mr Semple is a good man at cross-country running when he is in England,' said Gavin.

Miss Loveday looked at him closely:

'I know not why you should ask me that,' she said. 'It is

well known that John Semple is a very fine cross-country
runner. He is a footballer beside. And now, farewell.
Atalanta – or should I say Diana? – must garb herself for
the chase. Will you all come to Loveday's to dinner? The
pig has arrived and looks inviting. I have good apples
stored. There will be crackling. My brother shall provide us
with sherry, and there will be brandy later. What say you?
Shall we toast the gallows together, Mr Policeman?'

'Look,' said Gavin, suddenly. 'What was Mr Pearson
doing on the night of the murder?'

'How should I be expected to know?' enquired Miss Loveday. 'Wear football stockings. We negotiate brambles and
gorse,' she added, turning suddenly towards Mrs Bradley.

'But I wasn't proposing to accompany you, and neither
does Mr Gavin care greatly for winter exercise,' said Mrs
Bradley firmly.

*

An enthusiastic bevy of boys from other Houses hooted
rudely at Mr Loveday's boys and loudly cheered his sister as
the cross-country runners set out at just after half-past one.
Miss Loveday was wearing a pair of football boots, a hat
tied under her chin, and had kilted her skirts to the knee.
Mrs Bradley and Gavin watched the procession from a
window.

'And now,' said Mrs Bradley, 'I suggest, my dear David,
that you borrow a bicycle and go at once to Mr Pearson's
house at the other end of the village. Pedal fast; you must
get there before Miss Loveday does.'

'What for?' asked the mystified Gavin.

'I think you will know when you see her,' Mrs Bradley
replied. 'Micklethwaite, I fancy, is the one material witness
for whom we have waited so long.'

'I wish we'd tackled him earlier, then,' said Gavin.

'The psychological moment did not arrive earlier, child.'

The runners had crossed the road and were stringing out
through the woods which lay between the School and the

river. Gavin, on a bicycle borrowed from Mr Wyck's butler, waited until Miss Loveday, in the wake of her boys, had disappeared among the trees, and then he turned into the roadway and pedalled for all he was worth in the direction of the village.

He arrived at the Pearsons' house in time to catch Marion at the front door as she was about to walk to the village.

'I won't keep you,' he assured her. 'The fact is, one of the masters has gone to Ireland to visit his father, who is very ill. We want to get in touch with him, and wondered whether by any possibility you may happen to know the address, as we want some information we think he can give us.'

'I don't know any addresses in Ireland except the address of a small hotel in Galway where I spent a holiday once with my father,' Marion responded. 'Is it John Semple who has gone?'

'Yes, it is.'

'We were once engaged. I didn't know his family lived in Ireland. I thought they were London people. They used to live in Hampstead, I think. I never met them. We weren't engaged long enough for that.'

'You wouldn't know their address, then?'

'No, I'm sorry. And now I must go, or the shop will be sold out of biscuits.'

Gavin went with her to the gate and pretended to cycle back towards the School. He had great faith in Mrs Bradley, but there was still no sign of Miss Loveday or any of the boys, and he thought Mrs Bradley must have been mistaken in supposing that Miss Loveday intended to visit the Pearsons.

However, he thought he would hang about for a bit and see what happened. The first thing that happened after Marion Pearson had left him was that a stream of boys crossed the road from a field adjacent to the Pearsons' house and plunged in among the sodden yellowish bracken on the opposite side of the way.

After these came stragglers. In the rear of the party came

Miss Loveday, going, all things considered, remarkably strongly, Gavin thought. At the Pearsons' house, however, she glanced round. Gavin by this time had hidden himself and his bicycle in a clump of laurel bushes just inside the Pearsons' boundary fence. She let down her skirt, untied her hat-strings, and sauntered towards the Pearsons' beautiful garden pool and rockery.

She glanced at her watch and then up at the top-floor windows. She seemed impatient, and, for so masterful a personality, somewhat irresolute. In a few moments, however, she lifted her chin as though she were listening, and hastened towards the garden gate. Gavin, to his surprise, saw what he took to be the hares. Two big boys came into his line of vision, each carrying a bag of what Gavin took at first to be the scent for the paper-chase.

To his astonishment they strolled up to Miss Loveday and, dropping the bags from their shoulders, they opened them and each took out a large chunk of granite. Under Miss Loveday's direction they placed them on Mr Pearson's rockery.

Miss Loveday turned and saw Gavin, who was strolling towards her.

'We meet again, Miss Loveday,' he said, as he raised his hat. 'Have you given up the run so soon?'

'By no means,' Miss Loveday answered. 'All right, gentlemen. You may leave us. I stopped to find out whether Henry Pearson was going to join us. He usually likes to do so. He is as fond of a pipe-opener as I am.'

'Well, it is my sad duty to request you to accompany me to the local police station,' said Gavin. Miss Loveday nodded.

'Both right and proper of you,' she said briskly. 'You will find little to prove against me.'

'And, of course, that's true,' said Gavin. 'She's only got to stick to her story that she merely got her boys to put a couple of stones, out of neighbourly kindness, on Pearson's rockery for us to be stymied so far as she and her brother are

concerned. No jury is going to convict an eccentric old girl
like that of being an accessory after the fact of murder.'

'I am glad to hear it,' said Mrs Bradley sincerely. 'Mis-
guided she may have been, but criminal – never!'

'Still, we've got Pearson all right,' said Gavin with great
satisfaction. 'Moreover, he's confessed to knocking Mrs
Poundbury on the head. He wrote a note to her, but
deliberately put *Mr* instead of *Mrs*, warning her that her
assignation with Conway was no secret. There was no such
assignation, of course, for the night of the murder, but
Poundbury naturally saw red and went chasing after the
fellow. Mrs Poundbury thought for a long time that he was
guilty of the murder. Bennett Kay, of course, was down at
old Mother Harries's, learning more of her charms and spells,
so that *he* was under suspicion too, and old Loveday's
bicycle was actually borrowed by Poundbury to get to the
town where, according to the note, his wife's meeting with
Conway was to be. Kay heard the bicycle go by before he
set out for Mrs Harries's cottage.

'When Pearson heard from little Ingpen – his nephew,
you remember – that the note had been found, he guessed
which note it was and was afraid it might incriminate him
in some way. He was determined to get it back if he could,
although he expresses great contrition that he had to hurt
Mrs Poundbury. What he refuses to tell us is exactly what
his motive was in killing Conway.'

'Oh, I can tell you that, I think,' said Mrs Bradley. 'The
champagne party in the Common Room seems to have
startled and upset Mr Conway. I think there is not much
doubt that matters had gone so far at Mrs Harries's cottage
between Marion Pearson and her lover that Mr Pearson,
far from continuing his opposition to the match, was only
too anxious that it should take place. When Conway told
him after the champagne party that he was not going to
marry Marion, the father's self-restraint failed, and he put
into practice the detailed plans for Conway's murder which
he had had in his head for some time. Miss Loveday's well-

intentioned efforts in getting her boys to return to him the incriminating evidence of the stones which had weighted the body failed in its object, but that was hardly *her* fault.'

'How did you get on to that?'

'I thought it jumped to the eye. What more convenient way could Miss Loveday find to disguise the two pieces from the rockery? I think it was a brilliant idea. Had she or her brother been guilty, she would have returned them before.'

'I think you have a criminal mind,' said Gavin. 'You had better use it to help me tidy up the loose ends of this beastly case. It's a funny thing, you know, but a bloke like your son, Sir Ferdinand, would have been able to get Pearson off if the fellow had left the body in the pond and sworn that he'd only knocked Conway out and the drowning was accidental. It was trying to incriminate the Lovedays that did for him. I suppose he didn't allow for Mr Loveday's panic and indignation at finding a body in his precious Roman Bath. Pearson, of course, had cut himself a key to the Bath. It was an easy thing for a woodwork and metalwork craftsman to do. He says he ran the body by car up that lane at the other side of the Bath beyond the boundary fence. Queer coincidence that the Lovedays should have visited the Bath a second time that night.'

23. *Aroint Thee, Witch*

*

I was always very curious in my Liquors.

IBID. (*Act 3, Scene 6*)

'So we part,' said old Mrs Harries, motioning Mrs Bradley to a seat by the fire. 'But before you go – '

'Before I go, I *would* like to know why you told me that lie about the beautiful woman with the golden voice,' said Mrs Bradley.

The crone chuckled.

'That was no lie,' she averred. 'I was wrong to let you think she had come with him to this house, but I was not wrong in coupling them. They had enjoyed themselves together. I knew that when you brought her here.'

Mrs Poundbury's connexion with Lecky Harries having been disposed of, the two old women sat still, each intent upon her thoughts.

'You are putting ideas into my head,' complained Mrs Harries at last. 'You want your book. I see that you mean to have it before you go.'

'No, no,' Mrs Bradley replied. 'I have spent time enough on the book. I would like to make you a present, that is all. You may perhaps remember me by it when I am gone.'

She put into the earthy old palm which came, gipsy-fashion, towards her, a witch-ball. The witch studied it gravely, as though she could see. She then looked at it more closely. Her lips drew back from her gums and her mouth opened with a long dribble of saliva. This dropped on to the witch-ball. Mrs Bradley leaned forward, half-anticipating what was to follow.

There in the witch-ball was Mr Pearson's garden with the pool and the rockery, and there was Mr Pearson himself crouching at the edge of the pool and holding under the water the head of an unconscious man.

With an effort Mrs Bradley dragged her eyes from the ball. When she looked at it again, the horrid scene had vanished and the dribble of spittle was trickling on to the edge of the crone's brown hand.

'And now,' said Mrs Bradley, 'it's my turn.' She leaned forward and spat accurately and neatly on to the crystal ball.

The witch started up, and put her free hand before her sightless eyes.

'No! No!' she cried, in the trembling tones of an old and frightened woman. 'Not that! Not that! Take it away! Take the water away! Oh, I drown! I drown!'

Mrs Bradley took out a spotless handkerchief and wiped the crystal clean. She tossed the handkerchief into the fire.

'There you are, then,' she said. 'But I want you to make a contract with me. I am a student of mental phenomena, and your mind interests me. I want to experiment with it. What do you say?'

To her delight, the witch agreed. It was with regret that she rose to leave Mrs Harries, but their future, she thought, held possibilities and had considerable interest.

'And now,' said Mrs Harries, when her guest reached the door, 'you will do as I told you before. In my front parlour you must put your hand well up the chimney, but beware lest you get burnt – I wish you no particular harm.'

Mrs Bradley, half-sure of what was in store for her, did as she was requested. She stretched as far up the old chimney as she could, and her fingers touched sacking. At the same instant she felt as though she was touching red-hot iron. She was sufficiently prepared for this to grasp the sacking firmly without withdrawing her hand or flinching from the pain of the burn.

She drew out the book of which she had been in search. She knew what it was the moment she saw it. Her hand, of course, was not burnt, and nor were the precious volume or its sacking cover. She went back into the kitchen. Mrs

Harries's old face was wrinkled with the mirth of Satan.

'It is yours. You have won it fairly,' she said. 'These eyes will never read another word of it. I always meant you to have it. It would bring me no luck to sell it to you, either. You shall inherit it from me, for, saving yourself, I have neither kith nor kin upon the earth.'

'I will come again to-morrow,' said Mrs Bradley. She went out, bearing the magic book of her ancestress, Mary Toadflax. She stepped carefully aside to avoid Paddock, her hostess's familiar, as he squatted in the very centre of the narrow garden path. As she opened the garden gate, a small hedgehog remained motionless. Then it lifted its tiny snout and whined three times.